A Worl

There was a rustle like white noise, and the mirror was pulling at her. Rebecca stared at the figures in the reflection, and in the reflection the vine branches seemed to writhe.

But they couldn't be.

She looked again at the Queen, seated in three-quarter profile with her sleeves flowing and her skirts spread. And the Queen turned her head to meet her eyes, and parted her lips.

Me, the Queen said, her voice deep and inside Rebecca's head. You...*Us*

Joanna O'Neill
December 2010

Also by Joanna O'Neill

A World Invisible

A World Denied

JOANNA O'NEILL

Wooden Hill Press

For David, Peter, and especially Simon

Published by Wooden Hill Press

First Edition 2010

Copyright © Joanna O'Neill 2010

The author asserts the moral right under the Copyright, Designs and Patent Act 1988 to be identified as the author of this work.

All Rights reserved. No part of this publication may be reproduced, stored In a retrieval system, or transmitted, in any form or by any means without the prior written consent of the author, nor be otherwise circulated in any form of binding or cover other than that in which it is published and without a similar condition being imposed on the subsequent purchaser.

ISBN: 978-0-9564432-1-2

Prologue

16:07 Eastern Standard Time:

Two hundred yards from the highway, in a shallow dip where the grass grew a little sparser and the frosting of snow had fallen a little closer, molecules moved.

A snowflake tipped and nudged the next, which slid and took others with it: a micro snow-slip. The tiny crystals changed the angle of reflection of the rays from the low sun.

The light moved.

A pair of white-tailed deer startled, lifting their heads and staring before bounding away across the pasture, and a snowshoe hare crouched with flattened ears and then leapt into a run toward the trees.

Another snowflake stirred.

21:07 Greenwich Mean Time:

In a cottage in the grounds of a country hotel a pencil rolled across the table.

A man raised his eyes from the journal on his lap. He hadn't jogged the table, yet the pencil ran smoothly to the edge and dropped off. The man frowned slightly, and then became aware of a faint rattling.

Faint but close by, and persistent.

He set down the book and his coffee mug and opened the door to the passage.

Louder.

He followed the rattle – or a thrumming, perhaps – and opened the door to the smallest room, where one wall was covered by speckled mirrors in old frames.

The mirrors were moving slightly, trembling; almost shivering.

And then they were still.

9:07 pm:

The wind soughed across the island, its cold song familiar to the cattle and sheep and ponies where they grazed. It ruffled the heather and caused the pines to sway, and sighed and thumped around farmhouses and barns.

Beneath the glass of the cabinet in the castle drawing room, where no wind could possibly reach, torn and faded silk shimmered briefly, catching the moonbeam from the window and making the light waver.

On a hillside a thorn bush shivered, scratching against the stone without and the stone within, and the fragile bones on the floor shivered too, and the feathers drifted and then settled.

The wind passed by.

Seven minutes past nine in the evening:

The television set in the back room of the Ferry House crackled and the picture jumped.

'It's the wideband.'

'It is *not* the broadband.'

'What's up with Milly?'

The two old men watched the tabby cat as she slipped down from the armchair and slunk low-bellied between the chair legs and into the kitchen. They heard the cat flap slap. It slapped again. Then it slapped for the third time.

They exchanged looks.

It slapped one more time, and both breathed again.

'What's got into the cats?'

Their companion, emerging from the kitchen with the tray, stared at the stuttering screen and then at the curtains closed across the north-facing window.

The signal steadied and the sound returned.

He put down the tray.

'Well it's nothing to do with us.' He lowered himself with a sigh into the armchair in the corner. 'Who are we voting off tonight, then?'

Chapter One

As before, crossing the threshold rocked his balance, and as before, he stumbled sideways and went down on one hand and one knee.

This time the ground under his palm was ice-cold and powdery with snow, and he stood quickly, brushing his hand against his worn jeans and staring at the unfamiliar landscape.

The grass was too short for moorland and the country too open, too featureless for a park. Pasture? Very big pasture; he could see no cattle or sheep but there was a line of posts, probably supporting wire, downhill to the left. Was Shropshire like this? Or Wales?

He was reluctant to turn round and look back the way he had come, but he forced himself, tensing his stomach for what he should see.

But there was nothing, just the single lump of rock and a gentle dip in the turf where his footprints began, as if the earth there had sucked in its belly, and under the dusting of snow the broader, flatter leaves of a plant that resembled ground ivy, clinging fiercely to strange soil.

Then lifting his eyes, he followed the slope of the land to where a dark wall of trees marked the end of the grass, and breathed sharply in as he saw the great steep of the mountain rising to the clouds, and its dense cladding of evergreens.

Not Shropshire then.

And it was freezing.

Roy Colvin drove with the side window open three inches despite the bitter air, so that the smoke was drawn out of the cab and he could knock ash from his cigarette from time to time. October, and the first snowfall had come early. The road was freezing over, but the way was straight and level and driving took little concentration.

He jettisoned ash again and frowned at the dark figure ahead, walking at the side of the highway. When he drew close, he braked gently and allowed the truck to roll to a standstill a couple of strides ahead. He leaned across the passenger seat to wind down the window.

'You need a ride, son?'

It was a convenience question; the kid was in a thin tee-shirt and sneakers, hunched and shivering.

'I'm sorry, I didn't–'

'Climb in.'

Roy stretched further and pulled the lever to open the door. The kid clambered into the cab, slamming the door on the cold air and winding up the window quick.

Roy eased the pickup back into motion, sliding only a little on the thin ice. Glancing sideways, he guessed the kid was probably older than he'd first thought. He looked about the same height as Robby, but Robby, like all the Colvins, was tall. This boy was shaving, dark stubble emphasising his sharp jaw and high cheekbones; and his shoulders were wider than Robby's.

'Roy,' he said. 'Roy Colvin.'

The kid turned to meet his gaze, and kind of – landed in the present, as if he hadn't been there before.

'Sorry. I'm – Daniel…Passenger…Daniel Passenger.'

Roy offered his hand and they shook awkwardly across the gear-shift; the kid's fingers were dead cold.

'So, Daniel, d'you know where're you headed? Nothing much out here but farms.'

The snow-covered fields sped away to either side, too fast to focus on. The truck can hardly have been doing more than, say, thirty, but the motion made Daniel's head ache. He fixed on the road ahead instead, straight and inexorable, the post and wire fences each side sucking him towards an unknown vanishing point in the dusk.

'Where are you headed?' the guy had asked, very reasonably. How to answer? *I don't know because I don't know where I am.*

So cold.

He'll think I'm a junkie.

Daniel dragged his remaining resources together into one massive, combined effort, an all-out attempt at normality. He drew his hands out from under his thighs where they were trying to thaw, and forced his back to straighten and his shoulders to drop. Hardest of all, he hauled his eyes off the darkening road to look across at the driver instead.

Roy. Roy Colvin. He wore a baseball cap with the peak curved and a padded jacket, the outer skin creased and scuffed, as weather-beaten as his cheeks. He looked like someone out of an American movie, a minor character at a gas station or diner. He was leathery and smoky, and English men in their seventies just didn't wear jeans and baseball caps, or at least, didn't look at ease in them.

His accent wasn't English and the steering wheel was on the wrong side.

This is America.

But had he landed up in the United States or in Canada? He didn't know enough about accents to guess.

Oh God.

The question still hung there, and for certain the suspicion.

Daniel took a breath, hating that it shook.

'Mr Colvin, I – I think I've been stupid. I had a lift with some people and they – chucked me out. They took my coat. My wallet.'

'Where're you from?'

'I...A long way. I'm not sure even...where this is.'

It sounded so lame, but the driver just said, 'You're in Antler Hollow. Burlington's behind us, about twenty miles.'

'Burlington...'

'Burlington, Vermont. You've been in Vermont for the last eighty miles, Dan.'

'Okay. Right.'

Daniel faced front again, the flanking lines of wire keeping him grounded and contained at least to a degree. He felt the old man's eyes on him, out to the left.

'Guess you'd better come along home with me.'

* * *

Nothing much out here but farms, the guy had said. The road was practically empty; they passed two pickups going the other way, headlights yellow in the dusk, and a giant lorry *('That'll be his last drop today')*, and were overtaken by a motorcycle *('Some fool on this ice')*. That was all. If Roy Colvin had not stopped to give him a lift he'd have frozen to death.

They passed a couple of turnings, each marked by a signboard that Daniel couldn't read in the gloom, and then slowed and took a right into a road that curved and swooped around a snow-covered hummock and finally delivered them to the shelter of buildings grouped around a yard. Roy cut the engine and sudden quiet rolled over them. It had been snowing again, lightly, the large flakes chased off the windscreen by the long wiper blades, and now the air was muffled as Daniel dropped down from the cab and winced.

His feet in the wet trainers ached.

He followed Roy across the yard and round the corner of a single-storey building, and into light falling across the snow from the windows of a house.

Roy led him through a side door into a room full of boots and winter coats where Daniel shed his soaked trainers, and then through a second door into the warmth – oh, warmth – of a passage where a striped rug covered polished floorboards and framed aerial photographs hung on wood panelling. A television was on somewhere nearby, voices overlapping one another excitedly, and there was the shocking smell of meat cooking, salty and rich, so that Daniel almost gasped. His guts creaked and he swallowed the sudden rush of saliva.

'Patty!' Roy's fingers on his back prodded him onward. 'We got company!'

Daniel found himself in a kitchen where saucepans were steaming and the smell was strong enough to undo him. He swallowed again, feeling suddenly faint, the voices muzzy. He put one hand on the back of a chair. A straight-backed woman with iron-grey hair hooked behind her ears was saying something, but somehow he couldn't catch the words.

Then his hand lost the chair as someone pulled it out and pressed him down onto it, and he dropped his face into his hands, his elbows on his knees, letting his life move on around him by itself for a moment. He couldn't make any more decisions right now.

'Son?'

A hand on his shoulder and another smell to ambush him: chocolate?

'Here.' The woman, Patty, held the mug until he had his hands firmly on it. 'It's not too hot, you can drink it straight down.'

Daniel sipped and then gulped the thick, warm liquid, part chocolate, part coffee, mostly heated milk, feeling his fingers itch as the blood returned to them against the hot china. The mug was white with large black letters: LOOK OUT HILL, HERE I COME, and on the other side, red numerals: 40.

A plate arrived on the table in front of him, a blue rim framing a saucer-sized cookie. 'Dinner's not for thirty minutes,' Patty told him. 'So eat up.'

Nobody was asking any questions, and everyone was being so kind. Daniel pictured fleetingly his own home, if you could still call it that, faced with a situation like this – the chilly, cramped kitchen, fish fingers and peas in the freezer, the twins staring, his sister harassed…But of course his father would never have rescued a stranger to begin with, just sworn at him for walking on the road and driven by.

Don't think about him. Them.

The business of the household flowed around him. A lanky boy brought him a pile of clothes and led him to a shower room along the hall where he changed and washed his hands, the fresh jeans and tee-shirt and zip-neck fleece – and *socks* – scented from laundry detergent and puckered from the pegs that had hung them to dry. Putting clean clothes on made Daniel feel faint again, and he waited another minute, leaning on the wall, his forehead on the smooth wood.

He was ashamed of his own clothes, worried that they smelled, and worried that he smelled too. He wanted to take a shower, but should you do that, uninvited, in a strange house? He hadn't shaved for three days and the face in the mirror over the basin was awful, hollow and grim, the bones accentuated by the beginning of a beard. His hair was wild, down past his shoulders and greasy. He ran his fingers through it, pushed it behind his ears, and then tried to lift his brows and even smile. He looked manic.

Oh God.

If he lingered any longer someone would come looking for him, checking on him. He unlatched the door and found his way back to the kitchen, his old clothes in a bundle under his arm. 'What should I…'

There was a second woman in the kitchen now, younger, wearing jeans and a sloppy sweater. 'Well, hi,' she said, casual and smiling as if he was just a regular person. 'Oh, just put those in the washer, will you? In the mud room, where you came in? They can go with the next load.'

Daniel found the washing machine next to the rack of coats and worked out that the way in was through the top. He dropped the bundle in and was closing the lid when he remembered, with a sickening jolt of shock, and pulled the jeans back out; he found the hip pocket and rescued the cards.

God, that was close.

Aware he was trembling, he slid them into the pocket in his borrowed jeans and returned along the hall, determined to be normal, or at least to act normal.

Forget it all for now. Think about it later. Just…try.

He walked into the kitchen to face the family.

Chapter Two

Rebecca set down her pencil for the tenth time in an hour and rubbed her hands together, massaging each set of fingers in turn, then folded her arms across her chest and buried her hands in her armpits.

The warmth was too slow coming, though, what with two sweaters and her fleecy dressing gown on top. After a few seconds she wormed them up inside the loose sleeves, each hand gripping the opposite elbow.

It was November and it was *freezing*. Too cold to draw.

Rebecca slipped off the high stool at her drawing board and padded to the kitchen to put the kettle on, leaning on the counter by the window while she waited. The early frost had vanished so it couldn't be actually freezing, but with no heating in the flat it felt like it.

The circulating pump that fed hot water to the radiators had died and the gas service people didn't carry spares. The replacement they'd ordered for her was supposed to be in by Friday, and if it wasn't she'd have a miserable weekend.

In the back garden Roly Pidgeon, the wonderfully named tenant of the downstairs flat, was moving about behind the beanstalks. He had been raking leaves earlier, of which were there a lot, courtesy of the giant lime trees bordering the road, but was now busy at something or other probably involving pots and string. Something autumnal.

Rebecca was not a gardener but she admired people who were, especially in cities. The Pidgeons managed to draw vast quantities of actual, edible food out of the small patch behind the house, and often had surplus beans or tomatoes or greengages to share with her. It gave one pause to consider what could be packed into a few square metres tucked away between buildings.

Now what did that remind her of?

Rebecca made coffee and wandered back to the drawing board, fingers tingling against the hot mug.

What are all those molehills?

She was an artist, more specifically an illustrator, and a good one at that. Even at twenty-two she had one major award to her name and had been shortlisted for others, which was all the more astonishing given that she had pig-headedly dropped out of art college early. Rebecca believed, or half-believed, that she knew the source of her precocious talent, but it was not something she cared to think about.

She was currently in the preparatory stage of researching and trying out landscapes for a children's collection of legends. There would be arched, stone bridges for trolls to lurk beneath and cliffs and ruined abbeys where wraiths could drift in shadow. She had spent the morning composing combinations of moorland, dry-stone walls and woods, and somehow the grass always turned out tussocky – little hummocks filling the foreground, like molehills.

Pretty enormous moles though, and the hills had funny ridges round them.

Rebecca took her coffee to the saggy brown sofa and wriggled her feet under the cushions. Every little helped.

At least the sky was blue and the sun was out. Rebecca was aware of the weather more than ever before, now that her studio was this room with its wonderful, floor-to-ceiling bay window.

She had been drawn to it at first sight, intrigued by the arched glass projection facing the road, like a miniature conservatory at first-floor level; north-facing, of course – almost certainly the row of terraced houses had been built as artists' studios.

The first time she had come to the flat she had been desperate to see this room and find out what the window was like from the inside, and had felt cheated when she was guided instead into the smaller back room. Now she was living here, her drawing board set up near the lovely window and the sofa dragged round to share the view.

The room was large enough to give plenty of space for living as well as working, and she preferred it to the back room, which was lined with books and furnished with curious, mismatched chairs. That room still felt too much like Michael's, probably because of his books, like a substitute for his presence. Rebecca's own collection – embarrassingly small by comparison – was packed into three short shelves in the studio.

Sometimes she felt like a transient, a temporary tenant passing through. She knew she ought to give thought to the future, decide whether she really wanted the flat and then talk to Michael about how to arrange it or, if not, find somewhere of her own.

But it was complicated. For a start it would require her to go up to Derbyshire as it didn't seem right to ask this without seeing him face to face. And then he, Michael, would have to get active and do things, and it didn't seem quite right to demand this of him either.

So here she was, three years on, still caretaking the place while its owner sat in a cottage in the Peak District reading a different library, the one built by his – their – ancestor.

And what else is he doing?

Rebecca grunted and sipped her coffee. That wasn't a good train of thought: steer away, too many ghosts.

But you can't always order your thoughts. Before she could deflect it, the image had come flashing into her mind's eye, squeezing her stomach as it always did, dragging at her spirits...

Connor.

Where was he now?

With fingers too cold to draw and cosy in the cushions, Rebecca gave in to reflection. She usually managed to avoid thinking about anything difficult, her nature steely and wilful, but there were occasions when the past would demand her attention, payment, perhaps, for allowing itself to be subdued the rest of the time. Then she would accept her lot, allow the memories in, stare out of the window without seeing the houses opposite, and dwell on the strangeness and the secrets.

Three years ago – it seemed incredible it was so long – Rebecca had had a chance meeting with another artist, Michael, while they were both drawing in the Victoria and Albert Museum. In the days that followed, life – Real Life, as she thought of it – had been put on hold and weirdness took over. She discovered that she and Michael were distant cousins and, together with another, shared a responsibility to find a very particular location and then – well, guard it.

This was always one of the trouble areas. Rebecca herself had not completely believed in the idea until she was there, in the cottage, her eyes straining to see through the swirling light into another world. Nobody sane would give it credence.

But it had happened, it really had. Between them, they had found the cottage and, what's more, discovered that they were heirs to the great house and its estate. That was the nice part. Leasing the mansion to a hotel chain had produced a head-turning pile of cash which had opened all sorts of doors of a different, a metaphorical, sort. Rebecca had been able to move out of the bedsit at the top of her great-aunt's house and, since Michael had moved into the cottage, take on the rent for this apartment, which was palatial by comparison. And without the pressure of having to take the first paid job she was offered, she had been able to pick commissions carefully. She had blossomed as an illustrator and stunned the publishing world with her talent and youth.

Thanks in part, she was sure, to those other-world genes.

And all that was fine, rosy, an adventure to be proud of with an outcome to celebrate.

But there had been a third team member, another distant relative: Connor. And Connor had disappeared through the door into the invisible world and not been heard of since.

This was the bad part. This was where Rebecca's stomach contracted and she found she was frowning. She rubbed her face and sighed.

Neither she nor Michael had realised what was in the boy's mind. They knew he was unhappy; they guessed that his home was wretched and that he was intending to leave as soon as his GCSEs were finished, but not that he was so desperate as to leap into the unknown.

Guilt had plagued them both, and Rebecca knew Michael suffered more than she did. He was older, and had kicked the whole thing off, so would carry the greater burden of responsibility. She worried about him when she had time, buried deep in rural Derbyshire, surrounded by the legacy of the traveller who had arrived in this world in the reign of Queen Victoria. She wondered whether he was working on making the doorway usable again.

However, he had moved his woodworking tools up there, had a workshop built and was once again making his beautiful, strange boxes. He couldn't be ill, could he? Not apart from colds and the like. But he was difficult to talk to, somehow – too reserved; kind but much too calm.

There was no one else to discuss him with. Nobody knew about this, not even her father; not even Steph, apart from a little superficial stuff: nothing that would disturb her equanimity.

Steph! Oxford and the Ashmolean! That was the link with Roly Pidgeon's garden.

She excavated the layers of clothing to reach her phone and check her diary: pretty open for the next month, just a meeting of her craft co-operative group and a hair appointment. She was letting her hair grow out of its crop and for the first time in her life was involved in six-weekly haircuts to reshape it. It was fun in some ways – felt very *celeb* to have a professional on her case instead of having someone just run clippers over her head periodically; but it was a bind to have to take over an hour out of her day each time.

Rebecca ran her fingers through her hair while she waited for the call to connect. She pinched a lock and pulled it down, squinting. Four inches, about; definitely needed a trim.

Steph was her dearest and oldest friend, and had stayed on at Oxford to do a doctorate on the presence of humour in eighteenth-century French poetry; not an interest Rebecca could share. They had agreed months ago to visit the Ashmolean Museum when it reopened after its massive rebuilding, and then forgotten about it. This Sunday's colour magazine had included a review of the ground-breaking glass structure that had been shoehorned into the site, and there had been tantalising photographs.

'Steph, it's me. When are you free for the Ashmolean?'

Twenty minutes later, her spirit refreshed by human contact and her fingers warmed by the coffee, Rebecca settled herself back at her drawing board and returned to work. She peeled off the top sheet and laid it on the stack at the side.

What *were* all those molehills?

Chapter Three

'Daniel, do we have a full half-dozen of Hildy's yet?'
'Yes.' He'd filled the last dimple in the carton that morning.
'Good. Janey Harper's coming by today. Well done.'

Well done... It was typical of Patty Colvin to praise him for something that was hardly of his doing. She ran the family much as a good infants' teacher runs a class, with judicious allocation of tasks, careful monitoring and continuous feedback: *That's right. Perhaps you should put it there. Good boy.*

That wasn't fair; she hadn't said 'good boy'.

He had become the farm's temporary egg collector, a suitably low-skilled job like sweeping the yard and doling out hay to the cows. Indoors he unloaded the dishwasher, vacuumed the floors and peeled potatoes. The Colvins got through a lot of potatoes just as they got through a lot of eggs, with omelettes and hash-browns for breakfast every day, although the delicate, minty-green eggs produced by Hildy Hen were saved for sale.

Hildy was the Ameraucana hen; the others were either Leghorns (white eggs) or Rhode Islands (brown). The cows were Jerseys because the dairy barn, which was old like the farmhouse, had been built too small to house the modern, larger Holstein breed; and the two flop-eared goats kept for cheese were Nubians.

Daniel was learning.

The problem was that he knew practically nothing about farming, about animals, about the countryside. The fact that this was the United States and not England was neither here nor there; he'd have been just as lost on a dairy farm in Sussex. He knew where milk came from but had never before lost himself in the placid, forgiving eyes of the cow that supplied it. He had never held in his hand an egg warm from its chicken. It invited re-evaluation.

The Colvins' business was dairy, although for a brief few weeks each year they harvested maple syrup, too, producing sweet amber liquid in the sugar shack up the hill near the tree line. *Colvin Milk and Maple,* announced the painted board by the highway at the end of the drive. Then the farm was busy and could have offered him a job, but the sap only ran in the spring and now, at the dead end of the year, there simply wasn't the work for an extra man.

'Sorry, son, but we don't have the budget for another hand.'

Daniel could see that. Roy and Patty were the oldest generation still working in the business – Roy was in his sixties, not seventies, Daniel having been misled by the farmer's weathered face – but their son, Buddy, and his wife Kim were full time too, and there were still their boys, Robby and Brandon, to share the chores. His predecessor as egg collector was eleven-year-old Katey, who was delighted to hand over the job.

It still amazed Daniel that the family had taken him in, seemingly without discussion, certainly without investigation. That first evening they had been so kind he had come horribly close to weeping. Perhaps they knew.

He had been given a room they called 'the little back', although it seemed large to him, but despite his tiredness that first night, sleep wouldn't come. Some time after midnight he had moved barefoot through the silent house until he found the study, where he stole a blank card from the Rolodex on the leather-topped desk.

After that he managed to get a few hours' sleep, and in the morning he had showered, shaved, and asked how he should get into town.

'You sure you're ready, Dan?' Patty asked, beating eggs for breakfast.

Her use of his name made him uncomfortable. 'I'll be fine. I'd just like to know which direction to walk.'

'Walk? Honey,' Patty shot him a look, her mouth twisted with amusement. 'You can't walk it. You can hitch a ride the next time one of the boys goes in. Now, you like tomatoes with your omelette?'

It seemed nobody needed to go in for days. Daniel suspected a conspiracy, but it was a conspiracy of the most benign kind. And he did feel unfit in more ways than the obvious.

As well as being unused to physical exertion – which included merely walking – he had to rediscover his voice, the language, how to react to people. He needed time to get rid of the dreams, to know that when he went to sleep his brain would rest instead of replaying, over and over, the worst year of his captivity. Strangely, this hadn't afflicted him while he was still being held but had emerged in the last few weeks, and he dreaded the idea that the dreams would plague him forever.

Heaven knew what the Colvins made of him. He was horribly conscious of how he must seem – Patty finding him stalled in front of the Dairy Farmers' calendar hanging on the side of the fridge, for instance, or recoiling from the huge tabby cat when she first came in.

'Never seen a Maine Coon before, Dan? What do you think of her – pretty neat?' Kim had asked.

They'd had every right to think he was wrong in the head.

Kim cut her sons' hair, deft with the scissors and clippers, and when Daniel daringly asked if she would do the same for him she threw the nylon cape over his shoulders and got to work.

His head felt lighter and his neck colder. He hadn't worn his hair this short since primary school, although the last bit of growth had been exceptional, but the face that looked back at him from the mirror was closer to some kind of normal. He'd stand a better chance of getting a job, at least.

He couldn't stay suspended like this, leaning on the kindness of strangers, ignoring the passage of time. He needed to get to England, and for that he needed money. And he needed his passport.

At least he need not berate himself for that. Who would have imagined he'd need a passport when he set out? It was breathtakingly bizarre, when you came to think about it, but awkward too. He would have to telephone his sister, and that was not going to be fun.

After breakfast, Daniel brought the box of cool green eggs out of the cold store and left them in the kitchen for Patty to clean up, then laced up the work boots borrowed from Brandon to go out and hay the cows for the last time.

Chapter Four

Steph's house was warm; even the hall. Rebecca hung her coat on top of someone else's and pulled off her boots. Even the *floor* was warm. She followed her friend into the living room, where kitchen units ran along one wall.

'This is lovely. You have no idea.'

'Yeah, well...We turn it down during the week, but someone's always here at weekends.'

Rebecca perched on the corner of the table and watched Steph boil the kettle and take down mugs.

'How long has the heating been off?'

Rebecca grunted. 'Since Tuesday. They're telling me early next week.' There had been an error in the order for the pump, it seemed, and the gas people were now waiting all over again. The weather was forecast to stay sharply cold; it was a bleak outlook.

'Well, you can always stay here if you like. Nobody'll mind.'

Steph lived in private rented digs, sharing an Edwardian house with three other post-grads. Compared to her austere student budget of a year ago she now had a small income and was comfortably set up; compared to Rebecca's little fortune, she lived in penury.

Warm penury. It was tempting although Steph's communal lifestyle felt alien to Rebecca, who had lived alone for three years now. First in halls and now this shared house, Steph managed to rub along with her flat-mates in a way Rebecca doubted she'd be able to. The current ones were Steph's close friends whom Rebecca had met before, and everyone seemed able to take the best from their situation and close their eyes to the bad – for surely there must be some bad?

'Cards?' Rebecca queried, sweeping them aside and stacking them neatly to make space for the mugs and biscuits.

'Ben's teaching us to play Bridge,' Steph said. '*Trying* to teach us.'

Exactly: sharing skills and having fun.

'Although I could have done with a free evening yesterday,

but they needed a fourth.'

Ah: and there's the rub. Best to live alone and be safe.

'So what are we doing and where are we going?'

The Ashmolean was amazing, like no other museum space Rebecca had experienced – a gloriousness of air and light playing stage to the artefacts. Whereas the Victoria and Albert, Rebecca's long-time favourite, presented a labyrinth of corners and staircases and secrets, the new extension of the Ashmolean allowed each gallery to be seen, tantalizingly, from the one before, pulling you through the rooms, drawing you ever onward – *Look here! And here! And look, there's more!*

In many ways it bore the atmosphere of a coolly classy fashion store, with the result that you felt almost like a consumer. Rebecca wasn't entirely sure she liked that, but it was a wonderful building any way you looked at it.

After a satisfying wander, they boosted their energy with coffee at the café in the undercroft, and then went back out to the street to shake themselves up with a brisk walk. Strolling is always tiring.

The air was still crisp but the sun was out and the sky was powder blue with only minor, unobtrusive clouds. The pavements were packed with Saturday shoppers.

'Where do you want to go?'

'Grass would be good.'

'Christchurch Meadow? Actually that's helpful as Joe's probably training and I could give him the key back…'

Compared with London, Oxford despite its city status felt like the countryside to Rebecca, especially these days when she drove rather than took the train and was aware of the open fields either side of the motorway.

Her windfall wealth had allowed her to pay for driving lessons and then, glory of glories, a BMW Mini, postbox-red, which lived in a resident's parking space on Trentham Road ready to take her on day trips at a moment's notice. Yet even now she rarely left London, confined by her work schedule. She was ambitious.

Opposite the wrought iron gates to the meadow Rebecca's

attention was caught by a painted board in the shape of a rabbit wearing a waistcoat – *the* waistcoat-wearing rabbit. He was propped against a shop front, staring at his watch on its chain. 'The Alice Shop,' she read, and gave a little huff of disapproval.

Steph noticed. 'What? Alice? What's wrong?'

'I've never liked it. Kind of Victorian Roald Dahl.'

'Oh no, you didn't like him either, did you?'

In literature they had very different tastes. Rebecca shrugged. It was true she hadn't found much to enjoy in Alice even as a child, but worse was the concept of falling into another world where who-knew-what could happen, which was deeply uncomfortable now. She really didn't want to explain.

'Okay, so falling forever is not a nice thought,' Steph was saying, 'but climbing through a mirror is fantastic, isn't it?'

Not *fantastic* as in *good*, Rebecca thought, although intriguing, yes. It had its appeal. Although *mirror* was sadly another of those no-go concepts these days.

She carried altogether too much baggage.

Dogs were tearing up and down the sandy path, a Dalmatian bounding about with two terriers and a little hairy thing streaming in its wake; joggers and cyclists wove amongst the walkers. Rebecca noticed a woman sketching near the river-bank and automatically followed her gaze to check out her view – a couple of dank red cattle loafing near a tip-tilted water trough beyond the rail fence.

Steph looked too, and when safely out of earshot said, 'Weird – she's got the cathedral on one side and the river on the other, and she's drawing cows in mud.'

'But that's what you do. You don't just draw the pretty stuff, you record what is there and then fiddle with it later if you need to. I'm collecting landscapes at the moment...I keep drawing molehills.'

'*Molehills?*'

'And thorns.'

Not vines, though, so that was a relief.

Steph ran up the outside staircase of the boathouse to where a couple of extremely well-built guys were being impressive with weights, and Rebecca went and stood on the pontoon, partly to feel the strange movement of it and partly to get a different view of the bank. Gloucester, Steph's college, shared a boathouse near the end of the row; beyond, the Cherwell met the Thames at an angle, shadowed by willows. On the very edge, a little apart from the others, a tree Rebecca couldn't identify caught her eye.

It was striking – three trunks emerging in a gentle fan from the wide bole, clearly hacked across years before, and another two leaning further out. Double trunks are common enough, maybe even triples, but five was rare, surely?

In fact, not just rare; there was something wrong with it. Rebecca paused and frowned. It looked different...

But there ought not to be a baseline for the tree to be looking different *from*. It wasn't as if she'd been here before. Yet the sloping trunks and trailing boughs seemed unwontedly familiar, as if seen recently. Very recently.

Déjà vu?

And yet the angles seemed wrong, or the background did, or...

'What are they up to?'

Steph had come back out.

Rebecca followed her friend's gaze across the river to where three figures were grouped around the wooden porch of another boathouse, standing alone on the opposite bank.

Three men, bizarrely all wearing gowns over their coats – a touch over the top, Rebecca thought.

'Who are they?' she asked.

'Well, they're academics, obviously,' Steph said.

'Academics? You mean Dons?'

Steph shrugged. 'If you like. It's a pretty loose term, I think. I know the tall one – I went to a lecture he gave on Shakespeare's lost years. Missing years, I mean. Weird stuff. I think he lives somewhere around here, but what they're doing at the boathouse, goodness knows.'

They watched. The three old Dons seemed a bit excited,

although it was impossible to see what about.

Steph said, 'Found the rabbit-hole, perhaps.'

Rebecca shuddered. Clouds had been gathering and the sunshine had gone, taking its thin winter warmth with it. She pulled her collar higher against the chill.

One of the Dons glanced across the river in their direction and for a moment seemed to stare. Rebecca met his look, disbelieving that he could really be interested in her. She saw him jab his elbow into his companion's ribs and point, and realized, with a little dip of shock, that they were both – all three now in fact – definitely looking at her.

Or Steph, surely?

'They're looking at you,' Steph said. 'I wonder why.'

Rebecca's stomach felt cold. She started walking back up the towpath.

'No, they're not.'

Not still, anyway; surely not still?

Walk away. Walk away.

Back on the street, Steph said, 'So are you staying?'

Rebecca thought about her icy bed and then Steph's toasty sitting room, kettle, cards and all. She deserved a quiet weekend.

'Yes please,' she said. 'That will be nice.'

Chapter Five

The kindness hung there right to the last.

'Keep that number safe and call if things don't work out,' Roy told him as they pulled up next to Wilson's Supermarket and Pharmacy.

'I will.'

'Dan, I mean it.'

'I know. I will.'

And he would, if he absolutely had to. But he'd have to be on his knees first.

The Colvins had finally relented and allowed him into town. He was still kitted out in their charity, wearing a sweatshirt and boots from Robby and one of Buddy's old coats, a heavy-duty canvas job with padding and deep, bellowed pockets. His jeans and tee-shirt were his own, and he had ducked the gloves. It had seemed a matter of personal dignity that he not be given gloves as well, although it would probably turn out to be a mistake. Well, he'd just bury his hands in his sleeves.

How he'd return them he didn't yet know.

'Don't worry, those things are all grown out of anyway.'

It was true the Colvin boys were both taller already than he was but there was principle at stake.

However, letting him leave wearing what he had arrived in would have been tantamount to manslaughter, so Daniel had accepted it all, even the fifty dollars in bank notes Patty tucked into his pocket.

'Just to get you started. Pay us back when you can.'

Burlington was the largest city in Vermont, with a population according to Roy of around forty thousand. It was large enough and busy enough for casual jobs to be on offer even for the utterly unskilled, but the University of Vermont stood on the edge of the town, which meant it was a student city and Daniel would have competition. And unlike the students, he didn't have anywhere to stay.

The day was grey; temperatures had lifted since his sudden

arrival. 'That's Vermont,' Patty had said. 'People round here say *if you don't like the weather just wait five minutes!*' The air was mild and rain had replaced the snow, which was both good – drier underfoot, less chilling – and bad – gloomy and without charm. The road from the supermarket was wet from the morning shower and few pedestrians were about. Daniel turned up the corduroy collar of his – Buddy's – coat and stuffed his hands deep into the pockets.

What could he do? He'd have a go at anything but what could he offer in return – what selling points did he have in his favour?

Willingness; the ability to learn; *need.* Was need a selling point? Would a potential employer notice?

He was stronger, at least. His work on the farm had built up quite quickly until he was pulling his weight – or almost – at the purely manual stuff. He knew he was much fitter even after only a fortnight, and being fit had the knock-on effect of lightening his spirits.

Despite the clouds and statistics, Daniel felt cheerful.

For a while.

The gas station had no problem with his lack of experience but wasn't hiring; next door, Madsen's Tire and Service Center was hiring but couldn't use anyone unskilled. There were a couple of small factories which had no casual jobs going, followed by a bakery and an electrical wholesaler likewise, and then he was pretty much in the centre of town and the shops had started.

Nobody wanted a sales or stockroom assistant.

Daniel worked his way along, going into every shop and eatery. The restaurants made his guts growl, and at two o'clock he lodged himself next to a downpipe in a narrow alley and ate his way through Patty's tuna sandwiches, leaning against a brick wall.

He had no idea at all where or when the next food would come.

No joy at the bookshop (wouldn't that have been nice?) or Mike's Cameras or a shop full of country clothing and sheepskins, but the next building was Papa Angel's Restaurant and Bar, and Daniel struck gold.

* * *

'Geoffrey, thank you, it has been so lovely to see everyone again, you're looking *very* well, such a sad occasion.'

Another little old lady patted his sleeve. No idea who.

'Look after yourself, Geoffrey. God bless.'

All these women who seemed to think they knew him.

'Good turn out for the old girl!'

And a few old codgers.

'Lovely sermon.'

Lovely sermon, beautiful flowers, wonderful music…

'Excellent spread, old boy!'

Oh yes, and good sandwiches.

Foster had booked The Rose for the wake, one of the smaller hotels between the cemetery and Finchley tube station, on the basis that most of the guests would be on foot – 'mourners' seemed too strong a word for the chatty bunch tucking cheerfully into smoked salmon and cucumber. A fair number looked decrepit and had taken taxis; perhaps he should have booked a minibus. His aunt clearly had a lot of friends.

Or acquaintances, at any rate. She had been an enthusiastic committee member with tentacles in practically every animal charity you could name from saving the sloth to re-homing battery hens. Quite a lot of the guests had stray hairs on their black coats.

He had had the cats put down.

'Such a shock for you, Geoffrey. Will you be alright?'

It had been unexpected, but a surprise more than a blow. At barely seventy his mother's sister had been in robust health and enjoying her husband's fortune after his coronary. He remembered her as a game old girl, much more assertive and confident than his mother, no doubt the influence of fifty years married to a wealthy man in charge of his own business rather than the middle-management man his father had been.

Then her hired holiday car had been met head on by a drunk driver in Provence. Both parties were killed outright, but the authorities didn't have much doubt where the blame lay.

Quite a hassle to bring the body back, but it had seemed the decent thing.

The real shock lay in discovering that he was – bar the smattering of bequests to fur-and-feather charities – the sole beneficiary of her will, including a very marketable house in Camden Square.

Not the company, though, which had been sold on his uncle's retirement; shame, as he'd have quite fancied a go at that.

Geoffrey sneaked a surreptitious glance at his watch: four fifteen. Well, their lookout if they got hung up in the rush hour. He would be at Camden Square overnight, a short walk away.

The discreet navy-blue figure of the functions manageress materialised at his elbow. 'Is everything satisfactory, Mr Foster?'

'Yes, yes,' Geoffrey said. 'Very satisfactory indeed, thank you.'

The phone was in Angel's office, up the stairs between the potted palms, overlooking the yard at the back. Angel pushed the phone across the desk and left him in private.

Daniel was once again adrift on the tide of American kindness toward strangers. He had asked for the cost of the call to be taken out of his wages, but Angel, third-generation with dark eyes but no trace of an Italian accent, waved this aside. 'Your sister, right? Letting her know where you are? The call is free, but then you get yourself a phone, okay?'

Angel was the Papa Angel of the business, as his father had been until he died. This Angel – Angelo Conti – was, at thirty-four, unconvincingly young for the title, but he had three daughters under the age of ten, so it wasn't a lie.

And he had a paternal spirit.

Daniel had arrived the day after one of the restaurant's dish machine operators had broken his leg playing ice hockey and landed himself in traction. Never having operated a dish machine before, Daniel was not ideal, but Angelo took a chance on him.

It was washing up, basically, only using machinery. There was a lot of it to be done, and he and his work partner fed the steaming steel chamber by conveyor belt and removed the hot crockery and cutlery and glasses at the other end.

There were rules, of course. You had to stack carefully so that the sprays could reach all areas, and you had to be careful not to handle the clean stuff where it would come into contact with food. You had to check for chips and cracks, and you had to learn to add cleaning and water-softening chemicals at the right rate. He was kept surprisingly busy.

It helped him avoid thinking.

Astonishingly, when he asked Angelo where he might find a hostel his new boss solved that problem too.

'Where you living now?'

'I'm – I don't have anywhere. I just arrived.'

Angel scowled. 'You ain't running away, Dan? You ain't in trouble?'

'No, nothing like that. I was robbed by some people I hitched a lift with, that's all. I need to work to save up enough to get home. To England.'

He had perfected the story now.

Angel scratched his head. 'Well, we got a spare room. If you can work a couple more hours in the shift, you can have the room free.'

And so Daniel became live-in staff, with eleven dollars an hour cash in hand (no paperwork), pickings from the kitchen to eat, and one full day off a week when he could wander around Burlington's concrete pavements, marvelling at how few weeds were managing to push their way through the cracks, and plan his exodus. And the first step for that was to ring home.

Daniel dialled the international code and then the number he would probably never forget, and listened to the ringing tone, his heart banging in his chest. This was as hard a call as he had ever had to make. He might even faint, it was so hard.

He skirted the desk and dropped into Angel's revolving chair, just in case.

The ringing tone stopped. 'Hallo?'

His sister had picked it up, thank God, and her voice was so familiar, so unchanged despite all that had happened to him, that for a moment he was speechless. Then he croaked, cleared his throat, and started again: 'Hallo. It's me.'

Chapter Six

Rebecca's quiet weekend didn't last very long. The flat was certainly warm and the company convivial, but *quiet* went out the window just after midnight as she was drifting towards sleep in the warm cocoon of the sleeping bag.

They had cooked pasta for supper, a big pot as all three of Steph's flat-mates were eating in, and then the five of them had walked to the pub where they were lucky enough to grab the table near the hearth. The pub – The Explosion – was an independent, with books on the shelf above a proper log fire and a podgy Labrador that wormed its way around the chair legs, begging for titbits. Tom rubbed the Labrador's neck, massaging behind his ears while the dog winced his appreciation.

'How're you doing, Flash, old man?'

'Flash!' The dog didn't exactly look the running kind.

'He eats chocolates in a flash.'

College talk was kept to a minimum in deference to their guest, and when it did creep in – people she hadn't met, events she hadn't been to – Rebecca was content to sit back and enjoy the quirky atmosphere. Her local on Trentham Road was plush by comparison (carpets, polished mirrors, framed prints of fifties jazz stars) and also dead boring.

Most of her friends in London belonged to the artists' co-operative with which she exhibited, her small silk panels in box frames quite different from her illustration work, and the nearest of those lived two tube stops away. That was fine; Rebecca was used to travelling to seek company. But living amongst your friends was an appealing idea.

Although it might also be a nuisance at times.

Rebecca suspected she was, at heart, a loner.

The talk had come round to rowing, which both Tom and Steph were involved in at college level.

'How much training do you have to do?' Rebecca asked. Steph had always been pretty fit, going hill-walking in the Lakes with her parents, and even midnight rambling, she recalled.

Steph rolled her eyes. 'Some. Not weights. I run most days. I have to show up for Sunday morning training, though.'

'In the Third Eight just rowing more or less does it,' Ben said. 'Only First Eight train.'

'Do you row?'

'Used to. I've started liking my bed more.'

'Oh, yes, speaking of beds, can Rebecca borrow your sleeping bag tonight?' Steph asked, and the conversation had moved on.

Ben's sleeping bag was a serious one, made for getting trapped on a mountain, and Rebecca felt constricted and over-warm (which made a change). It was difficult getting sleepy to begin with, and then, as she felt herself beginning to drift, there was a shriek and a clatter from the street followed by shouting.

For a second or two Rebecca wondered whether she was going to ignore it, but as the noise continued she struggled out of the warm puffiness and padded to the window.

The street was well lit. Four doors down a bicycle was lying on its side half on, half off the pavement, rear wheel spinning slowly. A man – Rebecca couldn't tell what age – was standing in the road, his feet spread and his knees flexed, poised; his hands were splayed in front of him and he was facing the narrow path between the houses beyond the lamplight.

A car had pulled up a little further along and the driver was walking back, his car door left open. He seemed excited and was talking, but Rebecca couldn't make out the words through the double-glazing. When he reached the cyclist they both stood staring into the narrow opening.

It was chilly. Rebecca shivered and looked around for her sweater; over the back of the sofa. She pulled it round her shoulders, and returned to the window, twitching the curtain again.

Movement. Rebecca jumped and both men sprang back, and there was a scrabble as a dark shape, long and low, barrelled out of the alleyway and balked, dodging the men, before taking off up the road. Rebecca heard its feet as it passed the house, pounding.

What the hell was that?

It looked as though the men in the street were asking the same thing. Gestures were made and heads shaken, shoulders shrugged. Then the driver returned to his car and the cyclist picked up his fallen bike, checked the front wheel and rode off.

Rebecca closed the curtains. Bizarre.

Now her feet were cold.

She chucked her sweater back on the sofa and wriggled into the sleeping bag. Warmer than outside but it would take a few minutes to get back to that sleepy cave.

She fidgeted, found a good spot, and closed her eyes.

Whatever kind of animal had that been?

Between the walls, behind the bins that smelled of refuse, under the iron steps in the deepest shadow the boy crouched, controlling his breathing, not moving but listening. He heard the men's voices and knew that the tallixer was going to make her break a moment before she moved, and that he wouldn't be able to restrain her. He felt her draw breath.

He held his own.

Then she leapt, springing into the light and away, leaving the two men confounded and helpless to give chase.

Do not move. Do not breathe.

He waited until the men left with their wheeled vehicles and the street was quiet. Then he waited until there was no more movement behind the window across the way.

And then he waited some more, just to be certain.

'*What* kind of animal?'

'Big,' Rebecca said around her toast. 'Black. Fast.'

'Couldn't have been Flash on the loose?'

'I said fast.'

No-one else had been disturbed. The bedrooms were all at the back of the house, looking out over the tiny yard where the bicycles were kept alongside the wheelie bins and the rotary clothes-line. Rebecca suspected she was not wholly believed.

She had slept well eventually, despite the close fit of the sleeping bag, but remembered the animal as soon as she awoke. It had been...singular. It was disturbing that she still wasn't sure what the creature was. From the admittedly awkward perspective of the first floor looking down, it had appeared big, bigger than any dog except, possibly, a Great Dane, and much bulkier. It could have been bigger. It wasn't a pony, though – the feet hadn't sounded like hooves.

'Unshod?' Steph asked with the voice of experience because she'd ridden as a child and knew about such things. 'Take a horse's shoes off and they sound quite soft. Muffled. Not clip-cloppy at all.'

'It didn't move like a horse.'

Rebecca saw in her mind's eye the bounding run of the animal, the creature, with its round head and short neck. It wasn't a pony, she was sure.

'Oh well.' Steph shrugged. 'How long are you here for? I've got to row this morning but I don't have anything planned for the afternoon.'

The thing was that if you hadn't experienced it yourself, you wouldn't be gripped by the same excitement. Perhaps "gripped" was overstating it; "held", perhaps, was closer. But Rebecca was definitely held. A guy falling off his bike and another guy stopping to help, that was commonplace, but the creature, that – beast... It had been so *black*, like clotted shadow, like something carved from the night, like...like something mythical...

They were washing up the breakfast things when Steph had a call which made her catch her breath.

'You're kidding!'

It seemed whoever it was wasn't.

'Wow.'

Rebecca looked interrogative.

Steph said, 'The boathouse has burned down. Totally.'

'What, your boathouse?' Rebecca pictured the square, flat-roofed buildings they had walked past.

'No, no, not our boathouse; *the* boathouse: the University boathouse. On the other bank.'

Ah, the one all by itself, Rebecca thought, and felt her stomach drop several inches straight down.

The boathouse the three old Dons had been on; in; *at*. Why should that bother her?

Steph said, 'I'm off anyway. D'you want to come?'

Rebecca trailed after her, reluctant. 'Is that a good idea?'
'Sure, why not?' Steph reached for her boots.
'I might…get in the way.' It sounded lame even to herself.
'Okay, see you later then.'
But of course she went.

It wasn't yet ten o'clock but Oxford was alive with churchgoers and Sunday shoppers, and they were not the only ones to have heard about the fire. There were others with them on the towpath.

The chill wind was unpleasant in Rebecca's ears; the weather had sharpened overnight and she wished she'd brought a scarf.

The damage was catastrophic; the building had been made of wood and very little was left. There was a pile, not high but widespread, of blackened, ashy pieces and twisted, scorched stuff that hadn't been able to burn – the remains of the water tank, plumbing and kitchen things. The grass around was scorched and there was a smell of charred wood.

Sightseers had gathered and were watching from a distance as men in fluorescent jackets tied tape to posts between the back of the wreckage, furthest from the bank, and a building behind.

'That's funny,' Steph said. 'I've never noticed that before.'

It was a house, red brick and plain fronted, with sash windows and a central chimney. It must have been completely hidden by the boathouse in front and by the mature chestnuts either side.

Steph said, musingly, 'I'd have thought I'd have noticed it when I was rowing. But then you don't look sideways much.'

The tape was being brought down towards the riverbank now, where the pontoon floated wanly redundant on the dark water. The towpath beyond was temporarily closed off.

Steph needed to get to the Gloucester boathouse on the north side of the river, so they trudged back, climbing up to the street for a quick blast of exhaust fumes on Folly Bridge before dropping back down to the opposite towpath.

Steph ran up the stairs to join her crew and Rebecca began to follow, and then paused. There was activity on the far bank downstream of the wreckage which had been invisible before. In the space between the cottage and the heap of ruins, right up against the tape that had just been stretched across, someone was at work.

Rebecca peered, frowning. That wasn't just a pile of bricks, it was a structure. The man must be a bricklayer.

She watched, eyes straining, as the man added another brick to the row, and then another.

He was building a wall. A little wall, only two feet high and barely three feet long, but already there were two other little walls forming three sides of a square.

'What on earth…?'

Steph had come back to watch, but Rebecca ignored her. Her guts were squeezing and making her queasy. She watched the bricklayer complete the row and begin a new wall at right-angles – the fourth wall, which would complete the square.

No.

It was a stupid, purposeless, miniature room made of brick, one metre square, and the bricklayer was going to add a roof, she knew it. He was going to fix it tight and seal the gaps, and no doubt go home bemused but pleased with the cash for a Sunday morning's work.

It can't be.

But it was so like…

Rebecca dragged her gaze away from the brick cell and saw the three Dons, the tall one in the middle, wearing their gowns even now, even here. They were standing withdrawn, perhaps taking shelter from the wind, but there was no mistaking their interest.

Perhaps they lived there, in the red brick house; that would make sense. But sense of what kind?

As she watched, the Don nearest the bank, stoop-shouldered and crow-like in his black folds, turned to face her, and once again she felt his stare.

Chapter Seven

Daniel was counting seagulls.

They liked to congregate on the railings near the steps to the pontoon, and this afternoon there were more than usual: a Friday thing, perhaps. He hadn't seen his crippled friend recently and, stupidly, it was bothering him.

A one-legged seagull shouldn't figure in the broad scheme of his life, such as it was, but he'd have liked to know it was still in the game, hadn't been defeated by the unremitting grind of struggling on when the odds are against you.

The marina was quiet but in an hour the buzz would begin as the bankers and stockbrokers and lawyers arrived with provisions for a couple of days' sailing, or came to take stock of what was needed for a weekend of maintenance – stripping engines, repairing chipped wood, re-varnishing. Running a boat saw off a lot of free time, it seemed.

Daniel had been watching the marina for a week.

His passport had arrived by post thanks to his sister, who was still more or less on his side despite three years of silence.

(Yes, three. Think about that later.)

Along with the passport had come an international money order for three hundred and forty pounds, which was probably everything in his sister's bank account and which would enable him to buy his way to England. He would repay her, obviously, although he had no idea how.

One problem still remained. His passport did not show any record of his immigration into the United States, and if he tried to exit he'd enjoy a short, quick march to some kind of detention for suspected malefactors or even terrorists. At all costs he was going to avoid that ever happening to him again.

This lack of immigration processing had been a constant worry, eating at him all the time he was loading and unloading Angel's dishwashing machine and babysitting the kids, but he had a solution at last – he hoped.

A conversation between clients overheard by chance had

given him a lead. Two men were bidding each other goodnight, and one was saying that he'd soon be sailing to the Bahamas to over-winter.

'Call next time you're this way,' the other said. 'Say hi to Boston for me!'

Boston. So people sailed from Boston to the Bahamas in the autumn. Did the Bahamas need you to have a visa?

He asked Angel, in what he hoped was a casual, roundabout way, and Angel said no. 'People go all the time. Rich guys. All the east coast ports. Nice life, huh?'

Daniel had access to the internet these days, welcome to sit at the Conti's PC in the morning if nobody else needed it. He had offered to pay for the cost of logging in.

'*Pay?* Danny, Danny, you never heard of broadband?'

So now he was sounding even more eccentric.

Within minutes he had found more information on his small, specific area of interest than he had dreamed would be available: forums where enthusiasts offered advice to one another; FAQ pages run by yacht manufacturers; marina regulations. It was amazing.

People with yachts – *rich guys* – kept them at marinas on the coast, and many chose to avoid the snowy New England winters in favour of the tropics. They would make their way south close to the coast, wait about in Florida until the weather conditions were right, and then hop across to the islands in not much over a day and a night.

And this was the crucial bit: he could enter the Bahamas from the United States legally without running into trouble over his unmarked passport, and from the Bahamas he could get a plane home.

All he had to do was persuade one of these rich people to take him as a passenger – a non-paying passenger, because even with his sister's three hundred and forty pounds it was going to take most of his pay from Papa Angel's to buy the plane ticket, one of the reasons he'd been working every hour Angel offered.

He had collected enough, he thought, to give it a try. He gave Angel his notice and was shocked and overwhelmed to receive a farewell lunch after the main rush had finished, which included a tray cake, baked by Maria with *Adios Danny* piped in green icing across the top. He couldn't remember ever having had a party before, and it was difficult to stay light. He felt shaky, like on the day he landed in Vermont, and was relieved when Maria brought it to an end so she could pick up the kids from day-care.

He hitch-hiked to Boston, found a temporary hostel which was cheap – parting with any of his carefully hoarded money was painful – and began his stake-out of the marina.

And here he was, ten days later, on familiar terms with individual seagulls but still no closer to getting away from the mainland.

No-one wanted an unskilled deck-hand. No-one wanted a paying passenger either – they were by and large, as Angel had said, rich.

Not all of them though, or at least, not all filthy-rich. One of the yachts, *The White Rabbit*, was actually lived in. He had noticed that the family went the opposite way to everyone else, leaving the quay in the morning and returning at night. He guessed the parents were in their early thirties, and there was a boy and a girl, not yet school-age.

He had watched the family a lot, partly because they were there a lot to be watched, and partly because they seemed somehow more approachable, more sympathetic than the other yacht-owners. The father departed each day wearing a suit and the mother lived in jeans and a fleece. He even knew the children's names: Josh and Abigail, Abi for short.

He had overheard them talking about sailing to the Bahamas for a pre-Christmas vacation. If only they could have taken him along...

But he'd tried and the rebuff had been decisive. 'I'm sorry, we don't take passengers.'

'I'll work,' he had said. 'I'll help with anything.'

But if the positions were reversed, would he take an unknown tramp on board his family's boat?

At least his hair was short now, and he shaved. No-one would know he was wearing the same clothes under his coat every day, periodically washed and dried overnight. Apart from the look in the eyes that met him in the bathroom mirror, he presented a reasonable face to the world, didn't he?

The dog that roamed the quayside sometimes – he hadn't worked out who owned it – was sniffing its way enthusiastically along the wall of the marina office, pausing frequently to widdle. It was one of those short-legged terriers with fold-over ears, and like most dogs seemed to enjoy life. No worries, it seemed to say.

Daniel envied it.

Although there had been no rain, the sky had been overcast all day and low clouds threatened thunder. The children from *The White Rabbit* came into view first, allowed to ride their bikes on the quayside despite the drop to the water. Daniel supposed they had been well-imbued with harbour savvy since birth and probably swam like penguins. He had noticed that any friends that visited had to wear child-sized orange life-jackets.

Abi, the younger of the two, rode her pink and white bike sedately alongside her mother, plastic streamers dangling from the handlebars. Josh tore along the strip from the town with his knees pumping, throwing in the occasional showy skid.

In a way it was a pity that they were so competent around water. How would it be if, say, little Abi toppled over the edge into the deep, cold ocean, and Daniel leapt in after her? From where he stood on the edge of the concrete, staring down into the depths, the sea looked easily up to drowning a small child. Would that have earned him his passage to the islands?

But of course she wouldn't. She was now pedalling thoughtful, wobbly circles and singing to herself like Angel's daughter Karina. Her mother had reached their boat and was walking along the pontoon. 'If it starts to rain you come and get your slickers!'

Daniel looked up at the ever-darkening sky, where the storm clouds were piling up, heavy with water. He'd get soaked on the way to the hostel if he hung around much longer.

'Hey!'

There was a sudden scutter of doggy feet on concrete and the screech of skidding rubber, and something hit Daniel hard in both legs – left shin, right ankle. He had a lightning glimpse of the boy's face, close up beneath him, and the yellow bike at an unlikely angle, and then knew he was falling.

Easily up to drowning a child.

But I'm not a child.

As he hit the surface on his back, Daniel pictured Buddy's padded coat filling up with water, knew it was years since he had swum – swimming pools charge entrance fees – and thought, *but you never forget, do you?*

Then his head met something much harder than the water, and he ceased thinking of anything at all.

Chapter Eight

Rebecca, back in London and supposedly drawing waterfalls, stared out of the tall arched window instead.

She was not happy. Oxford had unsettled her.

It was not the stare of the three eccentric Dons that was distracting her; although that was bad, it was not the worst. What haunted her was that brick box, like a miniature cell built around absolutely nothing. Or at least nothing visible.

Or at least nothing visible *then.*

A story was going round about the statue, *The Head of the River,* a bronze Eights boat at an unlikely angle close to vertical, which needed, everyone said, to be back on a plinth as soon as possible for the sake of tradition.

So soon that a replacement plinth was being built for it before the ruins had even been cleared?

Oh well, maybe the enthusiasm was a little wacky but that was the thought behind it, end of puzzle.

Rebecca didn't believe it.

She had watched the three Dons watching the bricklayer, and there had been more than the honour of a statue at stake. There had been anxiety, or at least unease: something very uncomfortable indeed and connected to that space inside the rising walls.

And she thought she knew what it was.

Steph had emailed on Monday evening after Rebecca had left, saying the city was awash with sightings of a mysterious beast, almost certainly the animal Rebecca had seen through the window.

Rebecca had gone on-line to check the news and had been disturbed to find not only stories about sheep with their throats torn out and missing pet cats, but also a plea for information on a man who had been seen interacting with the animal believed responsible.

There were a handful of photos, most of which had been taken from a distance on mobile phones and were fuzzy and vague, and one rather better which Rebecca peered at closely.

His hair was dark, that was definite. And he was young. She

didn't recognize the clothes, though.

Rebecca sighed, put down her pencil and went to make a cup of coffee. The business of filling a kettle, spooning out granules, stirring in milk was always soothing. Mug in hand, she gave herself a break from working, or at any rate trying to work, and curled up on the sofa instead.

The pump for the central heating had been installed and the flat was warm again. She was happy to be there now, but the question was: should she go to Oxford and knock on the front door of that house that Steph had never noticed before – nor most people, it seemed – or should she drive up to Derbyshire and knock on Michael's front door instead?

Oh Lord.

The problem was that she wanted to speak to him, needed to speak to him, but was afraid. She had been to stay for a few days a year ago – no, fifteen months – and had found him too quiet, too polite, for comfort. He had always been somehow contained, but he seemed to have retreated even further into himself since the difficult days when they had been working together to find and then seal the...door. Gap. Whatever you wanted to call it.

It probably wasn't healthy for him to be living in the cottage where a wall covered with mirrors concealed the door to a stone room much, much too like the little brick cell on the Oxford riverbank. But he wanted to, and how could she interfere again when she had meddled so much already?

The basic problem was the one it had always been: she was, at root, a little afraid of him, and also, in her heart, a little in love with him. It wasn't a comfortable combination.

It was all made messier and more worrying by the fact that he had become very bad at replying to email, and despite the fact that mobile coverage was very poor at Ashendon he hadn't installed a land line.

I could just ignore it.

Rebecca sipped her coffee.

She could. She could turn the proverbial blind eye. Nobody else seemed to think it impossibly, ridiculously strange that the brick box had been built before the timbers had stopped smouldering. Steph hadn't wondered why the Dons had seemed to be staring at her.

Maybe it really was a plinth for a statue.

Rebecca drove to Oxford.

She hadn't told Steph. It was Wednesday and her friend would be working, although that wasn't the reason. She didn't want to have to explain or argue but just wanted to get on with it. If she was wrong and there was nothing going on after all, well, maybe then she could drop in at Wellesley Street and they could celebrate.

Rebecca walked briskly along the towpath, committed to her chosen course, afraid to hesitate in case her nerve deserted her. It was another dull day, with a heavy sky and a gathering breeze which chased the geese and moorhens along the river and set the bare branches stirring. She had waited until the afternoon, figuring it would give her a better chance of catching them at home, and dusk was going to come early.

The site of the boathouse was still taped off. She supposed it took a few days to organize clearing up a mess like this. The pile of rubble had stopped smoking but remained as black as she remembered; the terracotta bricks of the plinth – or cell – peeped over the top, new and jauntily orange. Rebecca noticed that the statue had yet to be set on top, despite tradition.

She turned her back deliberately on the rubble and strode up to the door.

It seemed ordinary enough, just a nineteenth-century brick house beginning to look a bit shabby. The ochre-coloured paint was flaking away from the windowsills and the downpipe at the corner was a touch off vertical. The curtains hung limp and motionless behind the uneven glass of the windows. A name was spelled in scrolling black iron letters screwed to the brickwork: *The Ferry House*.

Rebecca mounted the steps and stood on the coir doormat.

Do it.

There was a door knocker in the centre of the door – a mermaid, her tresses artfully arranged to retain her modesty, her scaly tail arching to coquettish flukes. Rebecca lifted her and let her fall on the plate beneath, then breathed in and out once very deeply and straightened her shoulders.

She waited.

They've got to be in. If they're not in...

A swish of wheels on the towpath behind her made her glance round. Two cycles: one speedy, ridden by a thin guy in Lycra, and one more sedate with a basket under the handlebars and a rider wearing a skirt. When they had gone it was very quiet – Rebecca could see figures across the river near one of the college boathouses, but otherwise she was alone.

Nobody knows I'm here.

She hadn't thought to tell anyone. Of course she wouldn't normally issue bulletins on her personal schedule, but this was...perhaps less than wise?

Rebecca was reaching for her phone when the door opened with a scrape of the latch. She span round and looked through the narrow gap into the eyes of the Don she thought of as the middle one – not the very tall one and not the little, thin one. He was carrying a bit of weight although quite tidily, and when he saw her his eyes widened.

'Ah!'

He opened wide the door.

'Come in, my child, come in!'

And there had been no time to call anyone.

Chapter Nine

Daniel watched the light dip and swing, gently dappled, playing over the varnished wood, swaying with a gentle motion that echoed the dip and rock beneath him. Sound informed him where he was: the distant, open-air cry of birds and someone calling on the quayside, and the close-up slap of water against the hull.

The light had been too bright at first and he had used his forearm to shield his eyes, but that had worn off along with the sickness and headache, leaving just tiredness.

Although by now the tiredness might be from lying down for too long. Daniel checked the green figures on the digital clock set into the wall beside him: 16:03. There was time for a walk on shore before dusk if he wanted one.

Carefully, he rolled over and inched his way to the top end of the mattress. The bed was built into the cabin, tapering at the toe where it fitted into the bows, and there was less than a metre of floor between it and the sliding door into the living quarters, which he had already learned was called the saloon.

The boat was precision-designed like a watch, or perhaps a Chinese puzzle box, every centimetre of space utilized to the max. Impressive.

Daniel had never been on a yacht before, nor really on any kind of boat, although when he was ten he and Andy, one of his very few school friends, had enjoyed – more or less – a brief trip in Andy's uncle's battered rowing boat, its outboard motor belching black fumes. It had been nothing like *The White Rabbit.*

He couldn't quite believe that he was here.

They had told him what had happened and he couldn't remember any of it. Slouching against the pillar where the lifebelts hung and wondering where his hopeless one-legged seagull had gone was the last memory he could drag up. The next thing he had been aware of was the cold concrete under his backside and the perpendicular ridge of the lifebelt stand against his spine, and his eyes being stabbed by the daylight. Try as he might, he could not recall anything about the marina dog taking off after a cat, barrelling across the quay and causing Josh to swerve at speed straight into him, apparently standing idiotically close to the edge.

He'd gone in and bashed his head against the outboard motor of the dinghy, which had knocked him out cold and given him mild concussion – at least, mild enough not to be forcibly admitted to hospital.

Laura – Josh and Abi's mother – knew first aid, as did her husband. *('Two young children living on a boat? Of course we trained!')* They were certified lifeguards too. Having dived in and retrieved his unconscious, sinking body she had then done all the right checks and asked all the proper questions when he came round two minutes later, sprawled on the concrete and freezing…including the question about medical insurance.

He vaguely recollected admitting he had none, and no family or friends either.

At that point, efficient and businesslike with the dopey, bleeding stranger on her hands, Laura had shepherded him onto her boat, manhandling him with impressive competence along the swaying pontoon and down the narrow steps into the cabin, where she helped him out of his drenched top layers and discreetly left him to get into dry clothes belonging to her husband.

By the time he emerged, still disorientated but slightly less queasy, she also had changed and had loaded her kids into the Volkswagen. Within sixty seconds they were zipping through the Boston streets to the walk-in unit of the huge city hospital. There, a doctor who looked and sounded as if she could have been Laura's twin shone lights into his eyes and interrogated him before pronouncing it safe for him to remain an outpatient.

The examination cost money, and Laura paid it.

'It's no big deal. Don't worry about it.'

'I've got some money.'

'Daniel, it was less than eighty bucks. Forget about it.'

So she had worked out that he was broke.

Even as he was offering to pay it occurred to him that his preciously hoarded money – and his passport – were probably at the bottom of the marina, lost forever in the mud six metres down, and he was back to square one, only worse.

But later, back on board *The White Rabbit*, he found the sealed plastic bag still in the zipped pocket of Buddy Colvin's saturated jacket, and the seal had held.

Miracle One.

After that the miracles followed thick and fast.

He had been allowed to leave the hospital on the strength of Laura's being a qualified first-aider and competent to recognize if his symptoms worsened over the next seventy-two hours. But the family was scheduled to set sail the following evening to begin the coastal hop down to Florida.

'Do you still want to come?' Laura asked him. Clearly she had remembered him asking for a passage to the Bahamas.

He had heard the discussion through the half-open door to the saloon: *'It was our son who pitched him off the side and it was our motor that knocked him out. How are we not responsible?'* and her husband replying, *'What if he starts vomiting or goes deaf half-way across?'*

'Well, if we're half-way across then we'll be half-way to handing him over when we make land. But he won't, Matt. He'll be okay, I'm sure.'

Which was Miracle Two.

So many photographs of him as a child: in prams, on swings, at the sea; Geoffrey in bright red shorts pedalling a tricycle; Geoffrey in the back garden posing with a cricket bat as tall as himself. He had had no idea his aunt had taken so much interest in him.

There were even a few school photos – the annual ritual, never quite daring not to smile because your mother was going to buy the result, mounted in a royal blue card with gold text: *Geoffrey Foster – 1974*. And the sports teams, ranks of scowling boys with folded arms and a master beaming away at the end of the row; pale knees, bad haircuts and spots.

At a guess, his aunt's childlessness had not been by choice.

After a while he stopped opening the albums. Clearing the

house was taking forever and he was tempted to throw the lot into a skip but something stopped him and he knew what it was.

What if...

What if the other branch of the Foster family had taken that course? Instead of coming through that local history society woman to him, James Josiah Charles Foster's diary would have gone to the municipal tip, and he would never have learned about the parallel world that was only an arm's length away.

Aunt Margaret hadn't been a Foster, of course, but a Warren like his mother. The likelihood of there being anything thrilling in her study or loft or bedside cabinet was remote to verging on impossible, but still...

Geoffrey kept looking. Just to be sure.

He had told them his name was Daniel, so he must have had some wits about him even if it was all hazy now. More strangers being kind. He wondered whether British people would react like this, like the Colvins and the Contis and now the Cliftons. Or maybe it was only people beginning with C.

Surnames beginning with C, that is.

The Cliftons were Bostonians, and both were imbued with wanderlust; instead of buying a house after they married they had bought a yacht. Neither seemed to think it extraordinary.

'We both love sailing,' Laura told him. 'We're not ready yet, but when we've got enough saved we're going to take off.'

Matt was a realtor, which was what Americans call an estate agent. That was ironic, given that he had no house of his own. Anyone less like the estate agent Daniel had met some years ago (three years? six?), it was hard to imagine. He was shorter than Daniel, blonde and stocky, with a sunshine smile like Neil Armstrong or Gene Kelly, quick to joke with the kids and fool around, upfront and straightforward, everything on the surface.

Laura was short too, probably not much more than five feet, which was an advantage below deck; Daniel had to remember to duck – especially since he had already cracked his head once. 'I'm keeping my eye on you,' Laura told him. 'I'm watching your pupils, kiddo!'

Odd-sized pupils were a danger sign, as was confusion, headaches and vomiting. He had thrown up once, immediately on coming round, and quick-witted Laura had seen it coming and aimed him over the edge of the quay. Since then he had been feeling gradually better and better, and by the following day, when they were due to set sail, he felt normal apart from being so tired.

'Very common after concussion. Take it easy, it'll pass.'

So Daniel took it easy. Frankly there wasn't much alternative as he knew even less about sailing than he did about farming, and quickly realized he could best help the Cliftons by staying out of their way.

He watched though, admiring their nonchalant competence as they moved around each other in the restricted space of the deck, utterly familiar with the equipment and the routine.

Once they were clear of the marina he was allowed out on deck to watch the mainland falling behind as they made their way around the larger vessels moored to buoys in deeper water.

'Hey look,' Laura called to the kids. 'Look who's there!'

Daniel followed where she was pointing.

'It's old Hoppity – d'you see him?'

On the rail of the fishing boat they were passing was a scrawny seagull with tatty feathers and only one leg, and as they moved away it opened its beak in a silent salute.

Miracle Three.

Chapter Ten

They sat in the drawing room and ate buns with their tea. Rebecca hesitated a fraction as she reached towards the plate, and then told herself that even if that particular myth was based in truth it was too late for her: eating their food in their house could scarcely entwine her in their doings any more than she already was.

The buns were good, too. The Don that looked like a vulture was good at baking.

'A speciality of mine,' he said, smirking a little from six feet up.

'All done in the bread machine,' said the one that looked like a tortoise in a loud whisper, ignoring the glare sent his way and cheerfully taking two.

The Vulture swept a game of Patience aside to make space for the plate on the table, and sat down in a wing chair with chintzy covers and a round cushion encased in crochet.

The room was extraordinary. It was small and crammed with furniture, most of it dark brown and heavily ornamented – curving pedestals, clawed feet and barley-twist legs, intricate arched panels and inlaid patterns of flowers and vines.

Especially vines.

The sherry glasses in the corner cabinet were kept corralled on the shelves by fiddly little rails decorated with wooden bobbles. The standard lamp was as loaded with shaping as a chess piece and the shade sported an elaborate fringe.

They must have been collecting furniture for decades, but it didn't feel like the home of a connoisseur, more a junk shop. There were scratches and scrapes, and here and there a sticky patch. Rebecca had looked carefully before she sat down.

The soft furnishings were equally mismatched: one cushion of silk patchwork, one of threadbare velvet, and one of yellow cotton with a cheery print of balloons. She didn't think she had ever been in a room before where the curtains weren't in pairs.

The house had an odd but not unpleasant smell – a little fusty but mostly herbal, as if all the windows were open and the sun were shining on sage and thyme and rosemary growing just beyond, although in fact everything was closed and the gas fire was toasting her feet.

Well, you might expect it to be stronger; Michael was eighth-part and these guys were half. She, on the other hand, was a miniscule one thirty-second part and if she wanted to smell of herbal shampoo she had to wash her hair in it.

She found it hard not to search their faces for traces of their heritage, but when it came down to it she had no idea what she was looking for, at least nothing specific. But she felt there ought to be some otherness, some visible trait of their mixed blood evident in their features or colouring or form.

Professor Viator was the tallest, several inches over six feet so that even round-shouldered as he was he loomed over his companions, and over her too. Rebecca instinctively kept at a little distance from him so as not to be cowed. The academic gown didn't help, its heavy folds reminiscent of wizards' and warlocks' robes – or in his case, a vulture's folded wings; Viator the Vulture.

She couldn't help noticing what looked like spills of candle wax on the shoulders of the Tortoise next to her.

Professor Lloyd, rather. But he looked so like a tortoise, shrivelled and bony, his bald head wavering on his neck as it projected from the carapace of his gown – although tortoises don't on the whole wear spectacles.

He munched his bun, crumbs clinging to his chin, and wrinkled his eyes in a smile at her.

Rebecca sighed.

'How did you recognize me?' she asked.

The third one was called Professor Peregrine. He hadn't taken a bun and therefore neither had to wait to swallow nor spattered crumbs when he spoke.

'My child, we always recognize your kind. Quite transparent when you know what to look for.'

'What *do* you look for?'

He waved a hand. 'A certain look; a certain attitude. A way of moving, an expression. All the more apparent of course once the individual has been woken up, you might say: made aware. Enlightened. Informed. As you have been, of course.'

'You mean I'm not the only one you've found?'

'Dear me, no! Forgive me, but how arrogant! My dear, there are hundreds of you, thousands of you; probably a dozen just here, now, in Oxford.'

'How much, did you say?' asked Professor Viator, the Vulture, his voice severe.

'One thirty-second,' Rebecca said. 'He was my great-great-great-grandfather. My grandmother's great-grandfather.' She had memorized her family tree.

'Mm. Well it does get tricky by about the seventh generation.'

Good grief.

Perhaps she should have suspected this all along. Was it likely that she, Michael and Connor should be so freaky, so rare? If that gap had been open, why not others? And if Uriel Passenger had squeezed through and sown a few wild oats before retiring to reclusion in Derbyshire, why shouldn't others have done the same? Folk tales were bursting with examples of just this sort of thing.

She was commonplace after all.

'You are certain of that, are you? Fifth generation?'

'Yes, definitely fifth.' She had counted the 'greats' many times and was sure of her ground. 'Why?'

'Just wondering whether there might have been, shall we say, a top-up somewhere along the line.'

The Tortoise at her elbow huffed. Rebecca glanced round. He winked and then nodded in the direction of the table.

Rebecca said, 'No thank you, one is plenty.'

'Not the buns! *Her!*'

'What?'

Professor Peregrine cleared his throat and brought her attention back. 'To return to our problem.'

Yes.

Rebecca had been right to have come – or seriously wrong, depending on how you looked at it. Find a few answers? Definitely. Zip back home with everything in place and an untroubled mind? Ah...

As she had feared, the brick plinth was not a plinth at all but a security device.

'Not entirely accurate,' Professor Peregrine had said. 'We will put the statue back so by definition…'

But that was a cover. The brick cell enclosed a rift, as did the stone room hidden behind the parlour wall at Ashendon Cottage, preventing anyone from accidentally stumbling between worlds. The three old Dons knew that the rift opened when light beams from the two opposing worlds became entangled, and enclosing the space in darkness kept that to a minimum; at the same time the walls would also contain any – accidents – that might nevertheless occur.

It appeared that this area of weakness, like that at Ashendon, became live for only a minute or two in every twenty-four hours, but that minute had been just after the boathouse had burned down, taking the old oak plinth with it and allowing the moonlight in.

Rebecca recalled again the thin beams of light she had seen in the stone room at Ashendon three years before, deflected calmly around one another by the arrangement of mirrors, and the cataclysm when the door had opened and the light had been disturbed. For heart-stopping seconds she had felt herself on the brink of existence, teetering on the edge of a world utterly strange and terrifying that should not have been there, and even now, in the safety of the Dons' drawing room, her skin prickled at the memory.

'Couldn't you have thrown something around it, at least temporarily?' she asked.

'Precisely.' The Vulture glared at the Tortoise, who waved a clawed hand vaguely.

'I only said I didn't want to use *my* eiderdown.'

Rebecca instinctively looked at Professor Peregrine as the least insane person present. After herself.

He raised his eyebrows. 'I was at the Cheeseman Memorial Dinner. I didn't know it had happened until an hour later.'

And by then it was too late; the rift had closed by itself according to its own strange chronology and the unfortunates who had fallen through were away and gone.

'Naught but their footprints in the sand.'

And disturbing footprints: one human, or humanish at any rate, in shoes, and one very like the great four-toed pads of a large cat; the kind of cat that could take down a sheep.

'So we are wondering what you are going to do about it,' Professor Viator said.

Rebecca tasted a forkful of the lamb hotpot tentatively, and then relaxed. The Vulture's culinary skill went further than just buns.

She was staying to supper because time had crept on and the story she was being told was fascinating; she might have said incredible, were it not that three years ago her credulity had grown beyond bounds.

The Dons were only half-human, the other half originating in the world which ought to run safely parallel to the human world but which sometimes became dangerously confused with it: half-human, half-fairy, like Michael's grandfather, who was also her own great-great-grandfather. And just as Michael looked barely thirty despite approaching fifty, they were, all three, stupendously old.

'*How* long ago?' she asked, mistrusting her ears.

'Eighteen twenty-seven.'

'And just in time, too,' Professor Peregrine said. 'After that the colleges got the taste for rowing and started mooring barges up and down the bank. If it hadn't been for us they'd have been mooring them this side too.'

It was the rift, the gap, that their father had come through, and collectively they had taken it upon themselves to stop him doing it again, or anyone like him.

'Arrant irresponsibility. He simply upped and left one day. Our poor mothers.'

They each had different mothers.

'He did put it about a bit.'

'But you found each other,' Rebecca pointed out.

'That was easy.'

So they had built the Ferry House, or rather rebuilt it, as there had been a dwelling there before, smaller and fallen derelict, popularly known as Ferry Cottage.

'Probably been someone here doing the job for centuries,' Professor Lloyd, the Tortoise, said comfortably.

'And was there ever a ferry?'

'No, no, shouldn't think so.'

Not wishing to dwell on that, Rebecca asked why they hadn't built the house around the rift, to enclose it. 'Why leave it out in the garden?'

'Would you want an alien portal in your kitchen?'

It seemed the Tortoise watched television sci-fi.

'It was quite safe,' the Vulture added. 'It was in the shed. Of course, when the shed blew down...'

And then in 1882 they were handed the solution on a plate. By then rowing had become the thing to do, and the colleges had begun replacing their barges, moored on the opposite bank, with permanent boathouses. The Dons had promoted the idea that there should be a boathouse for the University itself – the whole university, that was, rather than any individual college – and generously donated their own land for it, right in front of the Ferry House.

'Why?' Rebecca asked, mystified.

The Tortoise winked.

'Built a plinth for the statue over it,' Professor Peregrine explained. 'Perfect security. No blowing that down.'

'Good old Bollers put up the money. Well, he'd made enough. Sugar. Slaves in the cupboard with his skeletons, you know.'

'Useful hand at Bridge, though.'

'True, very true.'

The Tortoise shot her a look as he reached for the pepper. 'Do you like cards, my dear?' he asked, far too innocently.

Before she could reply, Professor Peregrine scooped the subject up again. He seemed less decrepit than his companions and more grounded.

In 1827 he had been the youngster, tagging along, not getting the jokes. Now he was Mother, and it was he who dropped the yoke across her shoulders.

'So you need to find this poor chap and get him home.'

'And deal with the beastie.'

'Yes, and deal with the beast.'

'But without drawing attention to yourself.'

'No, most unwise.'

'Or us.'
'No indeed, nor us.'
Just that, then.
At least the lamb hotpot was good.

Chapter Eleven

Life on board a yacht was strange, and strangely restful. For a start there was no clutter, absolutely none. The cabins and saloon were lined with cupboards and everything was put away, every bit, always. There wasn't much anyway.

Everyone had the minimum with which they could reasonably manage. 'Capsule wardrobes,' Laura said, and she didn't mean the cupboards but the few, carefully chosen clothes that met all occasions. They used the public library instead of buying books; the children were allowed only a few toys and only very small ones – Lego and drawing books and a few action figures from Star Wars and Shrek. The bicycles lived with their grandparents while they were sailing.

Daniel had asked how the yacht came to have such an unwatery name.

'She was called Alice when we bought her,' Laura told him, 'but we couldn't keep that because my Mom's name is Alice. So.'

'I wanted to call her the Slithy Tove,' Matt said. Laura elbowed him in the ribs. 'Or the Momrath,' he continued, dodging smartly.

'Yeah. So we settled on *The White Rabbit.*'

The fibreglass dinghy, essential when they were moored at sea, away from their own marina, rode on davits at the stern once they were in open water. That had a name too, stencilled carefully along the side: *Dormouse.*

Now that there was no danger he might need to be nursed, Daniel was given Josh's bed at the stern, Josh sharing with his sister. The deck was above and there wasn't much headroom, but as the stern was blunt the mattress didn't taper as the double in the bows had.

Matt lent him underwear and a tee-shirt to sleep in and within a couple of days his own clothes – his own courtesy of the Colvins – had dried, even the boots and the padded jacket.

As the days went by, Daniel grew gradually accustomed to life at sea. He was mildly surprised to find he could cope with being in such a small space, unable to leave; it even became rather nice. The Cliftons were cheerful and considerate, and then there were the children. Daniel found himself perpetually astonished at the way the Cliftons managed their kids.

Abi liked to draw and colour, and she had an iPod loaded with stories and music. She accepted Daniel's presence on board unquestioningly, despite the fact that he was taller than her father and took up an embarrassing amount of space in the saloon. She showed him her drawings, and on the second day from Boston plonked a book on his lap, climbed onto the padded bench beside him and demanded that he read to her.

He was not expecting it and felt his heart lurch.

In complete contrast, Josh was a tight ball of energy who fizzed below deck, rolling around on his bed dodging imaginary bullets, standing on the saloon table to balance as the yacht tipped, running up the steps, which were called the companionway, and jumping to the bottom over and over again. But he was boat-savvy, as Laura put it, and could be safely allowed on deck, although at sea he had to wear a life jacket.

Daniel would have been inclined to tether him on a chain.

He learned the terminology, if not the techniques of sailing. *The White Rabbit* was a forty-four foot Bermuda-rig sloop. Matt and Laura had bought her second-hand so she wasn't as up-to-the-minute as some of the yachts in the marina, but to Daniel's eyes she was impressive and beautiful. He didn't get seasick, which surprised him, and he found the idea of sailing appealed. It felt unscheduled and free, even though he knew the Cliftons had everything planned to the last degree, and (he saw the humour in this, just) there was no vegetation – no leaves or buds or tendrils or roots, only the water and the air and sometimes, when it rained, the two mixed together, wetting his eyelashes and getting into his throat.

And it was fine.

They worked their way south using the Intracoastal Waterway, the ICW as the mariners called it, stopping at ports along the way to stretch their legs and restock with supplies. They moored on buoys and used the *Dormouse*, and Daniel had a go at rowing and found he was good at it: another reason to like boats.

The weather grew warmer and the skies bluer. One day they moored at Miami and went ashore for the final time before crossing the Gulf Stream. The mood was different. For the Cliftons it was the prelude to the main holiday, the point of the voyage; for Daniel it was the first stage of another goodbye.

They brought back pizzas to bake on board and ate them off the cardboard packaging using their fingers. People on boats avoided washing up as much as possible.

The weather conditions were perfect so they would not have to wait but could sail at midnight.

They drank cokes with ice clacking in the plastic tumblers while the sun dipped, and Daniel felt again the unEnglishness of warm, dark evenings. Josh and Abi had bedtime stories and went to sleep, and some time later Daniel turned in.

Laura was at the radio and Matt on deck. Closing the door while they were quietly busy dragged forth long-buried memories from when he was very young and his grandmother had been alive – the comfortable business of a home well run by competent, kindly grown-ups. He remembered her leaving his door ajar so that he could take comfort from the landing light, and lying in bed listening to the murmur of the television in the room below, the muffled surges of audience laughter or the strains of a theme tune.

He switched off the light.

It isn't often one's life is turned around in a day. It had happened to Foster before, at the bank, when his career had plunged down the tube after that of his section boss, and with it the expectations he had nurtured of penthouse suites, fast cars and maybe even a boat.

And now it had happened again, but in reverse. The house in Camden Square was not smart – Margaret and Paul had had little interest in fashion, neither in clothes nor home furnishing – but it was clean (apart from the cat hairs) and in good repair, and the location opposite the gardens put it squarely into the highly saleable bracket. Its own back garden was laid to lawn, with a magnolia tree which would add to its appeal.

There had been investments too, bits and pieces here and there, as well as a few shares in the company, and after inheritance tax and costs had been cleared there was going to be – well, quite a bit. Quite a bit indeed. And with it came a whole raft of new possibilities.

Three years ago Foster had put his estate agency on hold in order to follow a treasure trail that had led to something amazing – a way between worlds, the stuff of fairytales. He had thought at the time that such a thing might yield knowledge which he could use for financial gain – if quantum physics had been involved he might have become the next mega-power in the computing industry.

In the end the reality had been frankly terrifying, and certainly uncontrollable. But it had been reality.

With a degree in physics and a job selling houses, Geoffrey had become bored with his life. The few short weeks he had spent playing with stratagems and dreams had awoken brain cells from torpor, and returning to work afterwards had been grim.

And now, Aunt Margaret's house.

He had had no idea she was leaving it to him; he wondered whether his parents had known. He had always supposed her wealth would end up on her husband's side of the family, along with the business.

He might have dropped in on the old girl once in a while if he'd realised.

Anyway, the temptation was irresistible. If he sold the Camden Square house – *when* he sold it – there would be enough liquid cash to set him up permanently almost anywhere that wasn't London. He could get out. He would sell his small house in Wandsworth too, and buy something modest but comfortable – new, low maintenance – perhaps in the midlands…or home counties anyway; he wasn't sure he wanted to be based too far north.

And the remainder would give him enough to live on. No more kow-towing to the rich and smug; his life to live as he chose, not as he had to.

And right now, what he chose was to research the actuality of this parallel world known only to the three of them – himself,

Michael Seward and Rebecca Mulligan. The old mad woman he could discount – she had been neutralized effectively by the social services – and the boy had disappeared through the portal.

Geoffrey took a last glance around the house. He'd get in decorators to paint the walls a cool, modern white and replace the carpets with pale wood flooring, replace the kitchen. The increase in value would more than cover the expense and the house would sell quicker too. A quick sale was what he wanted.

He switched off the light.

Nassau, in the Bahamas, and more goodbyes; Daniel was getting good at them. Better, anyway.

Laura gave him a final health check, peering closely into his eyes so that he had to steel himself not to back away, and asking a string of questions. Most of his memory had returned, and he could now recall the eruption as the dog bolted in front of Josh's flying bike. The butterfly sutures that had held closed the cut on the back of his skull were no longer necessary.

There was no problem booking a flight to Heathrow.

Matt shook his hand and Laura laughed, and then he was alone again.

He slept surprisingly well on the plane; perhaps it was the last that he could thank his concussion for. But when they touched down at Heathrow his relief at having made it to England was diluted by the awareness that he had to start making decisions again – big decisions concerning the future, not just day-to-day living.

Looking through the window as he waited in line in Immigration, he saw a sky that was powder blue with picture-book, cotton-wool clouds. It would feel cold outside after Florida.

A thin, sandy-haired official took the passport he held out, looked at the old photograph of the boy he used to be and frowned at the face he now wore.

'Name?'

'Connor O'Brien,' Connor said.

Chapter Twelve

Rebecca drove north through the night.

The weather had turned nasty again, raining hard and with sudden flurries of wind that rocked the car. The A46 around Coventry was grim, but once onto the M1 the traffic eased and the scarlet Mini zipped along in cruise control while the Strauss oboe concerto played. Steph was performing it next term and Rebecca wanted to get familiar with it; she wasn't musical enough to enjoy many things on first hearing.

She had set off on impulse, the decision taken before she reached the car park. Her meeting with the Dons had slashed through her plans leaving them in tatters, and once again she was being forced to abandon her life – her Real Life – to get involved in this murky, dodgy, surreal business of a parallel world.

Fairyland, as Steph called it.

'That doesn't help,' Rebecca had told her, shortly.

She had called in at Wellesley Road. Having decided she had to see Michael it seemed frustrating and wasteful of time and petrol to go home first; Oxford was at least a quarter of the way to Ashendon, probably more in hours considering the slow business of getting out of the capital.

But she needed supplies. Steph lent her underwear and a couple of tops, and even had a spare toothbrush tucked away in her travel bag, which was an unexpected boost.

Rebecca had never felt entirely sure how much her friend understood about her friendship with Michael and their adventures at Ashendon House. She had let one or two things slip out, she knew, finding it hard to be continually guarded with her best friend, and Steph's customary reaction was one of mild interest when utter astonishment would have seemed more appropriate. Rebecca sometimes wondered whether she could put it down to the academic life Steph led, but mostly she just thanked heaven for it.

She took the time to have a swift, sleep-busting cup of coffee before setting off, and as she swept aside a copy of the Oxford Journal so she could sit down, she was caught by two photographs:

one of a sheep's carcass tumbled in a ditch, and the other, blurred and indistinct, of a dark shape on all fours. *'Boars Hill Beast Causes Carnage'* ran the headline.

Nothing about the mystery man.

'Are you thinking it might be that boy?' Steph asked, and as usual Rebecca could only guess how much she knew.

'I don't know. Yes, perhaps. Oh God.'

'Your Michael will be able to help.'

But would he? Steph's words were meant to reassure but she had never met Michael and certainly hadn't seen how the last three years had affected him.

Don't think about him while you're driving.

Trying hard not to think, Rebecca drove through the rain.

The barn was silent, but both men felt the presence.

'He'll be at the back, behind the bales,' Owens whispered.

PC Darren Blackman stepped forward. The ellipse of his flashlight revealed the tipsy brick floor of the barn, which was old enough to be on the Listed Buildings Register. The light lapped at the corner of a tarpaulin, and further in, something heavy and mechanical; the air smelled of hay and old wood with a hint of motor oil, but not of cattle or pigs or muck, thankfully.

Darren was not a country boy, but the local beat officer was on leave, he had been on duty, and Boars Hill was not far out of the city.

'Come on out!' he called into the dark beyond his flashlight. 'No need to be afraid!'

There was a scuffle.

With a bit of luck it would be the chap that had been sighted in the city over the weekend, the one who had been linked to this escaped carnivore.

The place was buzzing with accounts of the Beast, and several people had claimed to have seen a man, long-haired and wild-eyed, close to the creature and acting suspiciously, by which they probably meant 'not being eaten by it'. Two sheep had been taken near Boars Hill and it seemed plausible that the stranger might be here too.

The constable wasn't sure whether to use 'sir' or 'lad'. His flashlight lit up a boot, and an ankle above it.

Another scuffle and the boot withdrew.

'It's alright, sir,' (probably best). 'It's the Police. Just come along out and let's have a chat.'

Darren loosened his shoulders, jigged on the balls of his feet a little to prepare, just in case, and stepped forward.

Huddled on the spilled hay, hugging his knees to his narrow chest, a boy stared up at him with strained eyes.

The constable relaxed.

'Hallo,' he said, putting all the reassurance he could muster into his voice. 'My name's Darren. What's your name, lad?'

(Definitely 'lad' after all.)

For a moment he waited, flashlight directed aside, his free hand relaxed and the muscles of his face holding a smile. Then, 'Jack,' the boy whispered, and was a mystery man no longer.

Rebecca pulled up on the gravel in front of the hotel just after half past eleven. The lights glowing behind the curtains promised comfort and hospitality. Thick, cushiony carpets and polished wood lay behind the door, she knew, with attentive staff and reassuring anonymity. It had been a long drive and she was tempted.

But she locked the car and took the path to the side, feet crunching on stones in the dark as they had that August night three years ago, taking her past the first of the walled gardens to the low door of the cottage.

The lights were on here too, so at least Michael was up.

She knocked, and breathed deep while she waited.

Don't be an ass, it's only Michael.

But that had never worked, and when the door opened her heart gave its familiar little backward flip because he looked the same as ever; and then a second little flip because he looked so different.

'Rebecca!'

'Sorry I didn't let you know.' *Although if I had tried you wouldn't have replied.*

In the soft light of the sitting room, Michael was shadowy, a little shorter somehow than she remembered. She watched him clear the chunky pine table, closing and piling books and stacking a notebook and a pack of cards on top.

Cards? He hadn't been reduced to playing Patience, she hoped.

Rebecca watched him, trying to see him with fresh eyes, searching for a sign that he was not quite like other men. The Dons said it was obvious once you knew what you were looking for, but they had not been forthcoming about precisely what that was.

She was aware of a faint herbal scent, the sense of fresh air even indoors, which had been a part of Michael since their first meeting; could that be it? But she didn't share in that, she was sure.

She said, 'How are you?'

'Fine. You?' Michael sat down. 'You're growing your hair!'

'Oh, well…thought I'd give it a bash.' Rebecca refrained – just – from touching her four-inch locks. Michael's hair was still long, hooked behind his ears, and very black – as was hers. Was that a sign of their strange genes?

He was still beautiful.

Rebecca shook herself mentally. 'Michael, something's happened in Oxford. I came up because I need to talk to you.'

She watched him drop his eyes. 'Ah.'

'You know what I'm going to say?'

'The Beast of Boars Hill? It made the national news one day. I did some digging on-line.'

'And the Mystery Man?'

Michael looked at her sharply. 'Mystery man? Who's that?'

It was a relief that he was interested, and that he still had the ability to be sharp at all, these reclusive, evasive days.

Rebecca sighed and leaned back. 'There's some guy they think has something to do with the Beast. Doesn't talk, looks wild, possibly crazy. According to the papers, anyway. Seen alongside the animal, whatever it is, so the police want to interview him. The thing is, though–'

'You think they've both come through a gap.'

'Yes. In fact I'm sure of it.'

'And is it Connor?'

There – it was said.

Rebecca shuddered. 'I don't know. None of the photographs is anything like clear enough. Maybe.'

Michael looked at her for a moment, swinging his foot, his fingers interlaced in his lap. Was he remembering the past? Thinking what to say? Trying to read her mind?

And then he had sprung up and was heading for the door.

'Can I offer you coffee? Or tea?'

'Coffee, please.'

In the kitchen Michael said, 'You are sure about the gap?'

'Absolutely!'

While Michael fixed coffee, Rebecca explained about the three Dons and the astonishing history of the house on the south bank of the Thames, downstream from Folly Bridge, and the doorway, the gap which had been protected for the last century by the boathouse. And that the boathouse had burned down.

'There's talk of arson,' she said, 'but it isn't confirmed, and even if it is, it's not likely there's any connection with us.'

'Mm.'

Rebecca narrowed her eyes. 'You don't sound surprised.'

'I've been working through Uriel's library. Let's say it doesn't amaze me.'

'You knew that there was another doorway?'

'Probably more than one.'

'More!' Rebecca was shocked; the implications were massive. 'How many? Do you know where they are?'

'Not in any detail.'

'Good grief.'

They returned to the sitting room, and Rebecca blew gently across the top of her drink. Michael, clearly able to take it hotter than she could, sipped and then said, startlingly, 'Do you play cards?'

'Cards? No! You're the second person to ask me today.' He was watching her with his head tipped back. *What?* There's something about card games now as well?'

'Not the games.' Michael put down his mug and fanned out the deck of cards, sifting through them. 'Cards are very interesting, common in only slightly different forms to many, many cultures. Ever looked at the court cards?'

'The what?'

Cards didn't interest Rebecca at all, or not since playing Snap and Beggar My Neighbour as a child. Now she watched Michael extract four cards from his pack and lay them face up on the table. He pushed them towards her.

'Look.'

They were the four queens.

'What about them? Two red, two black; Tudor dress. They're all brandishing roses. *What?*'

'Look properly.'

Rebecca looked. Why did he have to be cryptic? Why couldn't he just tell her what she was supposed to see?

The queens stared past her, left or right according to the whim of the designer. They had bags under their eyes and hooded lids. One, the Queen of Spades, appeared to have a lazy eye, her gaze not lining up properly.

'What do you notice?'

'Well, they're all different.'

'Go on.'

Rebecca stared at the four cards set out in a row, analyzing the lines and blocks of colour. Now that she was paying attention she could see that each queen's face was actually quite individual.

The Queen of Spades, she with the squint, looked plump and comfortable; Diamonds was sweetly pretty, a little childish, by comparison with which Hearts looked middle-aged and plain – maternal, but in a down-to-earth, no-nonsense way. And the Queen of Clubs was...

Rebecca frowned. The painted eyes seemed to consider, as if with an intellect she wished to guard. She was attractive but not *pretty*.

She looked up. Michael was smiling with one half of his mouth only, one eye creasing.

Oh, Michael...

'Now look in the mirror,' he said.

Chapter Thirteen

Connor laid out the four cards on the table, two by two. It was surprising they were so nearly matched in size and proportion, but perhaps that was simply the ideal size for a card to be held comfortably in a hand.

A human hand? Or any hand?

Connor leaned his elbows on the table, his chin on his knuckles. What were they telling him? What were they withholding? How was he going to extract it?

How am I going to do this?

'Move over, man!'

Connor swept up the precious cards just before a drink can landed, slopping, where they had been.

'Shit.'

Clarence, the enormous teenager from down the hall, lifted the can and licked the trickle running down the outside; Connor half expected him to lick up the spill too.

'Oh, man!'

The other one – Lyle? – arrived with his grating laugh and purposely jogged his friend's elbow. More spluttering and slopping and swearing.

It had been a mistake to expect peace and quiet in the hostel. The place where he had spent his first night in Oxford had been better – it was part of the Youth Hostel Association and was cleaner, more orderly – but it cost too much. This one, over a fishmonger's and a shoe repair shop, would keep him going longer.

Connor headed out into the street. He'd try one of the bookshops – most of the larger ones had sofas and coffee machines these days. Coffee machines were beyond his means, but he wasn't likely to be noticed there, at least for a while. And the smell would be nice.

Oxford was very different from the city streets Connor had grown up in. As well as shoppers, there were tourists with cameras, even in November, and people his own age who stepped through intriguing doorways to vanish into the underlying world of the colleges, invisible to those left behind on the pavement. Opposite shop fronts and around corners, set into stone walls like castles, the oak doorways seemed to be everywhere. They were panelled and studded, often arched, and occasionally one would be open, revealing the short flagged passageway past the porter's lodge and the grassed courtyard beyond: the quad – it was called a quad.

He hardly knew whether to take the quiet, cobbled back streets where every doorway he passed tantalised him, or stick to the main roads and deny himself the torture.

Connor had schooled himself from an early age not to compare his existence with that of other people. It didn't help. But it was so hard, now, to watch the casual, golden people passing him by, checking their mobiles and laughing with friends, seemingly blind to their privilege, their good fortune in being where they were.

One girl, in thick tights and a short, pleated skirt, plunged out of a doorway and brushed shoulders with him, off balance: 'Sorry, sorry!'

''S okay.'

She threw him a brief smile and was gone, swinging her bag over her shoulder, in a rush to be somewhere else. The glimpse of grass and stone slabs and ancient leaded windows remained for a moment, growing narrower as the heavy oak door swung back, and then he was shut out once more.

The decision to come to Oxford was one he was scarcely aware of having taken. It seemed inevitable. He had never seen it until he accompanied Rebecca on their quest to round up the hidden objects, but from that first morning the magic had seized him.

It was the way the institutions of learning jostled with shops and offices, the colleges scattered like crocus bulbs thrown onto grass. Half the population didn't even see them, he suspected, unconscious of the hidden life carrying on its business only a wall's width away.

Not just the colleges, either: the Bodleian Library, the Sheldonian Theatre, the Pitt Rivers Museum and the Ashmolean;

names that curled exquisitely in his mouth, redolent of learning and appreciation and steadfastness. The John Radcliffe Hospital and the Oxford University Press and Blackwell's...

There was a pain in him as if his stomach were empty, the yearning to belong here as desperate as physical hunger.

There were Blackwell's bookshops scattered around Oxford, but the main site was opposite the Museum of the History of Science, where he and Rebecca had carried out a little underhanded requisitioning what seemed like an age ago. Connor settled himself in the coffee corner upstairs and took out his four cards again.

He stroked his palm over the table top first, checking for splashes or sticky bits, and then lay the cards out in a row. The order didn't matter; they were four individuals, not part of a sequence, although together they held secrets...

The first was the photograph of his grandmother, taken when she was a little girl using a solid-plate camera and printed on spongy cream paper. It was soft of focus, the child's hair misty, and had been faded out to an oval around which someone long ago had drawn in ink a pattern of trailing ivy.

The second was equally worn, the corners as creased, the edges as furry, but instead of a photograph there was a coloured picture of a woman in long robes. She was depicted semi-stylised, her face drawn in simple lines, the colours – terracotta, peacock blue and ochre – reserved for her bodice and skirt. Her arms, as pale as her face, were bare and she held a long-stemmed flower across her shoulder. She was neither full-face nor in profile but gazed to the side, refusing to make eye contact with him. In the corner behind her was drawn a three-segmented leaf, like a cloverleaf.

The third card was the Queen of Clubs from a modern Waddingtons deck. She was there by courtesy of the girl called Anna who had managed spectacularly to throw hot chocolate over everything his first night in the youth hostel. Cleaning up the carpet had taken highest priority and by the time they got to the cards they were sticky and stained.

Anna threw them in the bin. 'A pack of cards only costs a quid. I'll replace them.'

Connor had picked about amidst the pizza packaging and teabags and extracted the one he wanted. She was barely touched. He rinsed her anyway, grateful for the card's coating of varnish, and dried her with kitchen paper.

And the fourth card was the one he had taken from the Colvin family's Rolodex. It lay on the table before him now, with his forward-sloping handwriting marching along the ruled feint:

Stand on the island of glass and look towards the great circle.
Put the numbers in order left from the lay of the land.
Cross water to a place of captivity and face the stone at half-light.

Connor opened his notebook and began brainstorming.

By four his stomach was begging for food and he finished up, stowing the notebook in his coat pocket and sliding the cards carefully into their plastic bag. He would find a sandwich shop and get a sub, which would do as lunch and dinner both.

Managing on two meals a day instead of three was another way to stretch out his finances. He had less than a hundred pounds left and was hoping, though without much optimism, to finish what he had to do before it ran out. It would be difficult to work around a job.

It was raining. Connor turned up his collar and thrust his hands into his pockets before stepping out.

As he left the shelter of the doorway the second girl of the day in too much of a hurry to notice where she was going walked smack into him.

Chapter Fourteen

Rebecca woke late to buttermilk wallpaper and William Morris curtains. The mattress was over-sprung and there were sheets and blankets instead of a duvet.

Then she remembered.

One of the problems about seeing Michael was that the cottage had only one bedroom and Michael was the kind of man who would simply not allow a guest, or at any rate a female guest, to make do with the couch. The first time she visited, Rebecca had felt miserable knowing she had effectively turned him out of his own bed *and* landed him with a load of bed linen to launder just for one night.

The good thing was that there was a hotel within a stone's throw.

He had argued, but she had won: *'It's a treat for me, you know I don't take holidays.'* Which she didn't, so it was half-true.

Ashendon House, now a country hotel operated by a small and exclusive chain, did her a deal when she ran across just after midnight. It was strange to wander through the corridors and climb the stairs between walls freshly emulsioned in neutral pastels, carpet quiet underfoot. It was a far cry from the gloomy Victorian panelling and bare floorboards of three years ago.

The junk, because most of it had been junk, collected by Uriel Passenger, their common ancestor, had been removed to a commercial storage unit in Matlock. Sorting through it all had been such a dim prospect she and Michael had mutually agreed to postpone the job, and it now looked likely to be postponed indefinitely. Rebecca felt a little guilty about that – some of the exhibits might be of value to museums of social history, but if so then the museums would have to wait.

Rebecca showered and checked out. Michael had finished breakfast, so she took her bowl of cereal into the living room.

The books were where they had left them the night before. The cards were piled roughly and Rebecca avoided looking at them.

What Michael had told her was ridiculous.

I am not the Queen of Clubs.

In fact she might just club the next person who mentioned cards to her. Had that been what the Tortoise had been hinting at?

In fairness, Michael had not said that Rebecca *was* the Queen of Clubs, but that Rebecca fell into a category of women *represented* by the Queen of Clubs. And not the Queen of Clubs here but over there, in that other place, the World Invisible that she had once naively believed she had finished with.

'So where are these other gaps?' she asked now, and Michael pulled a rueful face and shook his head.

'Uriel didn't know. He suspected there was something at Oxford, but was confident it was being looked after. Someone in charge, guarding it.'

'Three, actually.'

'Yes. Otherwise he had the idea that there might be one on an island, in a prison of some kind, and that possibly a landmark stone was involved. He's vague on that, I'm afraid.'

'A prison.'

Rebecca pondered. Suppose a gap opened up in Wormwood Scrubs? Convicts disappearing like lemmings over a cliff...

Michael said, 'I wonder whether he might be confusing *prison* with *cells*. I thought of Lindisfarne.'

'Cells?'

'Monks' cells.'

Rebecca pictured monks in heavy woollen habits leaping through the tangled light beams. She sighed. Was it likely that this weak point, this tear in the fabric should have gone unnoticed?

'No, not really,' Michael concurred.

'And what did he mean by a landmark stone? Some kind of monument?'

'Probably not. My guess would be a natural landmark, like a finger of rock or a single, huge boulder.'

That might narrow it down, Rebecca supposed. But in any case, how was she supposed to smuggle a wild animal that ate sheep into any prison – or monastery – single-handed?

Michael didn't volunteer, and she knew she wouldn't ask. He was insubstantial in a way she didn't understand but was aware of all the time. As if he had dropped out of life.

Before she left, he took her to his workshop, new and sharp-edged amongst the drooping winter stalks, and stood her in front of the cabinet where his beautiful, strange boxes stood on display.

'Choose one.'

'What is it for?'

She heard the smile in his voice.

'For you!'

'*Me?*'

'For Christmas.'

Rebecca stared at the boxes. Michael used wood with eccentric patterning, sometimes burred, often wavy where the bark had been. Some boxes were as pale as ashes in the grate, some almost black, many were variations of amber and honey. Should she choose a small one, out of tact?

But the box low down to her left was calling to her, tugging at her attention. It was perhaps a foot long and nine inches deep, with a crazy organic edge to the lid and exposed wooden hinges. The colour was deep ginger, like a conker fresh from its case, and Rebecca's hand twitched with a yearning to stroke its satin skin.

Michael lifted it and gave it into her hands.

'Open it.'

She raised the lid and saw the neat compartments, lined with close-piled velvet, chocolate-brown. Then she closed it again, and heard the soft *tock* as it shut.

'Are you sure?'

'Of course.' Michael took it from her, tipping it to look at the base. 'Three one seven. I'll just put it in the book.'

Extraordinary to think that Michael had made more than three hundred of these gorgeous boxes. Rebecca waited, hugging her gift, while he wrote her name against the number in the ledger, and then they crunched their way back along the cinder path to the cottage and Michael wrapped a square of felt around the box to protect its surface while travelling.

And now it sat on the back seat of the Mini, with Rebecca's coat tucked around it to prevent it from sliding while she drove back to start her hopeless task.

*   *   *

The studio in the mews had changed hands.

Geoffrey Foster frowned through the glazing at the shelves on the wall which he remembered filled with polished wooden boxes but which now held jugs and dishes in cream and muted grey.

'Can I help you?'

A woman in her thirties with an Australian accent had come up behind him and was unlocking the door. She was balancing a pack of printer paper and a couple of desk trays on her free arm, and Geoffrey reached out.

'Allow me.'

He followed her into the studio and set the paper and trays down on the desk. 'I was expecting someone else. Have you been here long?'

'No, just since August. You wanted Steve?'

'Steve?'

'Guy before me? Steve Cahill? Free-form porcelain?'

Geoffrey said, 'No. Michael Seward. He makes boxes.'

The woman looked blank. 'Must be before Steve, then. Sorry, can't help you.' Then she said, 'You interested in some mugs? I saw you looking.'

'No, sorry.'

'No problem. Remember where I am though, in case you change your mind!'

At the door, Geoffrey paused.

'Aren't you a bit over-crowded? There are two other potters here already, aren't there?'

'We're not all the same, you know!' She laughed, sounding relaxed and full of sunshine. 'Paul's raku and Theo's hand-built; I'm salt-glaze!'

In Oxford Rebecca returned the things she had borrowed from Steph and then went on to park in the city centre.

The internet is a rich source of information, but sometimes only books will do. Rebecca found herself in urgent need of information on myths and fairies in the British Isles, and if she was going to beat the worst of the rush hour traffic in London she had better be swift.

It was raining in Oxford although the north had been dry, and Rebecca dodged from street to street, tucking herself under projecting shop fronts where she could. Her mind was teeming. The last few days had reawakened all the anxieties she had been managing to suppress, and now once again she felt overwhelmed by responsibilities she did not want.

What might this Beast kill next? A farmer? A child? Where was the Mystery Man and how would she find him? If he was Connor – she had to face the possibility – what had happened to him, that he had become so wild? And if not Connor, how would she be able to communicate with him? What language would he speak, and would he trust her? Where was this gap-in-a-prison? Why could the Dons not knock down their brick wall instead?

What was she going to do to help Michael? Would he ever recover from the dreadful night when she had clutched his arm and stopped him from going through into the World Invisible?

And where, in all creation, in this world or any other, was Connor?

The rain increased as she reached Broad Street; she put on a spurt to get under cover and collided heavily with a man coming out of the shop.

Chapter Fifteen

They crashed, stepped back to recover, and stared.

'Rebecca!'
She looked so different with longer hair, blown about in the wind and wet at the edges, curling away from her cheeks. But he knew her immediately and his eyes drank her in: the most beautiful girl he had ever seen…and the person he had most wished never to see again.

'Connor!'
Even before he had spoken her name she knew it was him, despite the differences – his hair for a start, cut short and almost straight – and of course he was a boy no longer. She stared at him, marvelling at how the three years had changed the angles of his face and his mouth and his eyes, while all the time it was the same face, the same mouth…
Her stomach plunged, and she shivered.

Chapter Sixteen

'Not in the doorway!'

The man shoved through, ramming his shoulder into Rebecca to make his point. She grabbed at her bag as it slid down her arm.

Connor moved as if jumpstarted, and Rebecca clutched his sleeve. 'Don't.'

The rain was loud on the passing umbrellas; she heard it as if her ears had only just started working. She said, 'Where are you go– …' and tailed off as she realized that of all the questions she might ask, that was not the one. She began again: 'Where have you be–'

Connor was moving her with his hand on her elbow, into the bookshop and through the knot of customers near the door: those preparing to go out, those who had just come in, and the queue at the till. They walked between the tables where the offers were piled – '3 for 2', adventure and romance and science fiction, epics of self-discovery, mystery and tragedy – and climbed stairs.

Then she was dropping onto a sofa and it was suddenly quieter, and Connor, because there was no question it was Connor, was sitting opposite.

His jeans were faded and thin at the knees; he had serious-looking leather laced-up boots, scuffed but unbowed.

'Connor, I…'

That still wasn't it.

'I don't…' She swallowed and licked her lips. 'Connor, it is you?'

Stupid!

Connor nodded, with just the smallest, softest huff of suppressed amusement. Irony, perhaps. Then he said, 'Yes, it's me,' and his voice was the same too, roughly, although perhaps less…bitter.

Rebecca let out her breath. Her hands were shaking. She clasped them together on her lap.

'Okay. Tell me.'

Connor talked.

Later, Rebecca was to wonder what anyone overhearing would have made of it. People came to the coffee machine and went. Did they listen to what Connor was saying? Did they wonder?

The words came out so matter-of-fact. But Connor had been a poet from before they first met; he would choose his words with care and attention to the effect they would have.

Captivity he said, when he might have used *imprisonment*. *Wardens* in place of *guards*.

When he passed through the chaos of tangled light in the secret room of Ashendon Cottage three years ago he had walked into a wood, a forest, in which the small stone room amid the leaf mould was an alien thing, an anomaly, an affront to commonsense.

'Forests are common there,' he told her. 'Everything grows so fast. You have to work really hard to keep land open.'

What had it been like to walk through trees in a world that was not ours? What had Connor thought as he stepped forward toward the first people he would meet there?

He wasn't telling.

'The wood was inside a wall. Too high to climb. I just walked along it until I found a door, but it was barred on the other side. There was a knocker though, so I knocked.'

It sounded like a fairytale.

'And someone heard me, realized where I must have come from, and took me. And that was that.'

He had spent years locked up. It was a cruel end to his amazing adventure.

'It was a house, though, not a cell.'

Rebecca thought she detected a shiftiness. She said, 'Mm.' Then she said, 'Wait, though. *How* many years did you say?'

'I don't know for sure. Somewhere between five and six.'

'It can't have been. That's crazy.'

Connor shrugged. 'It's the truth.'

He had a watch, he had pen and paper. Thank God he'd had pen and paper, as without he would have gone insane. But he had kept a calendar with steely discipline, recording twenty-four-hour days by his watch, noticing time slip until a whole day and night had been lost – or gained, depending on how you looked at it.

'Their days are shorter, which didn't help.'

Then his watch battery had given up and after that it was down to calculations, recording the days as they passed and trying to compensate for the difference in duration.

'I'm bound to have made mistakes. So something over five, but probably not six years.'

He was twenty-two, or thereabouts. No wonder he had grown up.

Especially after what he had been through.

'They were mostly okay to me.'

There was a mountain of experience in that 'mostly'.

He looked so like Michael, and yet so unlike too. For all that he was younger, his life experience had been so different, and not just the five (or was it six) years in Fairyland. He had never spoken about his family but it had been clear to Rebecca that they were nothing like her own. She suspected that his father was violent, and knew Connor had been sleeping rough at least part of the time they had been trying to locate that dangerously unstable gap at Ashendon.

And now here she was again, about to start looking for another gap.

Connor had eventually been sprung from gaol by a group of activists who seemed to know about the gaps and wanted to send him back. There had followed a swift flight overland with the hounds practically baying at their heels, to a hillside where a monolith like a fist kept the rift closed. Once the stone had been levered aside they had had to wait for the moment when the light from our own world shone through, and then Connor stepped into it and out of it again the other side.

'So where were you?' Rebecca asked, thinking of the tramp and the sheep-killer.

Connor said, 'Vermont'.

'Vermont!' That was no help then. 'How did you get back here?'

'The kindness of strangers.'

They looked at one another. Already Rebecca was growing

accustomed to this new, older Connor, and the sixteen-year-old boy was becoming a little hazy. He had always been mature, not to mention dauntingly intelligent.

She had minded that once, but not for a long while; not even, she knew, towards the end of that strange treasure hunt, although she scarcely had admitted it to herself at the time.

The kindness of strangers. He was enigmatic, but someone must have helped him hugely if he had managed to get back across the Atlantic. Rebecca knew him well enough to realise any kind of debt would weigh heavily on him; his moral sense was highly developed. She sighed.

Then she sat up, energised. 'Connor! You don't know!'

'What?'

Rebecca leaned forward and put her palms on the table. 'You've got money! You've got actually a *lot* of money! Ashendon House is a hotel now and they pay a socking great rent to us!'

He looked nonplussed – as well he might.

'Rent?'

'Yes!' Rebecca grinned. 'Connor, honestly, you're rich!'

Chapter Seventeen

Connor retrieved his few things from the hostel locker and signed himself out. From the top of the stairs he saw Rebecca, standing waiting in the hall, utterly out of place. The hostel resembled a run-down Bollywood movie set, candy pink and peacock blue and purple, the paint chipped and grubby. Straight and slender in her black wool coat, Rebecca looked like aristocracy.

They had left Blackwell's around five, when the streets were dark. The rain had stopped, leaving the scent of wet pavements, and the traffic hushed through the puddles.

Rebecca had said he had money. He believed her, of course, but it was difficult to feel it. She said he could get a flat, and he tried to imagine it: his own flat that he could just *be* in, alone and silent and whenever he wanted.

'Michael set up an account for you,' Rebecca had told him. 'The rent from the hotel gets split three ways and yours has just been feeding in. It's held in trust, of course.'

Three years' worth of rent from the hotel, just in case he ever came back.

'Where are you staying?' Rebecca had asked, and he had sighed. He badly needed space to get used to this extraordinary notion of not being poor, and the prospect of returning to the noisy, communal hostel was grim.

He noticed she was twisting her mouth, as if weighing him up.

'What?'

She raised her eyebrows. 'Connor, how are you with cats?'

'You alright with cats, Jack?'

The man who brought him food was being followed by an animal that was too small but in every other way so cat-like it was impossible to believe it wasn't a cat. It walked behind with its tail just dipping below horizontal, and when it saw him looking the tail shot up straight, and it broke into a little trot.

Tentatively, helplessly, he stretched out his hand. The miniature nose was delicate and dry.

'Only some folk are allergic.' The man, the guard, put the tray on the end of the bed. 'Well, I'll leave him in here if you like, then.'

The cat – the man had called it a cat, so it must be one – was black with a white front and paws. Perhaps it was a special miniature breed.

The food was all cold – flakes of something in milk and slices of bread that had been toasted. There was plenty of it, more than he really wanted, but he ate everything anyway.

After that he lay on his side and stroked the cat with long, smooth strokes where it stretched out beside him, and it purred just like a cat, too.

'Do you like buns?' Rebecca asked him, cryptic but cheerful.

They were walking along a towpath, and in the dark their feet splashed in unseen puddles. Connor was listening, but flagging. It seemed he was not the only one to have had adventures, although undoubtedly his were more extreme.

Would there ever come a time when he would feel in charge of his own existence? He had been out of any kind of meaningful control for the past five – or six – years of his life, and definitely out of control since arriving in Vermont. He had come to Oxford partly because Oxford pulled at him and partly because it was where Rebecca wasn't and nor was Michael, and he had been desperate to see neither of them. But that hadn't worked.

It wasn't that he resented them, or blamed them – far from it. But in their own separate ways they represented a kind of life he could never have. They were both privileged, both talented, both cool and experienced and confident.

Both beautiful. Especially Rebecca.

Why had Rebecca been in Oxford this afternoon? He had been careful with his calculations, knew that her friend Steph would have graduated last year, leaving no reason now for Rebecca's presence here.

'Steph's doing a DPhil,' Rebecca commented, casually.

'A Dee Phil?'

'Doctorate. It's what they call a doctorate at Oxford. Too posh to call it a PhD like everyone else.'

Steph was doing a doctorate. So much for covering all eventualities.

And now he was being escorted along the river to present himself at the door of total strangers and ask for hospitality. Again. His helplessness was depressing.

'This is it.'

They had reached a cordon around some wreckage. Rebecca led the way past and knocked on the door of the house behind.

'Dons, you said?'

'Yes, Connor. Dons.'

And as the door began to open he'd have sworn she smothered a grin.

Chapter Eighteen

There were lane closures on the M40 and by the time Rebecca got home she could have done with the Vulture's hotpot, especially having skipped lunch. His buns wouldn't have gone amiss either.

She made do with an omelette with basil which was barely surviving in the pot on the windowsill, and filled up afterwards with three-day-old bread. The milk had gone off. Her domestic arrangements were falling apart.

Lucky I've got a long date on this commission.

She was still early in the preparatory phase of the myths book and could afford to take a few days off. Even more than a few if absolutely necessary.

She really hoped it wouldn't be.

How on earth am I going to round up this animal? And find the Mystery Man? He was suddenly a major problem again, now that she knew for certain he wasn't Connor.

She stared at the wall.

What if I just don't do it?

Nobody expected her to get involved other than the three Dons, and they were hardly going to come after her. No-one else even knew the problem existed; well, apart from Michael, whom she had told, and Connor, who would have been enlightened by now, no doubt. If she shoved it all to one side and knuckled down to work, who would blame her?

Strangely, though, she didn't exactly want to forget about it. Have it done and finished and behind her, yes, absolutely, no question; but leave it undone? Not really.

Perhaps it was a curse; she would retain responsibility for all paranormal happenings that occurred in the entire western hemisphere over the course of her lifetime. Outrageous and unfair, but…interesting.

How do you find, trap and then hold captive a wild carnivore the size of a Shetland pony?

Rebecca drew up her knees on the saggy sofa. The street

lamps shone through the great arched window against the backdrop of the navy blue night, and with no curtain she knew she might as well be on a lit stage, but she didn't care. She liked the dark outside.

So this animal. Finding out where it had been should be straightforward enough if it was leaving bits of sheep behind. There must be no end of Oxfordshire farmers eager to help her locate it. But then what? Shoot it?

Her stepfather kept a gun, of course, as most farmers did. He had been careful to teach Rebecca how to make it safe, and how to stay safe when using it, and she was no mean shot to tell the truth – marksmanship had held its appeal when she was a teenager. But it was years since she'd had a go, and the prospect of explaining to her stepfather why she needed to borrow it was not inviting.

In any case, the Dons had instructed her to return the animal, not kill it.

Enlist a vet, then? Whack it with a tranquilizer dart and hoick it into a cage for transport? But what was the vet going to think about a new species of creature arriving at the head of the food chain, and how would she prevent him from submitting it for scientific investigation?

But if, through some miraculous reserve of cunning as yet undiscovered, she caught it by herself, where could she keep it until she managed to return it, and what would she feed it on?

It all seemed so improbable. She wasn't even an animal person.

I wonder if Connor is.

Connor.

Rebecca closed her eyes as her insides twisted again.

Meeting him had been like a physical blow. In fact it had been literally a physical blow when they collided, but the psychological shock had been greater.

When they had last met he had been a boy, three years younger than her and out of the question, even after she had begun, reluctantly, to realise that in many ways he was more mature than she was. The three years might have mattered less now, nineteen to almost twenty-three, but if he had really been – away – for longer, had lived an additional two or three years, then he had caught up.

In any case, he definitely wasn't a boy any more.

Rebecca rubbed her face. *Concentrate.* What about this animal? *What about Michael?*

She had forgotten Michael.

She fetched her laptop and emailed him. Surely he'd respond now? She had to try in any case. And then she began searching for the latest reports on the Beast of Boars Hill, paying much closer attention to detail than before.

By midnight Rebecca had two sheets of spider charts, the result of concentrated brainstorming. She had also had an email from Michael – perhaps her recent visit had switched him back on – expressing surprise and relief at Connor's return but, disappointingly, not offering his services as trapper.

She had also sorted out her fridge and emptied the dustbin and packed her suitcase.

She had taken a decision. London was just too remote. She needed to be in Oxfordshire with her quarry (assuming neither had already moved on) and with people she could at least talk to about things even if they stubbornly refused to do anything with her. That meant the Dons.

And Connor…

In the police station holding room, Jack slept.

With nothing to do all day, he was extraordinarily fatigued by evening. After finishing the little beans and the sauce and the funny little fingers of meat, he stretched out on his side and went to sleep, the cat curled comfortably in the small of his back.

The constable collected the tray and noted that Biggles showed no inclination to leave the room.

'Anybody's friend, old Biggles, always has been,' the desk sergeant said.

'Well, he's not anybody's friend at the moment, just that lad's.'

The sergeant shrugged. 'Some people have a way with animals.'

True. It was a pity the lad hadn't been able to give them any information about the Beast. He had so little English it had been difficult to decide whether he was being deliberately obstructive or just knew nothing; or was simple, which was probably more like it.

Well, tomorrow Social Services would be taking him off their hands. In the meantime...

'Any more dead sheep today?'

Roly Pidgeon was knocking earth off his boots at the back door.

'Mr Pidgeon, I'm going to be away for a few days. Might be a couple of weeks. Just to let you know.'

There was no reason for the Pidgeons to be kept abreast of her movements, but they were a sweet old couple and Rebecca had long ago given them a spare key to hold for her.

The old man raised his hand. 'Just you hold on a tick, first.'

Rebecca set her suitcase down and waited, pretty certain of what was coming. The day felt holiday-ish, although the only real similarity with a holiday was the disruption; she certainly didn't have a swimsuit in her luggage.

Roly Pidgeon re-emerged bearing two knobbly brown paper bags. 'Got a few too many at the moment. Any use where you're going?'

Rebecca felt the weight. She opened the tops: a dozen or so earthy potatoes, cold and scented with the outdoors, and a richly green, frilly Savoy cabbage.

'Are you sure you can spare these?' It was a familiar routine, but one she felt bound to follow.

'Course we can. Ground throws up more than we know what to do with!'

Rebecca knew that, of course, and also knew she wasn't the only friend to get such gifts. 'Mr Pidgeon, how is it you're such a brilliant gardener?'

He coloured rewardingly. 'Oh now, it's the soil really. Good soil throws up a lot. I feed mine and look after it, that's all. Now you take care wherever it is you're off to, and don't make the cabbage wait!'

Rebecca made two trips to the car, stowing everything with precision in the tiny boot. There would be a way for cars to get access to the Ferry House, she was sure – the Dons might have brought in their furniture by handcart a century ago for all she knew, but there would have been deliveries to the boathouse before it was wrecked.

She found she was quite looking forward to surprising the unlikely old men by turning up on their doorstep again so soon.

Chapter Nineteen

Connor awakened to daylight, the spatter of rain on windows, and a deeply savoury smell that wasn't bacon. He lay still, allowing his senses to nudge his brain into gear.

He recognized the room instantly, knowing where he was from the feel of the collapsing feather pillow under his head even before he opened his eyes. After nearly three months of strange beds, in farmhouses and flats and yachts and hostels, waking each day to struggle to make sense of where he was and how he had got there, today he just knew and it seemed perfectly right.

Despite icy sheets and sagging mattress springs, Connor felt able to relax for the first time in months, or even years, and it was delicious.

He rolled onto his back and linked his fingers behind his head. Quite possibly, it might be for as far back as he could remember. The sensation was so novel, so luxurious, that he intended to enjoy it, not analyse it. Right now he felt like there was nothing he needed to do, nowhere he needed to go, and no-one he needed to deceive.

That last, especially, felt liberating.

It had been extraordinary, mind-blowing, when Rebecca introduced him to the three old men and they had been so unperturbed, so accepting of him, as if he and Rebecca and the whole story were commonplace. Having braced himself for scepticism and suspicion, he had suddenly found no need for it – nothing to push against, nothing to duck. It was almost like falling over.

Rebecca had delivered him and then driven back to London, where she still lived. The least ancient of the three ancient men, who was in the kitchen about to make tea or supper or whatever it was called here, simply added another pack of sausages to the pan he was putting in the oven, and an hour later Connor was eating toad-in-the-hole, the sausages deliciously charred and the batter squidgy beneath its dark crust. There was mashed potato and Brussels sprouts and a thin, winey gravy that married everything together, and Connor ate like a starved man.

Then they had talked.

Lying in bed, staring up at the ceiling, Connor began to smile.

You would think that after five years in an alien world he would be shockproof. He ought surely to have grown a thick, impermeable shell from which surprises would simply rebound. But the gradual realization last night that three of Oxford's Dons, three holders of college Fellowships, three professors who had been lecturing to students at the University for decades were only half-human and over two hundred years old had left him reeling.

'But we've retired now,' said Professor Lloyd, the one that looked like a starved reptile, as if that made it all right.

'Although *one of us* should never have been teaching anyway,' said the fierce one with the glare.

'I was colourful. I injected *zest*.'

'You were too lazy to graduate!'

Professor Lloyd nodded serenely. 'True, true.'

Connor said, vaguely aware that he was latching on to the least improbable aspect but going for it anyway, 'But if you didn't graduate, how could you–'

'We had *glamour*.'

Glamour.

The Don waved his hands in the air before him. 'Fairy glamour. Not Marilyn Monroe.'

The youngest of the Dons – or at any rate the least ancient – cleared his throat. Connor already thought of him as the head of the little family despite, or probably because of, being the junior member. 'I am a few years younger,' he had explained.

'He was the whippersnapper,' the reptile had added.

'It's a way of confusing people, that's all. It enables us to get by without drawing unwanted attention. It persuades people to forget how long we've been here.'

That would certainly help, Connor thought. He said, 'So you all just – walked in one day?' It shook one's faith in the University a touch.

'No, no! We studied as hard as anyone!'

'Two of us, anyway,' muttered the Vulture, Professor Viator.

'Went through the educational system such as it was in those days, put our backs to the metaphorical wheel, and in due course our academic achievements were recognized. All quite legitimate.'

'My mother was over the moon.'

'Your mother never learned the truth.'

'Of course not – why upset her?'

They were half-brothers as well as half-fairy, and their respective mothers had found one another and formed a kind of mutual support group around the time that Jane Austen was writing *Pride and Prejudice*. Deserted, the three wronged women had retained their full measure of pride and battled the inevitable prejudice, and their boys had grown up and discovered the gap between the worlds that their vanished father had used.

'Slap bang by the river on land owned by Cardinal's College,' Professor Lloyd said. 'So of course we had to become members.'

And so they did. At first they simply kept an eye on the position of the rift, building a house for themselves close by and enclosing the trouble patch in their front garden, so that no unsuspecting passerby would fall through it.

Quite a decent-sized house.

'My family had money.'

Connor asked, 'Wouldn't the gap have been safer indoors?'

Professor Viator said, 'Undoubtedly, but would we?'

Professor Peregrine cleared his throat again. 'If something came through in the garden, it could just jump the wall and be away. We none of us felt comfortable with waking to find a wild animal in the spare room.'

'Or a snake.'

'Had a tallixer once.'

Professor Viator said heavily, 'Twice, I think you mean.'

'A tallixer!' Connor was shocked. 'I saw a picture of one of those. They're meat-eaters, aren't they?'

'Certainly. Top of the food chain. Imagine a cross between a panther and a wolf.'

'I never saw one in the flesh.'

'Keep themselves to themselves in the main, but some fool people keep them as pets. Say they're for personal protection but it's a show-off thing really.'

The tallixer had provided the tipping point and in the early

1880s they thought of a cunning way to build around the gap without, as Professor Lloyd put it, risking being gobbled up by things that went bump in the night. They built a boathouse.

Competitive rowing was in full swing by then and the boats were kept on floating barges that shifted up and down the bank according to which college was top of the league. The three Dons planted the idea of building a permanent structure, which didn't immediately go down too well.

'But then we pointed out that it could be used for partying too, and that did the trick.'

'Fell over themselves to get it through. It was up and running by Christmas.'

The gap was sealed inside a hefty oak cube, ostensibly the plinth for *The Head of the River* statue, and for a hundred and twenty-eight years Professor Peregrine, as Senior Member of the Cardinal's Boat Club, kept a relaxed but constant eye on the thing.

'A hundred and twenty-eight!'

'Glamour, dear boy, glamour.'

And now the boathouse had burned down and the gap opened to the sky and by pure bad luck two large things had blundered through in the early hours of the morning, when the worlds had interacted and the moonlight over the Thames in Oxford had collided with light from the world invisible which was just next door.

Next door...

In the spare bedroom, Connor suddenly became alive to the fact that there was an element in the murmur downstairs that didn't fit. One of the voices was too light to be coming from the rusty throat of someone entering his third century.

Rebecca.

Connor dressed quickly, vowing to get himself more clothes before the week was out, and had a quick scrub-up in the bathroom. The tantalising smells from the kitchen suggested lunch rather than breakfast, and Professor Viator was setting out cutlery in the dining room.

He glanced up as Connor passed the open doorway. 'Good. I was just about to call you.' And beyond him, holding a glass jug of water, stood Rebecca.

* * *

Nobody answered the buzzer and the intercom remained silent, but just as Foster was about to give up, the door was opened by an old man in trousers one just knew went up past his waist. He looked nonplussed.

'Who are you?'

'My name's Foster,' Geoffrey said. 'I've come to see Michael Seward, but he doesn't appear to be in.'

The man snorted. 'Don't know him very well, then, do you? He's gone up north. Three years ago he went.'

'Ah. But his name's still–'

'That's because he's still the tenant. But he doesn't live here.'

'The flat's empty?'

'No, no, of course it's not empty.' The old man seemed exasperated; he closed the front door and shooed Foster ahead of him to the road.

So Michael had moved out, yet his name was still on the door and someone was using the place...

Geoffrey said, quickly, 'Is Rebecca living here then?'

The old man turned round.

'Oh, you're a friend of *Rebecca's?* Why didn't you say so?'

Professor Viator had cooked cottage pie with strong, dark cabbage, and there was blue-veined cheese and crackers to follow. How the old men packed it away was a mystery, but Connor was not averse to a cooked meal in the middle of the day. He noticed Rebecca took only a small portion. She said, 'Cabbage courtesy of Roly Pidgeon.'

'*Roly Pidgeon!*'

'The man who could feed the world. Lives downstairs.'

In London, she meant. She must have moved from the tiny bedsit then, as it had been her great-aunt who lived downstairs there, hadn't it? Another question to ask.

She had come to join forces, although it seemed her agenda was not the same as his.

'If I'm going to round up the Beast of Boars Hill I need help. And if this Mystery Man is part of the deal, I'll want help with him too.'

Two Dons attended assiduously to their cottage pie. Professor Peregrine cleared his throat. 'I think you will find that he is.'

'Thought so. Any ideas? Is this another Uriel Passenger having a jolly jaunt and up to no good?'

She was very blithe.

'Perhaps, but I rather think not.' Professor Peregrine helped himself to more cabbage. 'He doesn't seem to be coping very well. Hiding in sheds and running away from people. It rather suggests a disturbed mind, wouldn't you say?'

It looked like the Dons had shovelled the problem of the accidental immigrants onto Rebecca. Connor had yet to see a newspaper and had known nothing about the business until last night. But their problems now overlapped, since the Dons were adamant they shouldn't demolish the newly built wall around the boathouse gap.

'Dear boy, you should never go back the same way you came. At least, not once a few days has gone by. Always goes wrong – always.'

'Goes wrong how?' Rebecca asked.

Viator glared at his plate. Lloyd hummed at the ceiling. Professor Peregrine said, 'I don't think we want to go into details at the table. Trust me, my dear, it is simply not an option. This person and the tallixer need to find an alternative route. Would you pass the peppermill?'

'Okay then,' Rebecca said. 'Ashendon.'

'No.' Connor shook his head, a small movement. 'Ashendon just leads to prison. Captivity, I mean.'

'But you were – well, from here. If they belong...'

'No.'

Rebecca sat back.

Connor said, 'But there is another gap.'

'There are always other gaps,' the Vulture said. 'The problem is finding out where they are.'

'Yes.' Connor hesitated, but knew it was time. He said, 'But that's what I've promised I'll do.'

Chapter Twenty

There were known to be four gaps. Connor had been told this quite categorically by the people who had sprung him from his incarceration. They also told him that the locations of only three were known, and that they wanted Connor to find the remaining one and make it safe. And Connor, of course, had given his word, which meant that was now added to the schedule.

Rebecca didn't know whether she should be weeping, raging, or laughing hysterically. A week ago she had been drawing imaginary landscapes for mythological creatures to gambol in, and now she was about to strike out into the real landscape in search of *real* mythological creatures…or was that paradoxical?

I am leaving normality behind. Again. There are going to be huge swathes of my life which I will never be able to talk about because no-one will ever believe me.

Connor fished in his hip pocket and brought out a small plastic bag. He extracted a piece of paper, and as he tucked the bag away Rebecca thought she caught a glimpse of the small, all-over pattern you find on the back of a playing card.

He laid the note on the tablecloth. It had the punched holes of a Rolodex card, and there was handwriting on it in ballpoint pen.

> *Stand on the island of glass and look towards the great circle.*
> *Put the numbers in order left from the lay of the land.*

Rebecca was unable to refrain from commenting: 'That should be *lie* of the land.'

'It's what she said.'

She? Rebecca shot him a look.

> *Cross water to a place of captivity and face the stone at half-light.*

'That last bit ties in with what Uriel Passenger thought,' Rebecca said. 'But what's the rest about? What numbers?'

Connor didn't know. His rescuers had been operating not entirely from philanthropic motivation. They were a small team of political activists, and by a mixture of imagination, tight planning and sheer, cold nerve they had effected his escape. They knew of four rifts where the light from each world periodically spilled into the other and threw the way open, and they were intent on closing them off, because they believed that while even one gap could be passed through, then both worlds were under the threat of catastrophic infection.

'Infection?' Rebecca asked. 'What kind of infection?' Were they talking about the corruption of hearts and minds? Pastoral populations becoming besotted with the internal combustion engine and television game shows?

'Disease,' Connor said shortly.

'Ah,' Professor Peregrine said. 'Amazonian tribes wiped out by the common cold. No appropriate antibodies, you see. A very good point.'

Rebecca turned the idea over in her mind. 'What about midges? Fleas? Surely they could be getting through unnoticed all the time. Was the Black Death caused by fairy fleas?'

It came out funnier than she wanted. Fortunately nobody seemed to notice.

'I suppose so,' Connor said. 'I suppose it depends on whether at least one side is open to the air.'

So the gap at Ashendon was protected by virtue of the stone room having been built around it, and the one here in Oxford by its plinth. The third was in the middle of a Vermont pasture, but was protected the other end, Connor said. But that left one which hadn't yet been found, let alone made safe.

'It could be anywhere,' Rebecca protested. She couldn't devote years to this.

'No. Definitely Britain.'

Somebody had known something once. Why would people not keep proper records? It was the same old story of paranoia leading to wrapping the truth up in riddles, and then lack of interest meaning nearly the whole lot was forgotten.

Interestingly, it seemed to be much the same in both worlds, despite the continuing presence of magic over there. Connor's rescuers had been able to tell him only the sketchiest of half-remembered hints: two numbers that needed to be discovered and which would then confirm the location hinted at by the riddle.

'That's my guess,' Connor had said. 'She *said* 'Cross water to a place of captivity and face the stone' so I'm assuming we have to go to an island with a prison...'

Rebecca noticed that he had said 'we'.

'..and that by then it will be obvious which stone we have to face.'

But there remained that cryptic instruction: *Put the numbers in order left from the lay of the land.*

Which should be 'lie of the land'.

There had been too much salt in everything. Everything except for the breakfast flakes. Corn flakes. Jack liked corn flakes. But he had eaten everything and felt much stronger despite the salt.

Stronger, and able to work the Skill.

He chose his moment with care, waiting quietly while the lady in the trousers who had come for him spoke with Dave, his favourite. He could feel her attention on him even though she was talking and looking away – he thought she probably knew this moment was risky despite the room being full of people who would try to catch him if he made a break for it.

Dave was looking his way, smiling and being kind.

Jack smiled back.

Then they were outside and walking together on the paving slabs beside the road, which was smelly and noisy from the machines only an arm's length away. He preferred not to look, tucking himself between the lady and the wall. It was a good wall, high and strong and made of stone, and he wondered what was behind it and whether it would be better than here.

A little ahead of them the wall stopped and there was a doorway. Someone, someone in a skirt, came through it onto the pavement and crossed the road.

He readied himself. It could work. If he concentrated.

'My car is only five minutes away,' the lady said. She was looking forward, walking briskly, probably not thinking too hard.

Good.

He heard laughing and footsteps behind him, and when he

looked round he saw a bunch of people, quite a few, about to overtake. That would be confusing. Good again.

At the doorway, which was wide and deep with a little room on either side, Jack expelled all the air from his lungs, shrank into his clothes, and stepped sideways into the opening, away from the lady and the fumes and the noise. For an instant his guts clenched with alarm as the group following turned in with him, but then they had formed a wall of a different kind between him and the lady, which helped him to hide. They were ignoring him anyway, although whether because of the Skill he wasn't sure.

But he was inside, behind the stone wall and into the wide green space beyond; he slipped round the corner and kept walking.

Outside the college the social services officer span round.

'Jack?'

He had gone. How had he gone?

She backed up and hurried through the open door into the quad.

'Excuse me, madam, are you a member of this College?'

The porter, if that was who it was, had emerged from his office and come after her. So embarrassing.

'I'm sorry – Barbara Dobson, Social Services. The client I was escorting just ran through here…I think.' Honesty elbowed its way to the fore. 'I just need to–'

'I'm sorry, madam, the College is not open to the public. If you'd like to wait here I'll call the Head Porter and we can see what we can do.'

Not much by that time, Barbara Dobson thought. *The college is closed.* How demeaning. And it would be a whole lot more demeaning when she had to admit she had lost her client between the police station and the car park.

Oxford!

Steph was working at home. Rebecca made tea for them both and pulled out her Mac. 'What's the broadband password?'

She logged on. Having written two cheques, she needed to move some money across into her current account to cover them.

Connor's face had been a picture. 'What's this?'

She had told him it was just an advance. The arrangement Michael had set up would need a bit of juggling before they could access Connor's share, but in the meantime he needed some cash to live on. The cheque she had written to him had been for a thousand pounds. That ought to buy him a pair of jeans and a sweatshirt or two.

Connor was going to stay at the Ferry House, but Rebecca needed somewhere more sane. In any case, three cooked meals a day would kill her and the Vulture had already begun peeling potatoes when she left.

Connor had walked part of the way with her, and they went via St Aldates, where Connor would be able to pay the cheque into his Post Office savings account. Rebecca was glad to learn that he had one.

'I don't have the book, though.'

He could pay in but wouldn't be able to withdraw.

'But it's at home?' The word slipped out, but Rebecca let it lie. 'You can go and get it?'

She had watched the old, familiar, grim look fall across Connor's face. *Home* had never been a good concept with regard to Connor. But his sister had lent him money to get back to the UK, so not everything about it could be bad.

A thought struck Rebecca and she paused, catching Connor's arm. 'Hold on, you need to pay your sister back, don't you?'

'This will cover it.'

Rebecca set off again, brisker. 'I'll write you another one when we get to the Post Office. Don't argue, Connor, it's your money! You can reimburse me when it's all sorted.'

And that was the second thousand.

After her bit of banking, Rebecca settled down to browse. She Googled *island, prison* and *stone*, and ran swiftly through the non-starters – Zanzibar, the Rolling Stones, comics...

And then stopped.

Rebecca read the names, but the temptation to speak them was too great. Despite Steph's scholarly silence, she spoke aloud in the quiet room, 'Pulpit Rock and Nicodemus Knob'.

Chapter Twenty-One

Connor paused on the pavement outside the Post Office.

Turn right, and he could cross back over Folly Bridge and take the towpath to the Ferry House. But turn left, and he had all of Oxford before him.

The streets were wet and the cycles hushed as they passed, but for the moment the rain had stopped and Connor hoped Rebecca would make it to her friend's flat before it started again. The afternoon was drawing down; street lamps had come on while they were in the Post Office and most cars were using headlights, but it was too early yet to retreat indoors and close the curtains. The evening would be long enough as it was; the Dons could wait.

Connor turned left and headed north towards the city centre, content just to walk. After five years of being restricted to the barn and its yard, walking in a straight line for minutes on end was still a source of delight.

Hearing English too, spoken with English accents.

At the crossroads he turned right into The High and then left again into Turl Street, between smaller shops of stationery and second-hand books and past the open door of a coffee shop, spilling its giddy aroma of freshly ground beans. He continued onto The Broad, past the doorway of Blackwell's where yesterday, astonishingly, he had met Rebecca and all the pieces of his existence had been thrown into the air. The Broad became Holywell Street, running alongside the honey-coloured palace that was New College, and he turned right again into the aptly named Longwall Street and finally back to The High.

And now it was dusk and Connor, using the homing sense he took for granted, began to head for the river, but then swerved into one of the narrow, cobbled streets which wound between the main thoroughfares and served the backs of the colleges. The cars and buses were left behind and there were only ranks of bicycles tethered to railings, rain gutters bordering the cobbles, and the hush of distant traffic.

He recognized, with a little shock, the doorway into Corpus

Christi, where years ago he and Rebecca had stood and stared at a stone column with a golden pelican on top, and he paused for a moment, feeling the passage of time.

She had been so superior, unattainable for a trunkful of reasons, and so disparaging toward him. Her presence had been a perpetual, nagging trial, and he had wasted hours imagining all the sparkling, bitter things he could say.

He never said them, of course. It was odd and frustrating that someone so self-possessed, so confident, so *unreachable* should also seem so in need of being looked after, but she did. He had wanted to guard her even then, throw a cloak of protection around her which would see off any threat, and he still wanted to now.

The Queen of Clubs…or rather, of Clover. If it were true, then that would account for some of it.

A University student coming towards him turned casually, unappreciatively, maddeningly under the arch to vanish into his sweet, desirable, invisible world, and Connor moved on.

Oxford hurt.

Merton Street took a wriggle to the right and tipped him onto Blue Boar Street, and there, staring upwards, stood a boy with a cat, and it took two seconds for Connor to realise there was something seriously wrong about them.

He stood still and thought. He was afraid of butting in where he wasn't wanted, and he was also afraid of sparking a reaction that would be, well, unhelpful. But the boy didn't look great.

Connor followed the line of his gaze to the signboard swinging above the pub door, and saw the painted name – *The Boar* – and the painted animal that leapt from left to right, and which was really not a boar.

The cat sat down as if prepared to wait if necessary. Connor looked at it, and then at the signboard again, and then back at the boy, at the side of his face. He considered for a moment the things he might say, the first things that could be said to this person who was so badly lost. Then he made up his mind.

'Tallixer,' he said.

* * *

'Tallixer.'

Jack jumped, every nerve in his body leaping with alarm, and span round.

There was only one person behind him, a man maybe two lengths away, so it must have been him who had spoken. But he was standing at an angle, his eyes turned aside, his hands in his pockets, and when Jack looked he took a step back, away from him.

Jack breathed. Too late to use the Skill; but perhaps he didn't want to anyway.

Tallixer, the man had said.

Licking his lips, Jack said, 'Tallixer,' and pointed at the picture on the board.

The words felt strangely comfortable to him as they formed and were given voice. Connor was surprised; he half-expected the sound of the alien syllables to be frightening and depressing, but it seemed returning home had neutralized them. Now it was just another language, another ability, even an advantage. Definitely an advantage right now.

He had leaned on a bollard in order to lessen the threat and the damp was seeping through his jeans, but it seemed to be working. Jack – he said his name was Jack – was willing to talk, although he didn't seem to know much about what had happened to him.

Connor guessed that the police had picked him up and that he was probably being handed over to Social Services when he gave them the slip by darting into Christchurch College. After hanging about in there a while, no doubt aided by a little Skill, he had emerged from the back gate into Merton Street and almost immediately been frozen in his tracks by the sight of a tallixer on the pub sign.

Because it was a tallixer. Maybe once it had been a boar, but it was now way too feline for that. Odd. Perhaps someone had seen a tallixer near here centuries before the Dons took over the guardianship of the gap and thought to commemorate it this way. It would explain why a beast no more native to this world than a gryphon should be adorning a pub sign.

On the other hand, there were enough pubs called the Dragon or the Unicorn or the Mermaid...

At least it cleared up any remaining doubt about what the Beast of Boars Hill would turn out to be.

Connor, stretching his memory of vocabulary, said '*Come with me and meet the teachers*'.

The boy was shivering.

The cat stalked in front, its tail a waving question-mark.

Chapter Twenty-Two

Rebecca scooped a black and white cat off the armchair nearest the door and dumped her bag.

'I know where it is,' she said, 'I Googled and it's got to be.'

Then she said, 'Oh.'

In the farthest corner, standing with his back to the glazed corner cupboard that held the Dons' collection of mementos – a china donkey in a floppy hat, a frog made from shells, a commemorative mug from the Great Exhibition of 1851 – was a boy, a teenager, with a wary, suspicious stare that reminded Rebecca of her first ever meeting with Connor. He had dark corkscrews of hair way past his shoulders and was wearing a baggy black sweatshirt and jeans with the hems turned up. He seemed to shrink at least two inches in every direction when Rebecca looked at him.

'Ah,' said Professor Lloyd. 'This is Rebecca, Jack. Say hello to Rebecca.' Then he said something else, extremely fast and full of consonants Rebecca wasn't used to – strange sequences that made her think of eastern Europe – ending up with, 'hello'.

The boy said, carefully, 'Hello.'

'Yes,' Rebecca said, 'Hello.' Then she said, 'Right, who is this?'

'Jack,' the Tortoise said. 'He doesn't remember his surname, so we're calling him Jack Green. It's neutral, but quite appropriate.' He leaned towards Rebecca and spoke behind his hand in a hopelessly stagey whisper: 'I wanted "Jack Rabbit" but they wouldn't let me.'

Rebecca looked at the boy. He was a bit rabbit-like, crunched into the wall watching her. His edges seemed somehow blurred.

'Is this the Mystery Man?' she asked. 'Did he come through your gap?'

'It isn't our gap *as such*.'

So this was the Mystery Man. Well, that was one hurdle overcome.

You can't name somebody 'Jack Rabbit', though. That was

typical of the Tortoise.

The other two Dons had given themselves aliases in Latin, which was perhaps more cloak-and-dagger than had been necessary even in the nineteenth century, but they were straightforward enough in translation: Peregrine was an Anglicisation of *peregrinus*, meaning 'sojourner' (unfortunately a funny word in English) and *viator* meant 'traveller'.

The Tortoise, on the other hand, had named himself *Custos Calignosus Ostiorum Nefastarum*, which in English came out as 'Dark Guardian of the Forbidden Portals'. And when that proved too much of a mouthful he took the name Lloyd after Marie Lloyd of the Victorian music hall. ('*She was a poppet.*')

Rebecca sighed. 'Where are the others?'

'Tesco.'

'What?'

'Perry drives but V chooses the food. He doesn't trust us with root vegetables.'

'Connor?'

'Here.'

Rebecca jumped in a very small way, caught between relief and tension.

Connor closed the door behind him and poured a cat off his arm onto the rug.

'*Someone* left the door open!' the Tortoise said in a sing-song voice, gazing innocently at the ceiling.

Rebecca frowned. 'I did. Why?'

'There'll be a fight if Biggles gets in with the others,' Connor said.

'Why?' Rebecca asked again, mystified.

Everyone looked at her. Connor said, 'He's a stranger. You must have noticed him?'

'She noticed him alright. She nearly squashed him with her haversack.'

'It's a cat,' Rebecca said. 'There are enough of them here. And I didn't nearly squash it, I moved it first.'

'Not black ones. He's Jack's cat.'

'He brought a cat with him?'

'Well, yes and no. Not from there. He's a police cat.'

Rebecca stared.

Connor, speaking kindly and slowly, said, 'He's the police station's cat. Jack made friends with him, and when he escaped, Biggles followed him. It's alright, Rebecca.'

'I want a cup of coffee.'

Professor Lloyd sparked into action. 'I'll put the kettle on. There are still some fairy cakes from yesterday!'

Fairy cakes at nine thirty in the morning. Staying here would have killed her.

The supermarket expedition returned while the kettle was boiling and by ten o'clock everyone was cosy with a hot mug as if it wasn't barely two hours since breakfast. Auntie Edie had been like that, Rebecca recalled. Maybe it was age; although her great-aunt's eighty-odd years had nothing on the Dons.

Rebecca noted Connor got rid of one of the little sponge cakes with his coffee. Jack-the-Mystery-Man had three – she counted the frilly paper cases left on his plate.

Biggles the police cat smoodged down between Jack's thigh and the arm of the chair and tucked his paws under his furry chest. The boy stroked him, long, firm strokes from the base of his ears to the base of his tail.

Rebecca's great discovery had been annoyingly shoved aside by the newspapers Professor Peregrine had brought back. They had bought all three locals to get the full spread, but it was the same story in all of them.

'Beast of Boars Hill Devastation!' A photograph of a glum man in wellies standing next to something that could have been a dirty sheepskin rug but which was clearly not.

'Boars Hill Beast Strikes Twice!'

The rather more restrained Chronicle omitted the photograph: *'Farmers angry over lack of action to capture beast'.*

'Why don't they shoot it?' Rebecca asked.

There was a communal in-drawing of breath. The Tortoise hummed and waggled a foot. Jack in the corner quivered.

'What?' she said.

'It's Jack's tallixer,' Connor said.

'Jack's what?'

'Tallixer. The creature's a tallixer. A major carnivore

somewhere between a panther and a wolf.'

'But what do you mean "his"? You don't mean to say it's a pet?'

Connor sighed, which was unsettling, and looked at her slightly sadly, which was even worse. She nearly said 'what?' again, but caught herself in time.

'Elsa the lioness.'

'*What?*'

Rebecca whipped round but the Tortoise was hiding behind his mug.

Professor Peregrine explained. 'The Adamsons' lioness, Elsa, that they raised from a cub. They wrote about it: Born Free.'

'And a film.'

'Indeed.'

'Virginia McKenna. She was a poppet. *He* wore the pyjama trousers and *she* wore the pyjama jacket.'

Rebecca said, 'But–'

'The thing is, this tallixer is like that lioness,' Connor explained. 'She's tame, really.'

Rebecca flapped a newspaper. 'Doesn't sound like it.'

'She's just hungry. She hasn't attacked any people. But if she carries on taking sheep someone might try to shoot her, so we need to move quickly.'

He was very compassionate. Rebecca's thoughts took a little hop by themselves and suddenly she knew why the teenager's clothes were on the large side and looked so new.

He had always bested her.

'Alright,' she said. 'What do we do?'

There were elements of farce about it, like something from a comic, as unlikely in its way as balancing a bucket of water on a classroom door to soak the teacher. What do you use to catch a dog? – a bit of meat. What do you use to catch a major predator at the top of the food chain? – a really *big* bit of meat.

'Don't open them here,' Rebecca snapped as the Vulture presented his knife to the shrink-wrap. 'I don't want blood dripping all over me. We'll take scissors with us.'

Three legs of lamb, still safely vacuum-wrapped, went into the boot along with her rucksack and a carpet bag – made from actual carpet – which contained Connor's overnight stuff and some spare clothes for their Mystery Man, who was no mystery any longer but merely a fairy.

Or not.

'I don't think he is,' Connor said. 'He doesn't look right.'

The Dons agreed.

'If a very small child strayed through a gap and never came back, how much would he remember after, let's say, fifteen years?' Professor Peregrine asked rhetorically.

How terrible. Rebecca imagined the parents. They would never know what had become of him; they would invent all kinds of horrors.

She shuddered.

'But this gap was supposed to be safe under your statue,' she protested.

Connor shook his head. 'It doesn't work like that. Think. I went through in Derbyshire and came back in Vermont. There was only, oh, fifty miles or so between the gaps that side. Jack could easily have fallen through a gap a long way away and then landed in Oxford when he returned, even if he hadn't travelled far in the other world.'

So it wasn't just time that was out of kilter, although it was the time discrepancy that was so difficult to stop thinking about.

Rebecca watched Connor pumping up her rear tyres with a cobwebby foot pump he'd found in the lean-to behind the Ferry House. He had insisted on checking tyre pressures before they set off, apparently accustomed to maintaining his family – there was that word again – family's old car.

Connor's back was lean but wider than three years ago, and more...

Well, more. The short hair was novel and...nice. And the decent clothes. He had nipped into the city centre and come back with some things Jack could wear without getting lost inside, and a waterproof with a fleece lining. Connor himself seemed wedded to an old canvas jacket, and Rebecca didn't feel up to asking why.

There were still so many gaps.

She, Connor had said of his rescuer.

Professor Viator made them sandwiches, and Rebecca arrived in the kitchen just too late to grab the bread knife from him to cut slimmer slices for hers.

And then it was dusk and the three of them climbed into her car – four including Biggles, who it seemed was coming too – and Rebecca turned the key in the ignition.

Fill up the tank first and then big game hunting on Boars Hill.

Chapter Twenty-Three

Connor watched the road illuminated by the car's headlights, the ditches and hedgerows either side of the tarmac visible briefly and gone, left behind, over and over, as the Mini sped on its way. Rebecca eased off for the bends but accelerated again before they had quite come out, crisply and full of confidence. Connor suspected she enjoyed driving.

He had nearly climbed into the back seat to keep Jack company, the boy's silence and shyness awakening in him an urge to protect, but had decided that was too weird; Rebecca would think he was avoiding her. So he let Jack ride behind alone and slid the passenger seat back to give himself more leg-room. The Mini was compact, and a tallixer on board would be a challenge, always supposing Jack could really entice it to get in.

Rebecca said she had seen the beast but only from a window, across the street and in the dark. Connor suspected she didn't realise just how much space a large, feral predator would fill.

Boars Hill was a village south-west of Oxford and very rural. One left the city behind very quickly, and once outside the ring road the farms and fields took over.

Connor had no idea whether their plan would work. He had had very little experience of animals other than skinny urban cats slinking amongst the trash cans until he landed up in the Colvins' dairy farm and found himself feeding cows and chickens and goats. He had learned a lot in a short space of time and found it fascinating, not least the way that something that measured four feet high and six feet long could seem to take up so much more space simply because it was alive and breathing. The immense, hot, sweet-smelling bulk of a Jersey cow had been so much greater than its mere dimensions. He had the feeling a meat-eater would be the same and more.

He fingered the two whistles in his pocket, the dog whistle and the ordinary one. Jack seemed confident the tallixer would hear and come, and that the bait of a hunk of raw meat would be enough to induce her to trust a stranger.

'*She will not bite us?*' he had asked. '*This is safe?*'
Apparently it was.
He had noticed that Rebecca, despite her lack of interest in animals, seemed fearless.
She said something and he took his eyes off the road.
'Pardon?'
Rebecca raised her voice fractionally, using a kind of intense whisper. 'How much English does he understand?'
'Oh. I'm not sure. Not much at all if you speak fast.'
'Mm.'
Connor suspected she was going to be speaking very fast indeed from now on. He said, 'He's not dangerous, Rebecca. He's lost and quite scared, probably.'
'You said back at the Ferry House that he wasn't from over there, though.'
Fairly fast; not racing. Connor thought she was probably trying quite hard.
'I don't know. It's certainly odd that he has any English at all. But also he doesn't quite have the look...'
'The look.'
'It's hard to explain. Just something – other, I suppose. Nothing I can describe. But Jack looks too ordinary.'
Even we look more 'other' than he does, Connor thought. He and Rebecca, and Michael too, were not quite like other people. Rebecca for a start was the most beautiful girl he had ever seen, despite disdaining to wear make up or bother much about her hair, and Michael was, even to his eyes, pretty extraordinary to look at. His own face was just that: his own face, too familiar to be analysed, but he was aware there had been comments from time to time...
He hadn't had the chance to meet many people on the other side, but those he had seen shared a symmetry, a regularity, a harmony in their features which nevertheless was mixed with a kind of wildness...
Very hard to describe.
But Jack didn't have it; he just didn't. He looked like a kid, growing too fast, with bitten nails and big teeth. Ordinary. Yet he spoke their language, had very little English, and was walking

around with a tallixer.

And he had Skill.

I'll have to explain to Rebecca about Skill.

'Okay, this is Boars Hill.' Rebecca said. 'I need somewhere off the road to park.'

The lanes were too narrow to leave the car on the highway. They needed a drive or lay-by to park in safely – and hopefully to load a large animal in later.

'There?'

'Too late.'

The gateway had appeared in the headlights and gone before Rebecca could brake. Checking there were no cars behind her, she slowed to a dawdle and Connor strained to see ahead, beyond the headlights' beam.

'There!'

Rebecca pulled in to the cart track, the Mini bumping down the rough edge of the tarmac, and shifted into reverse.

'What are you doing?'

'Turning round. I want to be able to pull straight out later, not mess about doing nine-point turns.' *With a huge animal in the back* was what she didn't say.

Connor watched her twist in the seat, steering with one hand while she looked out of the rear windscreen; no girly stuff with mirrors for Rebecca. He smiled.

'Okay.' The engine died. 'So what now? The meat, right?'

With clouds hiding the stars, it was deep dark – not quite black, but nearly. Your hand in front of your face, yes, but you couldn't see your feet. Connor tripped on the rutted mud and felt a fool.

Rebecca opened the boot and three times Connor pierced the shrink-wrap around the joints and sliced downwards, holding the bone out in front of him to keep clear of the drips. In the open air the scent of raw meat was much stronger, more surprising, than in a kitchen.

'That plastic's not going back in my car.'

Connor met Rebecca's stare. She had a point. He looked

around, knowing there wasn't anywhere and that he was being feeble.

'Stick it in the hedge.'

Connor stuck it. He felt bad, but where else was there? In the grand scheme of things a single act of littering wasn't so dire, and in return they were going to remove a serious public nuisance. He shoved it deep into the twigs and then wiped his hands on the grass. When he straightened up, something cold and wet pressed against his knuckles. He flinched.

'It's a wipe. Use it.'

Connor rubbed the tiny wisp of scented wetness between his hands and chucked that into the hedge too.

It had dried up during the afternoon and was now crisply cold. Connor zipped up Buddy Colvin's jacket and followed Rebecca and Jack into the field.

His eyes were beginning to adjust, but the sky was still only a slightly lighter shade of dark and everything else was just black and deeper black. It was unnerving not to be able to see where you were treading. Connor stumbled a couple of times and then began to walk with an exaggerated action, lifting his feet high over potential hummocks and tussocks. No way to check about cowpats, unfortunately, and he realized he had recognized the open-air scent of cattle; his few short weeks as a farm hand had left him with some surprising abilities.

'Oh–' Rebecca beside him bit off an expletive.

'Lift your feet up.'

'I was lifting my feet up.'

'Well, lift them higher.'

It was ironic. Rebecca, although you'd never guess it, had grown up on a farm in Suffolk while he had been rootling about amongst empty beer cans and food wrappers on tarmac and concrete. Yet he seemed able to cope with a bit of rough grass in the dark while she was clearly aching for paving stones.

Jack, no doubt wondering how the grass could possibly be so short, had already pulled ahead, his silhouette skinny and slight up ahead. Connor wondered how far away the tallixer was, and how close it would have to be before it would notice them.

And how concerned it would be about them being three.

He said, softly, 'Jack!' and saw the silhouette pause.

'I think this is where we split.'

No reply.

Connor cursed himself. Much slower, he said, *'We – three – different ways. You go on.'*

He pointed ahead. Had he got the words right? He wasn't at all sure about that 'different'.

But Jack had set off again, moving quicker and apparently having no problem at all with the rough ground.

Rebecca was at his shoulder. 'It sounds a bit Russian. Eastern European anyway. All those *zhnyuh* sounds.'

'I suppose.' He wasn't much of a linguist; learning the little he'd got had been hard.

They watched the boy's shape grow fainter against the sky.

'The thing is,' Rebecca said, 'how close does it have to be to smell the meat?'

Exactly. None of them knew. Nor how far the whistles would carry. Jack himself seemed encouragingly confident, but it was all way out of Connor's realm.

'And,' Rebecca added, 'what do those headlights belong to?'

Connor looked at her, and then past her, back the way they had come, where the hedge enclosing the field was sparse enough to allow the wrapper from a leg of lamb to be stuffed into it and the beam of a car's headlamps to shine through.

Something had pulled up in front of the Mini.

The background throb of an engine died.

Chapter Twenty-Four

'And what do those headlights belong to?'

There were no street lamps out here and Rebecca had not left a parking light on because she had tucked the car nicely into the gateway, right off the road.

The silence doubled, meaning that a low background noise she hadn't been conscious of had stopped. Someone had turned off an engine.

Then the headlamps went off too.

Motionless in the field, she listened intently, filtering out the soft night-time sounds of the countryside and tuning instead to human sounds: footsteps and car doors and equipment being handled.

A car door opened, then shut; then again.

She glanced at Connor. Blast this dark, out-of-doors thing; Rebecca wanted a torch, but she had been over-ruled on the basis that artificial light really would scare the tallixer away.

'I'll go,' she said, and found Connor had said it too.

She followed up quickly. 'No, it should be me. I know what I'm doing. You go on.'

She felt rather than saw Connor concede, and started to move only to hear him hiss: 'Be careful. And be tactful.'

Be tactful! The nerve.

Rebecca made her way towards the gate. Whoever it was on the other side of the hedge was making no attempt to be quiet, and satisfyingly Rebecca was able to get right to the gate before saying, 'Hallo! Can I help you?' loud enough to make him or her jump.

Him. It was a man. He had a torch, which showed her his beard as well as a pull-on knitted hat and a fat, down-filled jacket.

The other thing he had was a look of shock. Rebecca beamed. 'Yes?' she said.

'Ah, sorry, wasn't expecting... Am I okay parking here?'

He took her for the landowner. Couldn't be better.

'As long as you're on the highway,' Rebecca said.

'Ah, right, yes. Are you–'

'Can I ask what your business is?' Rebecca said swiftly. She loved London and would probably never move out, but that didn't mean she had forgotten how her father used to approach trespassers: a brittle smile and a steely intent. It came easy.

'Journalist. Oxford Bugle. Looking for the Beast of Boars Hill. Third night, actually.' He looked rueful and Rebecca guessed it was not an assignment he would have chosen.

'And you're here because…?'

'Last sighting, wasn't it? That farmer that wants to shoot it reckons it's still around. Are you the, er–'

'Shoot it?'

'Yes, that's right. Up every night with his shotgun, apparently.'

Rebecca thought rapidly. 'Well, it's possible it's still close by, but I've already cleared this area. I'm heading–' (she made a quick calculation) '–north, but if you want to explore east…?'

She thought it was east, although the road had twisted a lot. With luck he wouldn't be any better at guessing the direction in the dark than she was.

The reporter glanced across the road. 'Oh! Right. Okay, good idea. Thanks.' He slung a serious camera bag over his shoulder. 'Cross your fingers for me.'

'Certainly. What's the use of a camera, though?'

'Infra-red. Not mine, of course, belongs to the office. See you!'

Rebecca watched him cross the lane and climb the gate into the opposite field.

Good riddance to that.

Perfectly tactful.

Connor heard Rebecca's voice, though not her words. The tone was unmistakable.

She'll be alright.

He'd rather have been the one to go, but she was right about knowing what she was doing. He was aware how intimidating she could be when she chose.

Jack was out of sight now, lost in the clotted shadow where the trees began. Connor pictured him, striding over the grass, confident in the dark. Did night vision get better with practice? It seemed unlikely, but Jack gave that impression. Perhaps he was just more used to coping with not being able to see since he hadn't relied most of his life on street lighting.

The countryside was dark in a way cities never were.

It was cold, standing still. Rebecca was having a conversation with the driver of the car. She hadn't got rid of him yet, but it didn't sound like there was trouble.

Connor left her to it and set off.

Jack walked fast...

Jack *Green* walked fast...

Why had they wanted to give him another name? Why did he have to have two names? The old men had been really insistent about that...

The grass was so short and he walked easily, his stride swinging, eager to get to the trees. Gira wouldn't be hanging around where there was no cover and no prey. If she had taken a sheep recently she wouldn't be too impressed by the hunk of meat in his hand either, but at least it ought to get her attention.

What she would make of the *car* was another matter.

He wished Connor could talk better. It was horrible having to struggle to communicate. It would be easier not to try, but some things had to be said. He wished one of the old teachers had come along.

He wasn't comfortable with *Rebecca* at all.

A bird called, hooting, over his head; he had reached the trees and now dropped his pace, working his way along the edge of the line of tree trunks, unwilling to enter the wood without a light to guide his feet. Disappointingly, he didn't seem able to make even the smallest light here; a little of the Skill had travelled intact, but light-making had clearly been thwarted at the border.

After a minute or two he found himself facing a hedge, and picked up a few scratches clambering across – the growth wasn't dense enough to support him and he went through as much as over.

What was wrong with this place? Why were all the plants so weak?

On the far side was more pasture, rising towards a spinney of slender trees on the brow of the hill.

Jack drew breath and blew into the whistle, hoping that the sound he could not hear would, if he was really, really lucky, be heard by a pair of finely-tuned, ever-hearkening tallixer ears.

Rebecca's satisfaction at having pulled one over on the reporter soon dissipated under the difficulty of negotiating the lumpy terrain in the dark. Holding a dripping piece of meat stiffly out to one side didn't help. If she was the one to meet the tallixer, she might just hurl the leg of lamb at it.

No, she couldn't do that or she'd have nothing left to persuade it to follow her.

The plan was to fan out, blow their dog whistles, purchased that afternoon, and hope that the tallixer would be within range and interested enough to approach one of them. Then whoever that was would signal success by three short blasts on the second whistle, the ordinary one, and head back to the car.

She'd have preferred to be able to call Connor rather than hope he could hear a whistle, but that was not possible because once again he had no mobile.

I should have sorted one out.

It was so difficult. One moment he was frighteningly experienced, mature, confident in his judgment and generally unassailable, and the next moment he didn't have a clue. And all the time he was…

Intriguing. A puzzle. A book of secrets Rebecca didn't quite have the nerve to open.

She allowed her mind to roam back three years and recall the Connor she had met in Michael's flat, which was her flat now: a silent, skinny, suspicious kid who drank black coffee and wrote poetry.

He was less silent now, but even so, what he said seemed to slide around on the surface. Not exactly social talk, but not personal either; just moment-to-moment factual communication. God forbid that he should reveal anything about himself.

Rebecca sighed. It wasn't relaxing, being in his company, so why did she look forward to it?

He was very protective of Jack.

There was a belt of trees ahead of her, and just as she reached them she remembered what the reporter had said about the farmer and the gun.

Connor realised he was enjoying himself. He shouldn't have been; this wasn't some midnight ramble they were on but serious business.

Still. The dark was much more comfortable than it had been at the start, now that his eyes had adapted. He had begun to pick up sounds too, where earlier the fields had seemed silent: small, intimate, wild sounds made by creatures that had no interest in humans. Somewhere distant a fox barked, hoarse and grating, and something tiny squealed briefly. Nature at work.

The raw meat in his hand smelled strongly.

Rebecca's nonchalance with regard to the tallixer had surprised him. She was putting a lot of trust in Jack's assurance that his pet would not attack a person. Connor felt a flutter of anxiety in his stomach which suggested he believed Jack with his head rather more than with his heart.

He recalled Roy Colvin speaking about lynx, wild cats three feet long that were an endangered species in Vermont. *They're not big,* Roy had said, *but big enough if one took you by surprise.*

They didn't take you by surprise, though, because they were shy and saw you coming before you saw them. A tallixer was much bigger, and this one had learned not to fear people.

In America, guns of one kind or another were commonplace. Did English farmers own guns? Connor suspected some did. Would an English farmer try to shoot an animal that was killing his sheep?

It was a question nobody had thought to ask. Now Connor faltered as the possibility gained weight in his mind. Would a farmer bent on protecting his livestock take the trouble to make certain his target was on all fours first? How could he warn Rebecca and Jack? It wasn't possible. Why hadn't he thought about setting himself up with a mobile phone like the rest of the world? Stupid, stupid.

And then he started and gasped as a gunshot cracked.

Chapter Twenty-Five

Jack jumped, his skin flinching, and he said quickly, 'Gira!'

For a terrible moment of suspended time he stood, arms out, his will straining to draw the great animal towards him while she stared away across the night fields where the echo of the report still hung.

Then she turned her great, broad head and met his eyes.

'Gira.'

The tallixer moved, shoulders rising and falling, her great tufted ears pricked.

Jack took a step to meet her and drove his fingers into the dense, greasy pelt of her neck, rocking her head gently from side to side. The predator sighed and slumped to the ground, raising one foreleg to give access for scratching – something people were useful for.

She didn't seem interested in the hunk of meat; another carcass somewhere, then.

'They want to catch you,' Jack told her in the language of their home. *'You have to go in a car.'*

He wasn't sure she would fit.

They should move, though. It wasn't comfortable leaving the cover of the trees without knowing where the shot had come from, but waiting until dawn wasn't an option.

'Come on.'

Jack set off along the tree line and the clot of shadow that was the tallixer followed him.

Before they reached the road, they heard voices ahead.

Rebecca plunged down the hill, the cold air hurting her lungs, vaguely aware that if there had been one shot there could be another but not prepared to give it consideration. She had no idea where the gun had been aimed, so made for the sound itself, as best she could. The lane was ahead of her, she thought, and she was possibly not far from the Mini. But what lay between?

It'll be alright. It's going to be alright. It was just a shot in the air.

There were voices – someone angry, no, two angry people. Men. Neither of them was Connor.

She had to run along the fence for a distance to find a way through, and then reached a gate and climbed over into the road. There was another gate opposite and she got herself over and ran back. She could hear words now: *Bloody idiot! No business! Completely illegal!*

And then someone new said, 'What the *hell?*' and her insides flipped over.

PC Blackman checked his rear-view mirror – an automatic habit, despite the total absence of traffic – and turned into the lane, not quite single-track but barely wide enough for two. He wouldn't like to have to pass one of those monster tractors they had these days, but that wasn't likely after midnight.

Once again it was his turn to sort out the yokels, but this time he'd been expecting trouble and had been patrolling the Boars Hill area on the lookout. 'I've done my best to warn him,' the beat officer had said, 'but he had that portcullis look.'

It was a good metaphor. Darren had enjoyed that experience himself – talk-talk-talking away to a landowner and watching the bars come down: *Yack all you like but I know what I'm going to do.* That was the trouble with the trespass laws in England – never really black-and-white.

Darren passed two cars huddled into the side of the road, one safely tucked away by a gate, the other tilted with its near-side wheels up on the grass, making the road even narrower. The farm he wanted should be on the right.

There.

Darren pulled over, his turn to narrow the road, and got out. There was quite a huddle of them, and all going nineteen to the dozen.

Oh well. You chose this career!

He weighed in.

* * *

Never before in his twenty-whatever years had Connor been so physically affected by fear. When she had walked up, her face white in the reporter's flashlight, the relief made him feel sick.

Having run towards the sound of the gun as best he could, he had come across an argument between two men, one of whom held a long-barrelled gun in his arm and one of whom had a camera. Both sounded aggrieved; the camera man sounded frightened too.

He had begun to speak but then saw Rebecca and lost the words.

His eyes met hers, and without fuss they withdrew, sliding away while the argument continued.

'Do you know where he is?' Rebecca whispered, barely more than a breath. She was very close, trying to make her words carry without sound. She had jettisoned her leg of lamb, just as he had.

Connor shrugged, then mouthed, 'Car key,' and held out his hand.

Rebecca rummaged, then dropped the spare key into his palm.

'Keep these two here as long as you can.'

She nodded, and he removed himself, slinking as silently as he could and heading back in the direction Jack had last been seen. It was all he could think of to do, and he suspected Rebecca would be more effective at stirring them up than he would.

Keep them here, Connor had said.

She did her best – put in lots of confusing irrelevancies *('But it was only eleven o'clock'* and *'I'm sure there were two people at the spinney'.* She was especially proud of *'Has anyone seen Clive?')*

When it looked like she would be collared for a statement, she began to withdraw in tiny steps, sidling in the direction of the gate. They were still arguing and she doubted anyone would give chase.

In the lane, she ran along the tarmac to where her Mini, offering refuge and safety, was lined up ready and raring to go.

Then the passenger door opened and Connor unfolded himself. Rebecca said, her voice low, 'Okay, where do we look for Jack?'

Connor pointed, and Rebecca realised she couldn't see the back seat of her car at all for what was crammed in there.

'Oh.'

'So let's go.'

'Yes.'

Rebecca slipped out of her coat and stuffed it into the boot. There was no space for it inside; she wasn't entirely sure there'd be space for her. She yanked the key out of her jeans pocket and slid into the driver's seat. Connor, she noticed, had drawn the passenger's seat forward so that his knees pressed against the glove compartment.

I should have hired a van.

It was true, but it was also too late. Trying very hard not to feel the breath on the back of her neck, Rebecca started the engine and pulled away.

Chapter Twenty-Six

It was a strange, surreal drive to Derbyshire.

The first miles were horrible. Rebecca took her seat forward a couple of inches in the faint hope of avoiding that breath, which made the steering wheel too close and the gear lever too far back. But the breath was just as bad, and the tallixer had expanded into the extra space so that she couldn't move back.

That she wasn't going to be eaten just had to be taken on trust: not so much trust in Jack, who was too young, skinny and silent to engender confidence, but trust in Connor, who she felt sure would not let her run the risk of being mauled. She justified this on the grounds that Connor was grown up, but knew she would have trusted his sixteen-year-old self as well.

However, once they reached the smooth surface of the ring road and the car was no longer rumbling over cracked tarmac and swooping round hairpin bends, the great cat stopped trying to shift its huge bulk around and settled. The little cat settled too, riding on the miniscule parcel shelf behind Jack's neck. It seemed remarkably cool about the presence of something which outclassed it so impressively in every respect.

Jack had to be squashed and sweltering with half the tallixer across his lap, but he wasn't in a strong position to complain.

The dual carriageway stretched ahead, with no tail-lights to be seen. At least there should be no traffic hold ups.

After a while a growly sound started in the back: snoring. Rebecca tilted her rear-view mirror: two bodies slack and loose; only the cat on the parcel shelf returned her gaze, unblinking.

'They're asleep,' she said quietly.

Connor twisted to see behind. He couldn't be remotely comfortable rammed up against the dashboard like that, but he too was unable to slide his seat back.

It was like being parents, Rebecca thought. Mum and Dad in front, the kids asleep in the back, and lots of driving to be done.

She said, 'I don't know what Michael's going to say.' She had tried, but as usual her call had not got through and there had been no reply to her email. 'I mean, what would you think if a sabre-toothed tiger appeared on your doorstep?'

Connor said, 'He'll be alright.'

Maybe, if by 'alright' you meant he wouldn't call the police or have a nervous breakdown; happy about it was a different matter.

A motorcycle appeared from out of the dark behind them, swooped past and vanished ahead, way over the speed limit.

It was half past one and there had been all that rampaging about and excitement. Rebecca said, 'You'll have to talk to me. I'm going to get sleepy if you don't.'

So Connor talked.

Later Rebecca was to realize that only their peculiar, enforced circumstances had led to the conversation they shared on that drive north. Close beside her in the car, voice low so as not to wake the sleepers in the back, having to keep going in order to help Rebecca stay alert, Connor had simply let the words come.

No doubt it helped that it was dark in the car and she had to keep her eyes on the road – her attention, too, and she missed details here and there when she had to think about junctions and slip roads and changing lanes.

As she listened, watching the dark road stretching ahead, Rebecca began to build a picture of her companion's missing years.

'It wasn't prison,' he had said. 'Detention, really.'

But *detention* wasn't a good word.

'Or captivity.'

That sounded like a zoo.

Whatever it was, it hadn't been freedom. The…people, the other kind of people (Rebecca shrank from calling them *fairies*) had been at a loss over what to do with him. The way back was sealed at the Ashendon end, and they were afraid to let him loose to wander, so they used an empty house.

'It was more of a barn, really.'

A barn, then. They used an empty barn and locked him up in it. For years. To begin with, he had been confined indoors.

'There was a yard. It took a few months, but they eventually grew a hedge around it that I couldn't get through or over.'

Being allowed access to the open air had been wonderful.

'What do you mean *before the hedge grew?*' Rebecca interrupted, confused. 'How many years were you waiting?'

'Not years, months. Just months. It's amazing.'

Everything grew far faster than in this world. You could watch it happening – buds swelling, blossoms popping, leaves unfolding, almost like a stop-motion film. 'Sleeping Beauty's forest,' Rebecca commented casually, and then shivered as she realized that the story had probably originated in that other world and migrated here, along with all those other ideas Michael had talked about three years ago – unicorns and dragons and mermaids.

'Did you see any animals?' she asked, curious.

'Some. Some are recognizable. Peculiar birds. Cats are much bigger, like – I don't know. Like spaniels. Like Maine Coons.'

'Maine whats?'

'Coons. Huge breed of domestic cats. I met one in Vermont.'

Rebecca paused; then: 'Unicorns?' She had to ask.

'I didn't see any.' Another pause. Then he added, 'But I think they're there. Not the mythical unicorn that purifies water, though; just horses with a horn. Ponies really, they're not big.'

Rebecca explored the idea that there were unicorns. Unicorns with an S – a plurality of unicorns.

'Not just one, then.'

'No, of course not. That's just story.'

'And not able to be trapped by having to lay their heads in the laps of maidens!'

Connor said hesitantly, 'There might be some foundation for that.'

'You're kidding!'

But of course he wasn't. He wouldn't. Not about this.

He had been able to see outside from a window in the ground floor. The upper storey, accessed by a ladder, had been to a sort of hay loft area without so much as a chink, and the hedge had grown too dense to look through.

All he had been able to see from his one window was a farmyard, and the comings and goings of the farmer and his family and their visitors. Seasons had come and gone and the trees blossomed and sprouted leaves, dropped them and faced the snows bare-branched, and then blossomed again. Petals drifted in sometimes.

'Weren't you cold?' Rebecca asked.

'There was a fireplace. They gave me wood. There's lots of wood there.'

'Did you have a chair? A bed?' Rebecca was off on a thought trail of domestic trivia. Essential trivia, though.

'Yes, they gave me furniture.'

'What was it like?'

Connor said, 'It was like Michael's boxes.'

Rebecca pictured the rows of beautiful, gleaming boxes in Michael's studio, and the one sitting on her chest-of-drawers at home; the swirling patterns of grain, the dipping, landscape contours of the lids, the sense of them almost having grown under Michael's hands rather than merely being made.

'Organic,' Connor added.

'Yes.'

The motorway slipped beneath them, its concrete crash barrier and gentle curves light years away from the twisting, knotty structures of the invisible world Connor described. So weird. How quickly one was able to accept the unacceptable, give credence to the incredible... Was she insane to be so calm in her knowledge of a parallel world full of magic? Probably.

Organic... Rebecca wondered whether her ancestry could be responsible for the undeniably organic style of her art, or whether it was mere coincidence.

Probably not coincidence. There were Michael's boxes too, and those recurring vines...

'Is there a lot of ivy?' Rebecca asked.

'Yes.'

Of course.

There was paper there and they had kept Connor with a constant supply, thank goodness. And ink – dark, black-brown ink that smelled of bark. He used a dip pen, but one that wrote smoothly. Rebecca had one of those, pinched years ago from the art room at school because she had bonded with it and felt it was her own.

So for years he wrote, and ran round the boundary of the yard, and observed the farmyard, and kept house...

'What about food? Did you cook?'

'They brought me meals. Mostly.'

'Mostly?'

'They are...absent-minded. Casual. No ill will, they just forget things a lot and aren't much bothered when they remember. It's just the way they are.'

Rebecca couldn't let it go. 'They just forgot to feed you? Often?'

'Not often. And not for long. It was okay, Rebecca.'

There he went again, soothing her. Rebecca realized her shoulders were tight, her hands clenched on the steering wheel. Three years ago it had been Connor who was like this – tightly wound, tense, perpetually on the edge of his nerves. Not any more. How could imprisonment have made him *better?* It didn't make sense.

Although he had been jittery the day they met in Blackwell's.

Rebecca snatched a glance at his profile. She said, 'What's it like staying with the Dons?' and saw him smile.

'It's okay.'

'Okay?'

'Good. It's good.'

There was a lull. Rebecca switched motorways, heading for Nottingham.

Connor, as if suddenly reminded of his duty as passenger, said, 'How is your aunt?'

'Aunty Edie? Oh, she's fine. As ever. Bonkers but fine.'

Connor had met, or rather glimpsed, Rebecca's aunt – great-aunt really – on the sole occasion Rebecca had allowed him into her home, the tiny flat at the top of the Edwardian house in Tooting. It was good of him to ask after her, but not surprising.

'And Celia popped it,' Rebecca added, thoughts of one old lady leading to thoughts of another. 'In the hospital. Massive coronary, apparently. Michael heard.' To everyone's relief, she thought, remembering the deep-rooted viciousness of Uriel Passenger's other descendant.

'And Michael's parents?'

'Going strong, so far as I know. Michael isn't very communicative these days.'

'And that estate agent,' Connor said. 'What happened to him?'

The estate agent: Geoffrey Foster, bane of their lives, or so it had seemed at the time. Connor wasn't to know that witnessing the opening of the way between worlds had flipped the guy's head and left him a very subdued puppy indeed!

'Gone,' Rebecca said. 'Gone without trace, never to darken our doors again. I'm sure he wishes he'd never got involved in the first place.'

The great cat woke and lifted its head when they left the major roads and entered the swooping helter-skelter lanes, but Jack snored on. Rebecca twitched her shoulders, the hot, meaty breath moist on her neck, and took the corners very easy.

Then the gravel was crunching under her tyres as she drew up in the car park, as close as she could get to Michael's cottage, and there was sudden silence as the engine died.

'Well.'

Connor said quietly, 'You go and break the news to Michael. I'll stay here in case Jack wakes up.'

Rebecca let herself out of the car, unfolding her cramped limbs and breathing in the cold, smoky night air. She stretched, her back and arms and her fingers too.

Okay, here goes.

Once again, walking along the path to the cottage in the dark hijacked her memories and drew them back to that night three years ago, and the astonishing events that had led to Connor's disappearance and the abandonment forever of her scepticism.

The movement and fresh, outdoors air had invigorated her and swept away the tiredness of the long drive. Rebecca felt alert and optimistic, and realised she was rather looking forward to springing the astonishing news on poor sleepy Michael.

The cottage was in darkness and Rebecca expected to wait for a few minutes while its occupant struggled to surface from sleep and stumble to the door. After two assaults with the knocker she heard faint sounds within of footfalls and then someone fumbling a little at the latch.

Rebecca smiled, planning her words; but they died in her mouth unvoiced.

In Michael's doorway, taller and heavier than she remembered and *wearing pyjamas,* stood Geoffrey Foster.

Chapter Twenty-Seven

Connor waited in the car, his hands in his lap, thoughtful.

Talking to Rebecca during the drive had denied him the opportunity to prepare for this. It had been reasonable of Rebecca to ask him to talk, and surprisingly it had been less agonising than he had expected to put into words something of those stagnant years. But it meant he hadn't had time to think about Michael at all.

The tallixer shifted her great bulk and sighed, as well she might; as well might they all.

Connor hadn't wanted to meet Michael again, any more than he had wanted to meet Rebecca. Yet events had conspired against him, and so far it hadn't been so bad.

He wasn't sure of the source of his reluctance. Guilt? He had misled them both in concealing his intention to use the gap as a doorway before it could be sealed. He had known, too, that slipping through himself would almost certainly mean Michael couldn't, or wouldn't. He had justified it by telling himself that whereas Michael was merely curious, Connor himself had been desperate, on so many counts – desperate to escape his oppressive, abusive home, desperate to end his sense of isolation, desperate to start afresh somewhere far, far away.

How selfish had that been?

Rebecca said Michael had changed; 'gone inside himself', she said.

My fault?

Rebecca was being a long time. Hauling his thoughts back to the present, Connor was about to get out and stretch his legs when he heard footsteps on the gravel.

Rebecca was crossing the ground towards him, and her face made him scramble out of the car.

'I'm simply pointing out that one doesn't normally admit a large, meat-eating predator into one's sitting room.'

'No you're not. You're dictating the use of *our* property, and what the *hell* do you think gives you the right to do that?'

Connor winced.

Rebecca had snapped, which wasn't totally unreasonable after having driven for three hours with that very predator breathing down her neck. She was tired and stressed and couldn't see the way ahead.

All of that went for him too, but he was more used to it, especially to not seeing the way ahead. That would be tough for Rebecca.

She was also hugely disappointed.

'Why didn't he let us *know?*'

Connor said, 'There's no signal at his parents' house, Rebecca. Remember?'

She turned to look at him. Perhaps it would have been better to have kept quiet.

The estate agent opened his mouth again and Connor got in swiftly before he could speak: 'But it doesn't matter because we all know what Michael would say. Don't we?'

He met the man's eyes, and thought about Skill, and about the little he had managed to absorb, practising month after month by himself in the barn. He knew really that it hadn't come across with him, knew that he no longer had it to use, but…perhaps just thinking about it, remembering it really, really hard, might, just might…

'Well, alright. I suppose you'd better.'

Connor smiled, and put sunshine into it.

'Thank you, Mr Foster. I'm sure you're right.'

The estate agent retreated grumpily and Connor felt his sleeve snagged by something. He looked round.

'What was that?' Rebecca had hold of his coat.

'What?'

'That. You did something. What did you do?'

Connor said, 'He just thought again. I didn't do anything. Look, Rebecca, get your bag and check in. Leave this to me.'

Rebecca, with characteristic foresight, had called ahead to book a room. She had suggested she book two. 'Jack will have to stay with this animal, but they won't need you.'

He had declined though, and Rebecca had accepted his excuse of being needed as an interpreter.

Now Connor walked her back to the Mini, trying to tread softly, conscious of the sleeping guests in the mansion.

The tallixer gazed through the window, a green, implacable stare. Giant cats had a self-possession that was off the register.

Rebecca, still cross, opened the boot and pulled out her bag.

'Well, good luck.'

'Yes. Don't worry, it'll be okay.'

'Oh I'm not going to worry!'

Definitely still cross.

Connor watched her reach the hotel door and waited until she had been admitted, and then leaned into the car.

'Jack? Wake up - we're here.'

Sleeping on the floor was no problem; Connor was used to strange beds, including park benches. The rumbling snore of the tallixer was strangely soothing in the dark. It probably helped that he couldn't see her.

Geoffrey Foster had retired to the bedroom and the scraping and thumping that had ensued suggested he had barricaded the door. Not an animal person, then.

Jack and his pets, the huge one and the little one, snuggled up together on the rug near the hearth, and Connor, knowing he was too long for the sofa, rolled himself up in his blankets at the other end of the room.

He had closed the curtains, lest any early passer-by caught a glimpse of what was inside the cottage.

Tomorrow the thinking would have to begin again, but right now he needed to sleep.

Just before the darkness took him, it occurred to Connor that he didn't know whether the tallixer was house-trained...

Chapter Twenty-Eight

Rebecca had been given the same room as last time – left at the top of the stairs and third on the right, overlooking the courtyard. She wondered hazily whether hotels kept records and referred to them when taking reservations: *likes to be near the stairs,* or *prefers east-facing.* Or more likely: *no complaints about being over the bar.*

Rebecca couldn't have cared less about being over the bar. She fell asleep in seconds, oversprung mattress, tucked-in bed covers and all, and struggled to surface when her phone alarm sounded a scant four hours later.

She won out, and a shower brought her fully awake. Today was not a day for lying in. She lifted a banana from the fruit bowl in reception and stepped out into a chill, misty morning.

But then she turned left, and walked around the farther side of the house, away from the path to the cottage.

The hotel aimed for the high end of the market: exclusive business conferences, large weddings and country breaks for people with lots of money. Walls had been taken down to make space for the restaurant and kitchen, and a conservatory had been built for breakfast and afternoon tea. Rebecca walked past the mock-Victorian windows of the conservatory and continued along one of the wings that stretched behind the house toward the gardens.

When Ashendon House had been a museum open to the public, this block had acted as a tea room. Now it had been converted to a gymnasium with a small but pristine swimming pool at the far end, and the courtyard itself was spruced up with ironwork tables and chairs and clipped yew in huge stone urns.

Beyond lay the sloping lawn and, farther, the walled gardens that had once fed the reclusive Uriel Passenger and his household of servants.

The hotel's lease included the grounds but Michael had retained one of the walled enclosures for the use of the cottage, and Rebecca made her way briskly past rose gardens and fruit trees and greenhouses, and unlatched a wooden door bearing the sign 'Strictly Private – No Admittance.'

That wouldn't be enough, though. She patted the door frame fixed to the stone: a bit splintery but sound. A trip to the hardware store, then; there was probably one in Ashendon Wyld.

Closing herself in, she stuck her hands in her jacket pockets and surveyed Michael's garden.

Chosen because it was the closest to the cottage, the garden was very little trouble to maintain because there was hardly any grass and nothing to be harvested or pruned. There was a winding path of beaten earth and loose shingle, and the rest was just a manic tangle of grey wood twisting through and spreading over and gripping a framework of timber poles and struts. In November it was bare and cold, but in the summer, Rebecca knew, the garden was a paradise of dusty lilac and chalky blue as great, falling cascades of wisteria clothed the wood. Utterly beautiful.

She set off along the path, shaking and tugging at branches as she went.

How much did it weigh? Although if broken wisteria trees were all they had to worry about…

The gate at the cottage end had been left ajar, despite its Private notice. Rebecca closed it and tramped between the scraggy winter beds to the cottage.

Connor opened the door to her, his face grim; behind him Rebecca heard Foster's voice laying down the law: *cannot possibly…where do you imagine…*

She raised her voice and announced breezily, 'Time to put the cat out, I think! Jack, let's go and show her the garden!'

The hardware store in Ashendon Wyld had once been the village smithy. Rebecca wound her way between the sacks of rabbit feed, bin liners and reels of string at the front of the shop to the counter at the back, where there were boxes of screws and brackets and wall plugs, and said, 'I need four really good gate bolts, please.'

She had to reject the really, *really* good ones as they were too wide to fit on the door frame, but the next size down was satisfactorily heavy and she bought a box of the right size screws to go with them.

As an afterthought, she also bought a screwdriver. She knew Michael must have one, but at the same time...This was on a very different scale from his lovely, delicate boxes.

By the time she was driving back to the house the sun had dispelled the mist and the sky was cloudless. Her spirits were revived by having had a little time by herself and she felt buoyant and positive.

Connor had refused to leave Jack to the mercy of Geoffrey Foster, and although Rebecca couldn't see the estate agent doing him any real harm, she could sympathise. Just what he was doing in Michael's cottage was almost beyond belief.

It interests me, he had said.

But not in the way it had interested him before, apparently. Then it had all been *money-money-money* – harnessing alien technology in the interest of financial gain. It had always sounded mad to Rebecca, but then so did radio waves and the internet. She had no idea how a television worked.

Now, apparently, all that had been set aside in favour of pure research. He said he wanted to observe and measure and record. He told them over breakfast that he had retired from business and would be investing his time in discovering more about the parallel universe.

Although not by going into it. He had seen Connor vanish and had no ambitions to follow him.

It all seemed so unlikely, and yet Michael must have believed him. At any rate, he had trusted Foster enough to leave him in the cottage alone when his mother had fallen ill and he had gone to Aberfeldy. That was a lot of trust.

It was difficult to work out whose surprise had been greater – hers on seeing Foster in Michael's house, or Foster's on coming face to face with the lost boy.

Rebecca grinned.

She had been to the supermarket too. Bread and cheese and apples for lunch, omelettes for supper, and a whole lot of planning in between...

Chapter Twenty-Nine

Stand on the island of glass and look towards the great circle.
Put the numbers in order left from the lay of the land.
Cross water to a place of captivity and face the stone at half-light.

Foster said, '*Lie* of the land.'

They were seated around the coffee table in the sitting room. Rebecca had taken one end of the sofa, which was deep and squashy and much to her liking, before realizing the risk she was running. However, Connor had taken the other half, leaving the chair to Geoffrey Foster. What a relief.

'It was what she said,' Connor replied, just as he had at the Ferry House.

'*She?*'

'Yes.'

Connor sounded prickly.

Jack was in the garden with his cats. The tallixer had spent the morning under the wisteria boughs while Connor and Jack each sat with his back against a door to block anyone opening it accidentally. They must have been terribly bored.

When Rebecca returned from the village, Foster fitted the bolts and the garden was now secure. Nevertheless, Jack plainly preferred the company of his pets, and he wouldn't have got far in the conference in any case, unable to follow their talk in his forgotten language. It didn't seem likely he would be able to contribute to solving the riddle.

The last line was the easiest, especially when corroborated by Uriel Passenger's suspicions about islands, prisons and landmark stones.

'This has to be an island,' Rebecca said, 'and one with a prison.'

'And a stone.'

'Yes. And I reckon it's either Portland or the Isle of Wight.'

Very pleasingly, both men turned to look at her. Rebecca said, 'Portland has a prison – actually two. And it has a couple of candidates for the stone: the Pulpit Rock and Nicodemus Knob.'

Connor frowned. 'Portland isn't an island, though, is it?'

Foster said, 'Pretty much. Definitely, if you discount Chesil Beach.'

'And I think we can,' Rebecca added.

She had researched online. Portland was an island two miles out from the south coast of Dorset. It was connected by a bridge, and also by the extraordinary bank of pebbles known as Chesil Beach that formed a permanent link to the mainland.

'But if the beach links it...' Connor said.

'Technically it links it,' Rebecca explained, 'but it only joins the mainland twenty miles away. Nearly twenty miles. It's just a heap of pebbles – you can't drive on it. Twenty miles of walking on a slope of sliding stones is just ridiculous. It would be harder than swimming.'

And Portland had a contemporary prison for young offenders *and* the old, abandoned Verne Prison. Portland Castle too, just in case that counted.

'And the landmark stones?'

'Nicodemus Knob is an outcrop of limestone, left after extraction. It's become a local landmark. Pulpit Rock is the remains of a natural stone arch. The Longstone on the Isle of Wight is a sandstone megalith. So we have two islands with prisons and landmark stones right there!'

She waited. Foster was leaning back, his legs crossed and his arms folded. Connor sat forward, frowning at the sheet of notes on the table.

'Well?'

Connor said, 'What about the Isle of Man?'

'Hopeless. Stone crosses *and* stone circles all over it. Too many.'

She waited again. Foster's foot wagged.

Connor shook his head. 'If it's that easy, why do we have the rest? What about these numbers?'

'Well, for a start they didn't know we'd have access to Uriel Passenger's diaries. It would have been a bit harder without that.'

'I suppose.'

Rebecca said, 'Oh come on! It doesn't always have to be hard, does it? Let's go to Portland and the Isle of Wight, anyway. We can probably do both in one trip. Let's just take a look.'

Foster cooked supper, proving to be able to turn out puffy, lacy omelettes as expertly as Michael had been able to fry eggs without ever breaking one.

The tallixer, Gira, stayed in the wisteria garden, not yet hungry again after the last Oxfordshire ewe she had consumed. Rebecca had stocked up on canned dog food and Foster promised to get in more when it was needed.

Jack, of course, had to stay behind.

'He'll be fine,' Rebecca told Connor. 'Bored, I expect, but you can't help that.'

At least he won't have to converse with him.

Conversing with Geoffrey Foster for any length of time was not an attractive notion. A good move of Michael's, to zip up to Scotland to escape.

Not a good joke.

Michael had gone because his mother was likely to die, and Foster's turning up the day before was simple coincidence. It was interesting that he had convinced Michael he could be trusted to care-take the Ashendon doorway, though; or had Michael been too worried about his parents to think clearly?

And that led to another thought. While Connor was explaining the situation to Jack, Rebecca poked about and found notes and letters of Michael's that she probably shouldn't have been reading but nothing connected to his parents' house in Aberfeldy. They weren't listed in the telephone directory either.

Foster already knew that. 'I looked for them once,' he said, unguardedly.

'I know. You followed Michael there. He knew where you were all the time.'

Foster looked shocked. 'How did–'

'He rang the hotel and pretended to be you checking your reservation.'

That had been very satisfying.

But there was no number for Michael's parents, and mobile signal was as bad there as at Ashendon. To all intents and purposes he was out of the picture; and that wasn't a comfortable thought.

Chapter Thirty

'Eight hundred miles to the next service,' Rebecca said. 'At this rate that'll be next week.'

She'd never done so much concentrated driving; it was just as well she enjoyed it. Even so, Derbyshire to Dorset was too far for a single hop, and they had stopped the night in Oxford.

Rebecca dropped Connor off near Folly Bridge and as she rejoined the traffic she caught a glimpse of him from behind, approaching the steps down to the towpath. He looked jaunty. A jaunty Connor. That was a first.

Climbing the stairs to Steph's flat was like stepping back into normality. It was disconcerting to note the ease with which she was moving between the real world and fairyland:

'What have you been up to?'

'Oh, just rounding up a giant magic cat with a boy who's seen a unicorn.'

'Coffee?'

'Yeah, thanks, no sugar.'

Ridiculous.

Next morning, batteries recharged, Rebecca collected Connor from the Ferry House. 'We're not going straight off. First you need to get a phone.'

And Connor, as if to prove there are no constants in life, said, 'Alright.'

Jaunty *and* a phone!

And a bank account, a proper one, with a cheque book and, soon, a credit card.

'I don't need a credit card.'

'Yes, you do. Not because you need to borrow, but because it gives you protection against fraud when you're buying something. And because hotels and things get nervous if you don't have one. It's just a tool, Connor.'

She didn't want to go to the solicitor without Michael, so for the moment Connor's income from Ashendon would just have to carry on accumulating untouched. Instead, Rebecca had moved some of her money around a bit so that Connor could open his new account with another nice big cheque.

'That's too much.'

'No it's not. I know you're going to pay me back. I'm still liquid, I haven't touched my investments.' She loved the terminology!

By ten thirty they had each other's mobile numbers stored in their phones, an OS Landranger map on the back seat, and were on the road heading south.

Rebecca had vaguely imagined Portland would seem smaller than it did. Still, four miles by less than two is pretty tight; living there must be odd. It was hard to see the appeal of an island; you'd get deadly bored of the causeway.

They had sighted long barrows on the last part of the drive. 'Fairy haunts,' Rebecca said.

Connor said nothing.

'Actually there is a promising tradition of fairies on Portland,' Rebecca continued. 'Plenty of legends. Apparently all the fairies fled the island the day the first church bell rang.'

Quite a while ago, then. Still.

They passed Weymouth Marina, climbed a steep hill between grey stone houses, and then dropped down again to Wyke Regis, the village at the end of the bridge.

There was a pub where the bridge sprang off.

'The Ferry Bridge,' Rebecca read aloud from the swinging sign. 'Do you suppose this is *ferry* as in *Ferry House*?'

How easy was this going to be?

Not very, sadly.

After stretching their legs at the quayside – not the pretty, seaside kind but a raw, concrete industrial site – they drove south, following the main road, and parked again near to Portland Bill, the southernmost tip, to eat lunch. Rebecca had bought a small salad box in Oxford; Connor had sandwiches like bricks stuffed with cheddar and pickle, and an apple *and* a banana, and a slab of fruit cake as well.

Then they walked past a war memorial, like a budget version of Cleopatra's Needle carved with the sad names of the fallen, and across a windy expanse of sand and short, dry grass to the lighthouse, which looked like something from a child's picture book, short and stubby and gleaming white with a broad, red, painted cummerbund.

A little further and they were scrambling over huge boulders to where a massive four-sided rock, its faces oddly flat, leaned nonchalantly like a ramp against the pinnacle.

'Pulpit Rock,' Rebecca said. 'Want to climb?'

Hand and foot holes had been carved out of the face. A nanny-ish signboard set into the stone warned that anything they did would be at their own risk, but it was like a climbing frame in a playground. Rebecca went up first, enjoying the stretch after all the driving, and then clambered on over the rough pinnacle to the plateau. The stone ramp was a ladder, just-off-vertical, bridging the sea between the pinnacle and the mainland.

She shuffled along to leave room for Connor. They sat side-by-side and took in the view – gunmetal waves on the right, the ragged shoreline and beyond it the downs to their left. The wind gusted in their faces, drying their eyes. Rebecca found herself very conscious of Connor next to her, his long thighs in the new jeans close to hers. She shifted slightly, and hugged her knees to her chest.

Connor angled his legs away. 'Sorry.'

''S alright.'

Say something quick...

'I do like the sea.'

Intelligent would be good!

Rebecca ploughed on. 'It seems so alien. It shouldn't do, I grew up near Southwold for heaven's sake. Weekend walks along the coast, you know... Well, occasionally...'

She was babbling.

'Anyway,' she finished, lamely, 'the sea always seems strange and...a bit creepy, somehow.'

Connor was silent. Rebecca dared to snatch a look and saw he was nodding thoughtfully – or was it absently? – as he gazed beyond her out to the horizon. His sharp cheek bones and straight nose and brow were clear and somehow *pure,* as if that was what people were supposed to look like: some kind of idealized masterform which had been corrupted over the generations – the black hair, dark, dark eyes and long lashes, the smooth texture of his skin very different from that of other men.

Not that she had much experience of other men; not close up.

It had been put to her in the past that she was scary. She was inclined to discount that as rubbish, but it was true she hadn't been exactly – sought after. Pursued.

Connor had never seemed remotely scared of her, even in the days when she felt he ought to be. A long time ago now.

Rebecca stared out to sea. She had been looking forward to this day, the two of them together with nobody else to dilute it, and now here they were, sitting on this rock in utter silence.

Pulpit Rock: they were there for a reason. Rebecca shifted in order to run her eyes over the land instead, the tumbled boulders and the windswept grass beyond. *Cross water to a place of captivity and face the stone at half-light.* That suggested this rock must be visible from the prison, one or other of them, and it wasn't going to be. Blast.

She sighed. 'I don't think this can be the stone we need.'

'No.'

Nicodemus Knob looked more promising, and as they drew near Rebecca's confidence rose.

The rock itself was not climbable – much higher and no friendly foot holes. But it was within a few hundred metres of the Verne Prison, which according to Rebecca's internet research had originally been a military fort. The depth of excavation of stone to build it had been marked by the Knob, which was simply a tower of stone left undug.

In addition, the prison had a gigantic dry moat and was said to be riddled with passages and doorways. Standing in this particular place of captivity and facing the stone was easy.

The problem was knowing what to do next.

'Now what?' Rebecca asked aloud.

Just standing there wasn't going to achieve anything. Surely they ought to see something that would indicate the presence of a gap? But there was just a stretch of scrappy grass and then the rock.

'If it's the passages,' Rebecca said, 'why do we have to face the stone?'

'It won't be the passages.'

'No?'

'It isn't likely there's a gap here if the passages were in use. The gap needs to be isolated.'

Rebecca mulled this over. It sounded sensible.

'Well, what then?'

Connor said, 'I don't think this is it either.'

'Oh.'

Rebecca gazed around. Maybe. In all honesty the spot was dank, cold, boring and uninspiring. Anything less meaningful it was difficult to imagine. And absolutely no magic.

'Alright. But before we go on to the Isle of Wight, I want to see this Chesil Beach.'

Chapter Thirty-One

There was a set of steps from the road alongside a grey stone pub. They climbed them and came out onto a wide, tarmac walk beyond which was the pebble beach. It was almost deserted; over to the left a child was squatting, playing with the pebbles; to their right, maybe fifty yards beyond the pub, a white rowing boat was beached on the stones; nothing else.

The wind was bitter. Rebecca zipped her coat up to her chin.

The stones were horrible to walk on. They slid about, giving way at every step, and were large enough to unbalance Rebecca's feet. The beach sloped, which made it worse. Walking along it for nearly twenty miles might save your life, but it wasn't something you would choose to do otherwise.

The pebbles themselves were lovely, though – smooth and flat, their angles vanquished by millennia of being washed together by the tides. They were shaded from mid-grey to white, with a subtle lilac tone en masse. It was impossible not to pick them up and feel their easy curves in your palm.

Rebecca hunkered down and tried out three or four until she found the perfect pebble for her hand. She caressed it.

'Did you see the sign?'

She looked up. Connor nodded towards an imperious-looking painted board announcing that removing stones from the beach was illegal.

'It's only one.' Rebecca pocketed the stone and stood up. 'Only one.' One stone in her lifetime.

Connor had moved on, keeping his balance easily on the sliding surface. Perhaps larger feet were an advantage. Rebecca took her hands out of her pockets, which helped a bit.

She felt reproved. Connor had always been straighter-than-straight. She remembered how he had squirmed at the prospect of liberating the telescope from the Oxford science museum, even though it had been hidden there over a century earlier specifically for them – or someone like them – to retrieve. He had wanted to ask the staff. At the time she had thought him naïve, but it had later transpired that he was right and they could have saved a little time and a whole lot of stress simply by asking for the hidden things.

To think that she had once suspected him of shoplifting.

And now she had disappointed him by stealing a pebble. She took it out of her pocket.

'Connor?'

He turned round.

Rebecca opened her fingers and let the pebble fall.

Chesil Beach curved ahead, a great, sinuous mound parting the sea and skirting the Dorset coast for farther than their eyes could see. A couple of fat seagulls stalked near the water's edge.

They passed the rowing boat, lying slantwise on the slope, a tarpaulin draped over one side. Rebecca said, 'What was the boat like that you went to the Bahamas in?'

'She was a forty-four foot sloop.'

'Right, well, that doesn't mean anything to me. What was it like inside?'

Connor told her. Rebecca tried to imagine living with an entire family in something hardly more spacious than a caravan, and almost shuddered. 'And they live on it all the year round? Even when they're not sailing off somewhere?'

'Yes.'

'Mad.'

'No. Just different.'

'I suppose.' Rebecca came to a halt. There didn't seem any point in struggling on much farther. She faced the sea, her cold hands stuffed back in her pockets. 'Have you thought about what you're going to do?'

'Find this gap. Send Jack home.'

'Yes, but after?'

Connor was silent. Rebecca risked a glance, prepared for the little jolt she was apparently doomed to get each time she looked at him. His profile was clear-cut against the pale sky, his brows drawn downwards in a slight frown, thoughtful rather than annoyed, his nose straight, his mouth firm, his Adam's apple exposed above his collar...

And there it came: the little, sinking squeeze of her stomach.

Every single wretched time.

It was ridiculous to feel shy of him when he was younger than her, even if only by a year now.

But he always seems older.

Say something!

Hardly knowing what words were going to come, Rebecca nevertheless opened her mouth and then dried up as Connor, without warning, leapt into a run and was away.

The loose stones under his feet sucked at his strength, drawing away his energy, negating all the spring; it was like running in deep sand, with the added complication of the slope threatening to turn an ankle. His calves strained.

Why hadn't he been paying attention? He'd seen it, just hadn't registered...

Stupid, stupid! And they'd gone so far!

Connor fumbled at the zip, which had got snagged; too much haste. He fought it, got his arms free somehow and let the coat drop.

Less than a hundred metres. The cold air ached in his chest. The water would be freezing.

Damn! Damn!

He managed somehow to keep his balance on the shifting downward slope, and then he was in the sea and instantly dragged back to a wading walk as the stones dropped away beneath the waves, the cold like a scalpel against his thighs and then taking the breath from his lungs as he threw himself forward and began to swim.

He'd been right: you don't forget.

Connor's muscles made the moves they had to make, while his mind whimpered at the cold; nothing at all like the public swimming pool...

But it worked; he wasn't sinking, and he had almost reached...

Connor drove his right arm forward and made contact; his fingers felt the sodden cloth and clutched, and he came upright and began treading water, gasping as he struggled to bring the child's head and shoulders above the surface.

And it was making a noise, wheezing and choking, but therefore breathing, and therefore not drowned yet.

He had never learned lifesaving techniques – lessons cost money – but he had seen movies. You swim on your back, one-handed, and tow the drowning person with your hand under their chin.

Easier to picture than to carry out. The shock of the cold didn't seem to have lessened, and it was so hard to keep moving, keep pulling the water under him, keep his legs kicking. The kid was small, couldn't weigh much, and the buoyancy of the water should help, yet it was like dragging a bag of cement...

The waves slapped his face and he swallowed salt water, sank a little and fought up again.

He hadn't come far out. Where was the bottom?

He gasped, swallowed water again, and coughed. On the shore Rebecca was standing, shouting...

And then his knee struck something and he was grounded, stones under his hand even while the waves slapped into his throat. Connor lurched up the slope until most of him was out of the water and suddenly weighing as if a walrus were sitting on him.

'I've got him.'

Rebecca was saying something – he could see her mouth moving and hear her voice.

'Connor, let go, I've got him.'

He watched her prise his cramped fingers open and haul the child off him.

He said, 'Use my coat.'

It was next to her on the beach, but she had unzipped her own jacket and thrown it over the little boy, wrapping it tight around him.

The wind, now he was out of the sea, was as cruel as the water had been. He wasn't sure he could move.

Rebecca left the child and threw the Colvins' coat round his shoulders. 'Put your arms in. Connor, *put your arms in.*' She sounded brisk and efficient and a bit scared.

Clumsily, he managed to find the right holes and shoved his arms down the sleeves. The cut of the wind lessened a fraction.

'Okay, come on.'

Rebecca put her arms round him and hauled upwards, and with a bit of effort and a stagger, he was on his feet.

Rebecca hoisted up the child, settling him on her hip with his legs dangling and set off up the sliding stones towards the tarmac. Shivering, Connor followed.

How long could you survive up to your neck in the sea in November?

Rebecca wrapped both arms round the child, sealing off the gaping collar with her spread fingers, pushing his face into her shoulder out of the wind.

She had no idea where she was going.

The pub was closed, she had checked that first. Down the steps and onto the street; there was no traffic, no pedestrians, not so much as a dog. No shops. There must be someone in one of these cottages?

How had Connor realized the dot in the water was the child they had seen on the beach? Rebecca had followed his direction and seen only a slight disturbance on the rolling surface – she'd have assumed it was a seagull.

Running after him on the pebbles had been nightmarish, although even thinking that struck a chord of guilt within her. Would she have plunged in like that, even to save a life? Rebecca could swim, but in safe, quiet swimming-pool water, not in full winter gear in the ocean.

Connor was shaking visibly, his boots making squelchy-sloggy noises with every step. He had taken his coat off before diving in but had not waited to untie laces.

The child was whimpering; that had to be a good sign, didn't it?

Where the hell were they going?

And then suddenly there was a woman bowling down the hill towards them, although Rebecca couldn't remember seeing her appear. She raised her arms in front of her as she ran, and instinctively Rebecca came to a halt to wait for her.

Let it be the mother. Please let this be the mother.

And, thank goodness, it was.

The cottage was small, the front door opening straight into the sitting room. Light from the low windows was already fading and the lamps were lit. There was a baby in a playpen under the window, sitting amongst plastic beakers and a shape-sorter box, staring through the mesh: the one that hadn't got away.

The mother – Jacqui – told Rebecca to make tea and then disappeared upstairs with the child, still in Rebecca's jacket. It would be damp and salty when she got it back.

There was a gas fire in the Victorian hearth. Rebecca turned the control knob so that the hiss rose in pitch and left Connor sitting on the floor in front of it.

If the child hadn't died from hypothermia, Connor wouldn't either. Would he?

She switched the kettle on, rootled for teabags and milk, found mugs. She loaded a good spoonful of sugar into Connor's and then a dribble of cold tap water too, and took the mugs through.

'It's not boiling, drink it straight away.'

Connor sipped obediently, and pulled a face.

'I know. But you're supposed to have sugar after a shock.'

Rebecca hugged her knees and watched Connor shiver.

'You saved his life, you know.'

'Should've stopped him going in.'

'How could you have stopped him?'

Connor said, 'We saw him on the beach. Should've taken him home.'

Rebecca thought back. It was true, but it would never have occurred to her to investigate, look for his parents, wonder why such a small child was apparently unguarded. She sighed. Failed again.

Jacqui's voice drifted down the stairs: 'You can have the bathroom now! He can have the bathroom!'

'Go on,' Rebecca said, 'and chuck your clothes out so I can rinse them through.'

She did, by hand in the kitchen sink while Connor was in the shower, and then shoved the lot in the tumble drier. His boots would have to stay sloppy for now.

The coat was okayish, the lining damp but not wet. Rebecca drew a chair in front of the fire to spread the coat open and saw a corner of paper sticking up from the inside pocket.

Paper and damp wasn't a good mix.

Rebecca drew it out. Not paper but card: three cards. Standing to one side so that she didn't fry, Rebecca looked at what Connor was carrying in his coat.

One was old, so old the edges were fluffy: a sepia photograph on thick, yellowed paper of a child in a smock. There were vines drawn around as a border. Hmm.

One was just a playing card, although Rebecca's breath caught when she turned it over and saw which one.

And the third...

Rebecca stared into the cool eyes of the alien queen, gazing back from her throne, her red-brown bodice the colour of old blood, her blue skirt spreading like water, vine leaves in her hair...

Connor slept on the drive home, his face angled towards her. From time to time Rebecca stole a look, until the last of the light had gone and the car was quite dark.

The southern counties passed beneath them and the evening wore on. Rebecca's stomach grumbled for supper, and she wondered what the mad Dons were cooking. She wondered how Geoffrey Foster was getting on with poor, wild Jack.

And she wondered again what had made her slip the Queen of Clover into her pocket.

Chapter Thirty-Two

Geoffrey Foster tipped the rice pan to check that the liquid had been absorbed and turned off the hob. He shrugged into his coat and walked briskly along the path to the door of the wisteria garden, where he thumped on the wood with his fist. 'Dinner!'

They had a system: he cooked food, Jack came in, Jack ate the food, Jack went back out again. It worked. And it meant he didn't have to waste time trying to communicate.

He had driven to a camping shop in Matlock and bought a three-man tent and an arctic sleeping bag. That enabled the boy to sit with his pets all day and sleep out there at night. He'd chosen a three-man tent in case the tallixer wanted to slip in too.

In the meantime he was working through Uriel Passenger's library of notebooks and journals, just as Michael Seward had been doing for the last three years. It wasn't duplicated effort; he was looking for information of a different sort, mathematical, possibly disguised or at least hidden in such a way that a non-scientist wouldn't notice it. Patterns, sequences, numbers…

At the same time he had been researching current thought regarding dimensions and String Theory, reading everything from Superstrings to Stephen Hawking. What he really would have liked was to get face-to-face with one of his old tutors, someone with a progressive mind, someone prepared to chew over the possibilities…

Not yet, though, not until he'd been through this lot. Besides, he was tied to the cottage at least until Seward returned, because that had been the deal.

Seward had been surprised, that was obvious, but easier to convince than Geoffrey had anticipated. It was purely fortuitous that the letter about his mother arrived the very next day – an unlooked for stroke of luck! Seward had even seemed relieved that Geoffrey was there to step in as caretaker in his absence.

The arrival of the refugees had been a shock though, and a nuisance. Although finding out that the kid, Connor, had found his way back…well, that opened a *lot* of possibilities…

The door opened and the new kid, Jack, came in, eyeing him as warily as ever. Foster nodded. 'Sit down. Chicken and rice, okay?'

'Numbers.' Rebecca spoke the word aloud, slowly, consideringly, inviting inspiration. It hadn't worked so far.

Put the numbers in order. But what numbers? There was nothing to go on at all.

They were seated round the table again, this time with the morning light coming through the side window and a teapot in a knitted jacket on a mat in the middle. There was a faint odour of fried breakfast hanging around, and Professor Viator was finishing up in the kitchen, clanking pans and banging cupboards.

Rebecca had arrived early.

'Let's try for the island of glass and the great circle,' Professor Lloyd, the Tortoise, said.

'Glastonbury,' Connor said.

He seemed none the worse for his dip. Rebecca was relieved. She had imagined all sorts of things which were no doubt medically unlikely, but still...

'Yes, Glastonbury,' she agreed. She had Googled it. First up there was an Italian island called Murano that was famous for blown glass production, but next on the list had been Glastonbury, originally named *Ynis Gutrin,* which was Welsh for *Island of Glass.* At least, according to Gerald of Wales.

'Who is?'

'Twelfth-century monk.'

Connor ought to know this stuff, it was right up his street. But of course he had never had a computer.

I wonder if I could buy him a laptop?

But she shouldn't risk coercing him. Although there might be a way...

Professor Peregrine, pouring tea, was expounding on the Arthurian legends and their link to Avalon and Glastonbury.

'...as good as an island, surrounded by marsh like that.'

'So what's the great circle?' Rebecca asked the room. 'I could only find a definition from geometry, lines cutting spheres in half.'

'The Riemannian Circle,' agreed Professor Peregrine, comfortably.

'But I don't believe that has any bearing on this.' Nobody disagreed. 'So I think,' Rebecca continued, 'we have to go to Glastonbury and do the looking. Glastonbury Tor, probably.'

Perhaps the great circle would become obvious once you were there. Although perhaps it wouldn't. It did seem a dreadfully hit-and-miss way to go about riddle-solving.

And then they were back to the numbers again: *Put the numbers in order left from the lay of the land.*

Lie of the land.

She, he had said.

Rebecca groaned.

The Tortoise said, 'Are there any biscuits?'

And Rebecca's phone rang.

The phone rang and Geoffrey Foster's hand went first towards a non-existent breast pocket and made contact with his sweatshirt before changing course. Some habits were deeply ingrained and he had spent years wearing suits. He leaned back to stretch out his leg and reached into the front pocket of his cords.

'Foster.'

It was Michael Seward, calling from a landline. Finally!

'How is your mother?'

Get the formalities out of the way, then drop the bombshell...

Forty minutes later Foster ended the call and put his phone on charge; he'd been getting too relaxed and had slipped out of the routine of charging it overnight. Ashendon was having a soporific effect on him, though it was debatable whether there was something in the air – the absence of exhaust fumes – or simply the cessation of normal life while he kept house and cooked meals without a microwave in sight.

Whichever, it looked likely to last a bit longer. The mother wasn't going to get better but she wasn't dead yet either. It sounded as if she'd been out of things for years anyway, but

Geoffrey supposed you had to go and show willing even if they didn't know who you were.

Still, handy to be in credit on the favours front; and the tallixer had to have earned him a few bonus points.

The tallixer had surprised Seward, who had gone very quiet at the end of the line while he was being updated. Foster couldn't work out whether he was seething with jealousy or just bored.

No, not bored, couldn't be.

He had run the three riddle clues past him as well, but Seward had no idea where they might find the numbers. He had one contribution to make though.

'Are you sure it says *lie* of the land?'

'Yes. Well, no, apparently they said *lay* of the land, but poor grammar gets everywhere.'

And Seward had said, 'Not poor grammar. It should be ley spelled L E Y. They're talking about a leyline.'

And that put a whole new slant on things.

Rebecca said, 'It's about leylines!' and all heads turned her way.

'That was Geoffrey Foster. He's spoken to Michael. It really is 'the *ley* of the land' – the leyline. The whole riddle is about directions.'

Foster had been at work. 'Numbers can give you a bearing,' he had explained. 'Give me two numbers and I'll work out what to do with them. But you need a start point as well.'

Now Rebecca said, 'The first instruction gives us a line. The second will provide us with a bearing away from that, which hopefully will give us a leyline. And the final instruction tells us where to end up.'

There was a pause. Then Professor Peregrine said, 'It sounds plausible. Then the numbers are absolutely crucial. What are they?'

But answer came there none.

Chapter Thirty-Three

There was an example at the front of the cheque book, written out to 'A N Other' and signed 'My Signature.' Connor followed it carefully.

Twenty-one – ish – and I've never written a cheque.

He signed, and flipped back to the front again to make sure it was correct.

He had already bought envelopes and stamps and there was a post box on the corner. The rest had to wait for this solicitor.

Connor walked.

It had begun to rain, cold, weighty raindrops you could see ahead of you as you walked into them. He turned up his collar and shoved his hands in his pockets but he didn't mind. Rain was good here; everything was good here. Oxford opened its arms to him, surrounding him with its bounty, the colleges and museums beckoning him...

And there was just a chance, a possibility, even if faint...

He crossed St Aldates and headed north. The Council had set up Christmas lights, arrangements of snowflakes and angels in silver and white projecting from the tops of lampposts, and to Connor they looked classier, more spiritual, than the garish coloured lights he remembered from childhood.

Why don't you come here? the Dons had said. Casually too, as if the idea weren't momentous, destiny-changing. As if they were asking what he had in mind for the weekend: *Going somewhere nice? How about the cinema?*

He'd barely been able to reply, but that wasn't a problem – the Dons were good at talking whatever the subject.

'It would be useful,' Professor Viator had said, the one Rebecca called the Vulture. 'We won't be here forever.'

'I'm going to be,' Professor Lloyd said, winking at Connor. 'Going to give it my best shot.'

'*Any* of us,' Professor Viator continued, with a glare. 'And the portal will always need a guardian.'

'I'd live here?'

'Eventually. Shouldn't advise it for a few years, though. You'll want to be in the thick of things.'

Connor had turned to look at Professor Peregrine, without doubt the sanest of the three. The Professor returned his look. 'Undergrad society. Bops and the Union and punting. Rowing. Do you row? You might want to row.'

'*Study* here?'

'Of course. Why not?'

Connor quickened his stride, overtaking the shoppers, dodging umbrellas.

Study here. Study *here*, despite having left school after GCSEs. It was crazy, but the Dons didn't seem to think it was a problem. Or at least, only a minor one.

'That was silly of you,' Professor Viator said reprovingly, as if he wasn't aware that Connor had been running away from his life when he crossed into the other world.

But he could enrol at the tertiary college and take A-levels, and then apply for a place at the University.

'I think you'll find you'll be offered one,' Professor Peregrine had said, with a steady look. Professor Lloyd had gazed at the ceiling and whistled a tune.

'But—'

The Tortoise broke off whistling. 'We read your poetry. Some of it. Won't turn that down.'

Connor had stared from one to another. Leave aside the fact that they'd been rifling through his stuff. 'I thought you – I didn't know you taught English Literature.'

Professor Peregrine sighed. 'A hundred and eighty years, dear boy. Plenty of time to dabble.'

There was a crocodile of school children on Parks Road; Connor stood near the kerb to allow them to pass, their faces bright, backpacks bouncing. They had been to the museums, probably; *learning*. So much information, so much knowledge, so much thought and creativity and endeavour, all here, available for anyone who wanted it.

Connor began to grin.

* * *

Geoffrey Foster stopped dead. His hand made a small, sharp movement on the page.

'*...placing my knife in the china cabinet for now.*'

'My knife'.

He read the paragraph again with mounting excitement. It was a page from the 1870s – Foster flipped back to check: yep, 1873, just twenty-odd years after the cottage was built around the gap.

Placing my knife in the china cabinet.

When you say 'my knife' you don't just mean any old knife. *My knife* implies something personal, something you keep with you. A folding knife presumably, a penknife...But there was more...

Foster stared across the sitting room. Outside the sky was white-grey and the branches of the plum tree in the garden formed scratchy black lines across the square of the window pane, but he saw none of it. The idea rolled around in his mind...

This was a knife Uriel Passenger considered part of himself; a knife he had probably had in his possession for many years. That was what he inferred from those brief words: unity; identity; history.

That knife had been his for longer than Ashendon. That knife had been his before he came here at all.

A knife that must, surely must, have come with him from the world next door.

What was it made of?

Foster shifted his position, sitting more upright in the armchair, and resumed reading.

Behind the dinosaurs, the Vulture had said, and the Tortoise had added, *Where the children aren't.*

Connor therefore walked past the skeletons mounted on plinths – not just dinosaurs, he noticed, but a horse and a dog and a very engaging elephant too – and immediately saw the arch and the steps leading into the dark, subterranean gallery that housed the Pitt Rivers collection.

He had read about it but he had never seen it: an extraordinary gathering together of items donated by a Victorian army officer–

cum-archaeologist, mostly displayed in their original nineteenth-century cabinets at a density more reminiscent of a white elephant stall than a museum.

And it was wonderful – crazy and muddled and hobbyish and even quite spooky in places: funeral masks and mummies lurked in dark corners and there were cases of strange little fetishes, clumsy pieces shaped crudely like pigs or whales with wrappings of clay beads around their bellies. Connor fed a coin through the slot of a glass cabinet and watched the wooden figures inside bow solemnly in thanks, their eyes lit red, invisible gears cranking.

Professor Lloyd had been right – there were no children in these gloomy aisles. Connor wandered, his eyes taking in raffia-bound spears, web-like silver amulets, banana-leaf stencils from the Pacific islands, and a medieval pack saddle with hooks for hanging things from. It was like an exotic version of the hoard with which Uriel Passenger had filled his house at Ashendon.

After a while he moved into the newly opened corridors beyond, where the walls were clean and empty and the light almost startling. There were lecture rooms and public lavatories, and a space for changing exhibitions. Photographs were on display there now, black-and-white prints behind glass: bearded men in Panama hats and tweed jackets posing above deep trenches, and broken pieces of pots arranged in tidy, labelled rows. Victorian archaeology.

Connor moved on, past photographs documenting studies and theories about the pyramids, Machu Picchu and the Easter Islands, and nearer home, the massive earthworks of Maiden's Castle, the dragonlike White Horse cut into the south downs near Uffington, and the greatest monument of them all, the extraordinary, baffling great stone circle that was Stonehenge.

Chapter Thirty-Four

Rebecca found the Pidgeons in the garden. Where else? It wasn't quite dark yet, after all.

Roly, in wellies and cord trousers, was bent over one of the beds while Alice held a plastic washing-up bowl and caught the handfuls of potatoes her husband passed up, destined no doubt for supper.

'Just to let you know I'm back,' Rebecca called from the gate.

'Right you are, love. Did you have a nice time?'

'Yes, thanks, very nice.'

Rebecca let herself in and dropped her bag on the floor.

Only herself in the empty flat: heaven.

She had come back to London because the resounding blank they had drawn on Portland had somehow dampened the prospects for the Isle of Wight, although Rebecca supposed they'd have to check it out some time. In the meantime there was nothing she could do in Oxford until someone worked out what the clues referred to and what these numbers were. Nothing she could do in Derbyshire either, and she definitely didn't want to get involved with Jack, the tallixer or Geoffrey Flaming Foster again until she absolutely had to.

Jack was difficult to communicate with and made her feel awkward, which she resented; Foster was still a smarmy big-headed, self-centred pain, made worse by the fact that sometimes he was useful (*never, ever let him know that*); and as for the tallixer...

'So what about the Beast of Bodmin Moor?' she had asked the Dons. 'Was that a tallixer too?'

'Almost certainly.'

All those farmers and journalists and day-trippers hoping for a glimpse of it without ever realizing it was ten times as unlikely as they imagined.

'Why is it always tallixers? Why don't small, ordinary animals fall through?'

'Undoubtedly they do,' Professor Peregrine had said. 'But

they don't cause the same level of stir. And then there are cats, of course.'

'Cats?'

There were cats in the World Invisible too, it seemed; they were a species common to both.

'Not sure which one they originated in, could have been either. Dual nationality, if you like.'

She didn't. The notion of cats zipping to and fro at will was disturbing. No wonder cats gave the impression that they knew something you don't.

But of course they couldn't be doing it that often, not if there were so few gaps. So few known gaps.

Enough!

This time Rebecca had stopped at the corner shop to stock up, and what she wanted now was coffee and the saggy sofa and the big, glorious window in the studio. Once ensconced, a cushion covering her feet and the mug in her hands, she could open her mind and let a few troublesome things in.

Michael's mother being close to death was one. Rebecca had not met Michael's parents, and although she appreciated that he would be concerned at his mother's likely demise, it was just what happened, wasn't it? If Michael was – she did a quick calculation – forty-eight (ridiculous as that seemed given what he looked like) – then his mother was likely to be at least seventy, possibly eighty. Eighty was pretty old. Didn't you start expecting things when someone got to that age?

Perhaps she was callous. Her own mother had died when Rebecca was only seven, and she had always found it difficult to get close to her stepfather. Perhaps she was warped.

If she was warped though, Connor ought to be twisted beyond recognition, yet Rebecca felt sure Connor would have proper, genuine sympathy for Michael if (when?) his mother were to die.

Her guts clenched again. *Damn it.* Every time, every blessed time.

Alone in her studio, staring into the dark city beyond the window, Rebecca said aloud, 'I fancy him *so* badly.'

It was undeniable. She was aware she planned opportunities to look his way when she knew his attention was elsewhere and nobody was around to notice. Everything about him sent ripples of flame coursing through her. It was ridiculous – she told herself it was ridiculous – but he was just so gorgeous.

She loved his wrists.

Rebecca examined her own wrist. Just another human wrist. Okay, hers was smoother and lighter-boned, it didn't have the knobbly bits, and her veins and tendons were better concealed, but it worked just as well; her forearm rotated obediently on cue; everything joined up and moved to order, she was as dextrous as he was, probably. There was no magic about it. Yet Connor's wrists, sinewy and strong, made her feel almost faint.

Sinews... Even the word made her stomach plunge.

It couldn't lead anywhere; how could it? They were utterly different kinds of people – Connor reflective and patient and long-suffering and *kind,* and herself intolerant and selfish and – and snappy. Snappy like a little, belligerent, snappy dog.

Rebecca sighed. *Know thyself...* but knowing oneself just led to regretting that you weren't better...

Suffolk was too far, but Tooting was easy enough. She would go and see Auntie Edie tomorrow.

'Dear God.'

Geoffrey Foster looked with dismay at the wall of cardboard boxes. Eight by twelve and *how* many deep? He was in for a royal few hours of shuffling space.

There had been no problem obtaining permission from Michael Seward, once again very quiet on the end of the phone line even though he must surely be interested. Suppressed or repressed? In any case, he had given his blessing, and Geoffrey had seen the kid into his walled garden for the day – it made sense to check that they were both safely inside before leaving them, an escaped tallixer the last thing he wanted to deal with – and then driven to the industrial estate outside Matlock where the Ashendon hoard was in undignified storage.

There were a hell of a lot of boxes.

Foster recalled the gloomy Victorian interior of Ashendon House before the hotel took it on, and the cabinets and cupboards and shelf-loads of bric-a-brac collected over many years by Uriel Passenger, the alien traveller from another world thought by his neighbours to be just the eccentric old boy on the hill.

There had been ancient musical instruments, grubby children's toys, costumes, glassware, clocks and telescopes, although nothing valuable as far as he could tell. There had also been big stuff – treadle sewing machines, looms, early bicycles and penny-farthings – and the walls had been covered with framed maps and charts and mirrors. And somewhere in amongst it all must have been Passenger's personal knife.

Foster read the label on the side of the nearest box. *Samurai costume. Horse brasses. Dog bowl.*

He should have brought a radio.

Rebecca took the tube to Tooting Bec; the underground was much quicker than driving through the heavy traffic, and she'd have been lucky to find a parking space on Manorfield Road anyway. Walking up from the station took her back three years – nearly four now – to the days when she had lived in the tiny bedsit flat on the top floor of her great-aunt's house while she was frantically putting together a portfolio and trying to break into illustrating children's books.

The days when she was visiting the V and A regularly to draw from the collection. Before she met Michael there.

Since then she had become published, inherited a serious amount of money, and received an award for her work which was almost unheard of for an artist of her age. She was a success.

How much of that was down to her peculiar genes? Accepted theories on Nature versus Nurture must surely be skewed beyond belief if one was part Alien?

Not for the first time Rebecca wondered whether her eccentric great-aunt had guessed any of it. The thing was that Aunty Edie was so hard to pin down. Where did eccentricity end and evasion begin?

There was a wreath hanging from a pin stuck into the front door, the faded decoration of nylon leaves and plastic berries her aunt pulled out each year. It felt too early for Christmas decorations, but Rebecca put it down to decades of decorating classrooms on the 1st of December.

The wreath had fewer berries on it each year.

I'll buy her a new one. A better one.

Rebecca rang the doorbell as a warning but then unlocked the door and went in without waiting for her aunt to get up. 'It's me, Aunty Edie – Rebecca!'

She passed the hall mirror with its branches of vine leaves inlaid in the mahogany frame and followed the soft hiss of the gas fire to the front room.

Edie was asleep, feet on a canvas-work footstool, head cradled in the wing of the old-fashioned armchair.

Okay. She'd get what she wanted first and then make a pot of tea.

When she had moved into Michael's flat only her drawing desk and chair had moved with her; the rest of the furniture stayed in her aunt's house. Personal belongings had travelled piecemeal, in bags and pockets as Rebecca had needed them, and some of them remained even now.

Wrinkling her nose at the fusty, closed-up air, Rebecca opened the chest of drawers and pushed aside her remaining underwear.

I suppose I ought to take all this.

At the back, pushed against the corner, lay the cold metal cylinder: a telescope; *the* telescope; the telescope she and Connor had extracted from the case of a grandfather clock in the Oxford Museum of the History of Science; the telescope that had enabled them to read the coded letter and find Ashendon House and its astonishing secret.

The telescope that had never revealed its primary purpose.

Rebecca looked at it lying in her hand. It was made of brass, perhaps twenty centimetres long, and seemed to represent all that was unsatisfactory about the link to the invisible world Michael had once described, so unsettlingly, as 'next door'.

Even after repeated explanations about quantum entanglement and photons and orthogonality, Rebecca did not truly understand how this fantastical stuff could happen. How could light from the two worlds colliding enable people to pass from one to another? How could it have been happening on and off for centuries before the Victorians put paid to it by erecting mirrors to deflect the intruding light beams and enclosing the lot in a stone room – or the plinth of a statue?

How had Shakespeare put it? *'There are more things in heaven and earth, Horatio, than are dreamt of in your philosophy.'* Rebecca had studied Hamlet at school, never imagining that the famous quotation held such resonance for her own future.

Each of the objects they had needed to collect had held two purposes, or rather at least two. Most of them did what you would expect them to do – the candle gave light, the clock told the time, the key unlocked a door – but had a secondary function as well which had been crucial in leading them to the location of the gap between the worlds.

But they had never used the telescope as a telescope. They had never looked through it at anything remotely significant, and that disturbed her. It was like unfinished business.

In amongst the tights and tee-shirts was a square of pale green brocade. Rebecca fished it out and wrapped the brass cylinder in it, folding over the ends and tying it with the length of gold cord. The three belonged together. Then she zipped it into her bag and looked around the room.

Anything else?

Outside the window the ivy cloaking the garden fence was thick, dark and succulent. All sorts of things were hidden in there, Rebecca knew: birds' nests, cobwebs, wizened apples fallen from the overhanging boughs, tiny creatures that waited and watched...

She went downstairs to boil the kettle.

Chapter Thirty-Five

The knife turned up almost four hours after Foster had opened the first box. Opening the boxes had been necessary because the labels gave only the sketchiest idea of the contents; that became plain once he had found the stuffed voles in a box marked 'Art materials and sewing equipment'.

Early in the afternoon, around the time he was thinking he'd break for a sandwich and a coffee, he rifled through miscellaneous junk in one of the smaller boxes to find, at the bottom, loose playing cards and a small folding knife, the metal spine of its blade visible along the edge of a worn wooden handle.

Wooden. Just as he had hoped.

There was a broken elastic band too, the rubber perished, which had probably been holding the playing cards together. Judging by the variety of the designs on the reverse sides, they had come from many different packs.

Foster turned a couple over. Court cards. He turned over more and realised with a small spark of interest that they were all versions of one court card: the Queen of Clubs.

Acting on impulse, Geoffrey scraped the cards together and slipped them into his jacket pocket along with the knife. He was certain this was *the* knife, the one he was searching for. It was comfortable to his hand, a greyish colour, with a pattern of leaves carved into it, although the carving was shallow and the edges smoothed. It had definitely been somebody's personal knife; it had to be Passenger's.

But God only knew why he had been collecting the Queen of Clubs.

Rebecca poured the tea and passed the cup to her aunt.

As usual, it was proving tricky to keep the old lady on track. She was brilliant when it came to reminiscing, less so when tackling the events of the day.

She had been no use at all on the numbers. *'A series? Like Fibonacci?'* But when Rebecca broached the subject of the island of glass and the great circle she went straight to it like a magnet to steel.

'The Island of Glass will be Glastonbury. King Arthur's Avalon. Joseph of Arimathea, the Holy Grail and the Holy Thorn.'

'The Holy Thorn?'

'It flowers twice each year. Once in spring as you'd expect, and again at Christmas, on new growth. Isn't that wonderful?'

Rebecca made a note.

'And what does the phrase *great circle* make you think of?'

Superstitiously, Rebecca crossed her fingers where they couldn't be seen.

'Great circle? Do you mean Stonehenge?'

Stonehenge! Rebecca jerked upright. She had only been once, and remembered the disappointment; she had pictured a long walk across a wild and windswept Salisbury Plain, the mammoth standing stones looming ever larger as she approached. Instead the monument was barely a stone's throw from two major roads and the car park was spitting distance away. The stones themselves were cordoned off.

But the size remained, if only you could mentally shut out the noise of passing traffic and concentrate – the unimaginable mass of the stones and the vastness of the human endeavour required to have brought them there and set them upright.

Great circle...it seemed promising.

'Druids,' Aunty Edie said, with relish. 'Plenty of magic there to get you started.'

'What?'

'Another cup, dear?'

Eccentric or slippery?

There were crumbs on the counter and the breadknife was in the sink; Jack had made his own lunch.

Geoffrey Foster crammed the shrink-wrapped meat into the fridge – canned dog food had proved not acceptable – and made coffee.

Half way along the passage he paused and opened the door to the small parlour. He set down his mug and surveyed the ranks of mirrors on the facing wall, their surfaces mottled where the silvering had perished, their frames dusty.

He went closer. In the reflection, the card table behind him was visible over his shoulder, the botanical design on the mug reversed; through the open doorway beyond, the passage was just visible, with its promise of the rest of the cottage extending – identical except backwards of course; it was strange how alien that made it seem…

Foster drew Uriel Passenger's knife out of his pocket and slowly brought it up to the mirror. He opened his fingers to reveal its carved surface to the glass. His eyes narrowed.

The ivy-leaf carving was reversed, the tendril spiralling in the opposite direction, and even now, even so soon, it looked surprising to him, somehow *wrong*, as if he had become familiar with it already. He stared, and slowly, before his searching eyes, the wrongness dissolved.

Just a knife in the mirror, and his own familiar face as he saw himself every day, which was of course the reverse of how others saw him.

Foster pocketed the knife and retrieved his coffee. But he couldn't quite suppress the memory, the impression that the mirrors had shivered oh-so-slightly when he showed them the wooden handle.

Rebecca closed Google Earth and shut her laptop. There would be no need to be disappointed by the tourists at Stonehenge all over again because there would be no need to travel there; nor to Glastonbury, although that was a pity because she had never been and Glastonbury Abbey and the Tor looked interesting and very drawable.

But if you interpreted the riddle as giving you something for a bearing to work off, then a map worked much better than being there in person.

Foster had said he needed a base line. Well, drawing with a ruler a straight line connecting Stonehenge with either Glastonbury

Abbey or Glastonbury Tor could be exactly that. Probably the Tor, being a high point and more visible from a distance.

Rebecca had no idea how two numbers could provide a bearing, but she believed the man; he was nauseating but competent.

I'm not ringing him, though. Someone else can do that.

She tried Connor, bracing herself, but her call went straight to voicemail, so she shelved it for the present and took a shower. She was going to make a foray into normal life and meet friends from the artists' co-operative for a pub supper. They had an exhibition coming up and needed to discuss arrangements. She felt guilty about her recent absences and hoped it was going to prove possible to put the crazy stuff on hold for a few hours while she gave the group her concentration.

Under the streaming water she ran through the checklist to be discussed: advance notices to the press; private view arrangements; design of flyers; who would be hanging the work.

They were exhibiting in a church hall in Hammersmith, and Rebecca had a fresh batch of embroidered pieces ready; she 'drew' with her sewing machine onto richly dyed silks, and these days she mounted the small panels in simple box-frames – classy and also easy for buyers to hang straight on the wall. There was a stack of them, carefully interleaved with corrugated cardboard, against the wall in the studio, but one, Rebecca's favourite, was propped on the bedside cabinet.

She knew why it was her favourite. All of them featured a central motif surrounded by a wide, complex border of botanicals – oak leaves and acorns, ferns, white-flowered hawthorn (although whether twice-flowering she couldn't say) and, in this case, vines.

Well…she always had liked vines…

She saw it behind her in the mirror while she was drying her hair, and her attention was caught momentarily by the reflected image. It looked – different.

Of course it was different: it was reversed. A mirror image, naturally. And yet…

Also propped up, cutting off the corner of the frame, was the card she had filched from Connor's coat pocket on Portland – his unsettling Queen of Clover. She also looked different in her mirror version.

Rebecca moved her hair-dryer slowly, focusing on the room she was seeing in the mirror, behind her mirror-self.

The card should have been too small to see clearly, and yet she had no difficulty in distinguishing the form of the figure, the folds of her gown, the lines with which the artist had represented her floating hair.

There was a flicker, a suggestion of movement and Rebecca's eyes leapt to the stitched vine tendrils of her own picture, and then immediately back again as she thought the painted cloth on the playing card had stirred.

Nothing.

The hairdryer sagged in her hand as she stared, and then stared closer.

The strange, sinuous patterns in the queen's falling sleeves were making sense, had turned into something no longer abstract. Like elements of an unknown alphabet, they still slipped and slanted across the painting, but they now formed, quite clearly, 2, 1, 9 and 7.

Four numbers.

Rebecca switched off the hairdryer and laid it gently down.

Two, one, nine, seven.

There was a rustle like white noise; the mirror was pulling at her. Rebecca stared at the figures in the reflection, and in the reflection the vine branches seemed to writhe.

But they couldn't be.

She looked again at the Queen, seated in three-quarter profile with her sleeves flowing and her skirts spread, and the Queen turned her head to meet her eyes, and parted her lips.

Me, the Queen said, her voice deep and inside Rebecca's brain. You... *Us.*

And Rebecca fainted.

Chapter Thirty-Six

'Yes. Hi. What?'

It was not what Connor was expecting, but it was Rebecca, which was a relief. After being diverted to voicemail three times he had started to worry.

'It's Connor.'

'Yes. I know. What is it?'

She sounded very tense. If he had still been walking, he would probably have stopped to give her his full attention, but in fact he had stopped before he made the call, still stuck in the past when the house telephone had been fixed to the kitchen wall.

Connor leaned against the railings of whichever college it was and said carefully, 'Are you alright?' He braced himself.

But there was just a pause and then Rebecca's voice saying, 'Oh...Yes. I'm fine. I just...I'm fine.'

She didn't sound it, but there's nothing worse than someone saying, Are you sure?, so Connor said, 'Good. Okay. Well, I was ringing about your message.'

Again the pause, as if Rebecca were lassoing her thoughts. Then: 'Oh yes. Sorry. Right. Well, it's just that I have an idea about the base line Geoffrey Foster wants. I've spoken to my aunt...'

As she talked, she seemed to warm up; the usual Rebecca came back, confident and informative and, it had to be said, just a bit heedless. Connor began to relax. She was okay after all.

'...suggested Stonehenge, and that sounds likely to me.'

Connor said, 'Me too. There's an exhibition at the Pitt Rivers Museum. It seems obvious.'

'Oh! Right! Well I reckon that's enough to try, at least. And,' Rebecca added, with something of her old swagger, 'I think I've got the numbers as well.'

'The numbers!'

Connor glanced up as he felt a drop on his hand, and saw the rain passing through the light from the street lamp across the road.

He heard the drops beginning to land on his shoulders, and started walking, shifting his hand to shield the phone from the wet.

Walking *and* talking into a phone, he thought drily – he was catching up.

Although listening more than talking. Rebecca had made a quantum leap of discovery. Her own designs and Michael's box label were almost identical despite having been designed quite independently. 'I hadn't even seen his label when I stitched this,' she had said. 'And Michael had definitely never seen anything of mine.'

She had checked the two embroidered pictures which included ivy, and the label on the base of the box Michael had given her, after something – she was cagey about what – had tipped her off.

There was a mirror too, apparently – some big, old family heirloom hanging in the house she used to live in that had a mahogany frame inlaid with a pattern of vine leaves. 'I rang Aunty Edie and she counted for me. Same numbers.'

Connor had arrived at the bridge. With his back to the rain, he fished for the cards in the inside pocket of his coat and drew out the soft-edged photograph of his grandmother.

There was just enough light spilling from the windows of the pub alongside for him to see.

He counted, and then counted again. Twenty-one vine leaves, nine tendrils spiralling, and seven bunches of grapes.

'Connor?'

'Yes.'

'What do you think?'

Connor drew breath. 'I think you're probably right.'

Rebecca stayed at home.

She rang Carrie, the chairman of the co-operative, after she had found that a cup of tea and half an hour had failed to mend her. She was half-truthful.

'I'm feeling a bit weak and wobbly, I'm afraid. Sorry.'

'Are you ill?' Carrie had asked, flatteringly concerned.

'No, no, it's just one of those things, I think. I'll be fine tomorrow.'

I hope.

Rebecca had never had concussion and didn't know what to look out for, but she took the robust view that if nothing seemed out of the ordinary tomorrow, after a good night's sleep, she must be okay, however fluttery she was feeling now.

And bruised. She had deftly managed to miss the rug and land on the polished floorboards.

Rebecca had never fainted before either, and it distressed her to think she could be so feeble. Had the entire episode been an illusion? The Queen of Whatever was back to normal now, looking politely over Rebecca's left shoulder without so much as a wink.

The design on her sleeves no longer writhed, but when Rebecca, with some trepidation, held the card up to the mirror, the motifs revealed themselves once more as the four numerals – 2, 1, 9 and 7. They reminded her of the text some websites require you to decipher in order to prove you are a human trying to log in and not a computer – the forms skewed and slippery but quite legible.

Legible in reverse; you'd never interpret them as numerals without the mirror. Had her story about the vine leaves and flowers been enough to convince everyone? Would she have their full confidence in the coincidence of the numbers without telling them about the queen to back it up?

Cards and mirrors…Now what did that make her think of?

She moved carefully around the flat, conscious of her newly discovered vulnerability and avoiding anything that gave back a reflection. She had scrambled eggs for supper, and got into her night things early, and was spoiling herself watching a thriller on Michael's tiny television when her phone rang.

Connor again.

Exactly how rude had she been? The thing was, it had been a shock coming round on the floor only minutes earlier with her legs bent one way and her arms another, twisted between the chest-of-drawers and the bed. She'd felt like Alice, stuffed into the house with her foot up the chimney and one arm through the door. She hoped it wasn't a bad sign that she couldn't actually remember their conversation.

'Hi,' she said cautiously.

She listened. Then she said, 'Okay. But could we do it tomorrow instead?'

Connor rang Geoffrey Foster to confirm a time and then gazed out of the bedroom window and thought.

It was unlike Rebecca to put anything off. On the other hand she sounded more or less okay. There was still something slightly out of kilter about her; she was being too nice, although that sounded harsher than he intended.

Her image floated into his mind, slender and straight and breezy, a touch scornful, as if perfectly aware she didn't suffer fools gladly and saw no wrong in it. Like a princess, but not a spoiled one, just someone who was regal and dismissive of it.

No, not a princess: a queen.

Why had she taken the card?

He was pretty sure she had. If he had lost the lot he'd have assumed they fell out on the beach, but the others were safely in his pocket. It was not likely that the kid's mother had gone through his pockets and stolen a picture card. So that left Rebecca.

But why? And did he dare tackle her?

Connor sighed. It was stupid, he was on a hiding to nothing. Cats and kings came to mind. To Rebecca he was and would always be a kid tagging along, a no-hoper in hand-me-downs foisted on her by events beyond her control. Someone she put up with.

God help him if she ever found out how he felt.

Geoffrey Foster pulled the laptop across the table and opened Google Earth. They might want to wait until tomorrow but he was getting started.

Glastonbury and Stonehenge. Obvious, really.

Twenty-one and either ninety-seven or seventy-nine.

It couldn't be an angle measured as 21 degrees and 97 or 79 minutes, because there are only sixty minutes in a degree.

So if you take them as integers *describing* an angle, then that angle could have a tangent of twenty-one divided by ninety-seven or ninety-seven divided by twenty-one.

Using the software tools in the program, Geoffrey drew the connecting line and began to measure.

Chapter Thirty-Seven

Rebecca gave herself a bit of time after she woke, slightly afraid of what she might discover when she sat up. But apart from the bruises, she was fine.

By nine-thirty she had her laptop open, her A4 pad and pencil on the table, and a tall glass of orange juice ready.

It was to be a conference call – of a sort.

The problem was that Skype was out because the Dons had not joined the computer generation. The Tortoise wanted to but was outvoted by the others, who had decided enough twenty-first-century technology was enough; television: yes, microprocessors: no.

So they had to go through Connor. She and Geoffrey Foster each called – she on Connor's mobile and Foster on the Ferry House land-line – and Connor passed information back and forth.

'He says the numbers don't work as latitude and longitude,' Connor told Rebecca.

'Why not?' Rebecca asked, and listened to Connor's voice, fainter, saying, 'Why not?' into the Dons' telephone receiver, the pause, and then Connor's voice louder again: 'He says they give you the Gulf of Mexico, the Pacific Ocean – one of the bits where there aren't any islands – Burma, and somewhere between – where was it?' Another pause. 'Right, between Australia and Malaysia.'

'Oh,' Rebecca said.

There was a roar of white noise.

'What on earth's that?'

'Hang on. Okay, say something.'

'Like what?'

A new voice, quite tinny but clear enough, said, 'Yes, that works.'

'Is that Foster? What have you done?' Rebecca asked.

'I've got both phones to one ear. We can all hear each other now, I think. Hope.'

It was smoother after that.

Having ruled out latitude and longitude, Foster had then assumed the numbers referred to two sides of a right-angled triangle.

'Why?' Rebecca asked. 'Isn't that just being unnecessarily complicated? Why can't they be a map reference?'

Connor made a small noise, quickly abandoned; Geoffrey Foster's voice, patronizing as usual, came in instead. 'You mean a grid reference.'

'Yes.'

'But which grid?'

'*The* grid. The grid we all use.'

'I don't think you use maps much at all, my dear.'

Swine!

'You're talking about the national grid reference system, but that was only introduced between the wars. When did these directions originate, do we know?'

Silence; nobody knew.

'Or do they get somehow updated to suit the recipient?'

That sounded uncomfortably like what Connor had found three years ago. One of the objects they had had to locate had been described to him as being in libraries that were both the old British Museum Reading Room, where the object had first been hidden, *and* the contemporary British Library at Euston, where all the stock had been moved to long after the clues had been set.

Magic.

Magic made Rebecca think again of the vines swaying in the mirror reflection, and the painted queen meeting her eyes…

Stop it!

She said, 'What do you do with the triangle, then?'

To describe a triangle, she was told, you only need to know three things: two angles and one side, or two sides and one angle. Therefore if you assume one of the angles is a right angle – ninety degrees – then they had their three bits of knowledge and could find both the remaining angles.

It would help to know which way round the numbers should be put: 97 or 79.

'Ninety-seven,' Rebecca said promptly.

'How do you know? If you've just counted leaves…'

'I've seen them written down,' Rebecca said, and then bit her tongue.

There was a pause.

'Written down where?' Foster's voice demanded. Connor, she noticed, stayed silent.

'I – I'll explain later. When we're all together. But that is the order.' *Hell – move on quick.* 'So what do we do with the angle?'

The angle could be used to give a bearing, provided you had a baseline – which they now did – and knew your start point.

'Do we know the start point?' Rebecca asked.

'Presumably either Glastonbury or Stonehenge.'

'Glastonbury,' Connor said. 'It comes first in the riddle.'

It still had to be determined which side of the line the angle had to be measured. Everyone waited while Geoffrey Foster did complicated things on his laptop up in the Peak District.

Was Jack watching over his shoulder? Rebecca pictured the skinny boy leaning over the arm of the chair, as if Foster were his dad or uncle. How peculiar to think of the estate agent – he would always be that to her – playing house to the poor stray kid and his ferocious pet.

And what about Michael? How was his mother, and when would he come back?

'Okay.' Foster's voice spoke again. 'I've extended both sets of lines and I think there's a problem. The final line of the riddle mentions a place of captivity and a stone, yes?'

'Yes.'

'One of the lines doesn't lead anywhere that could be considered an island.'

'And the other?'

'Assuming "left" means to the left while facing Stonehenge, the line leads to Lindisfarne, but unless this "prison" refers to the monastery that's a no-go. And the other side takes you where you've already been. Portland.'

Rebecca turned her collar up. It was raining again and the pavements were shiny under the street lights. Shop fronts glowed yellow and white, and Christmas trees, spruce and Nordmann fir, lay heaped outside the greengrocer's round the corner.

Rebecca let her eyes glide over the window displays as she walked. Everyone had made some kind of effort, although not much in some cases; the fashion stores boasted sparkling foam-board snowflakes half a metre across or giant silver baubles suspended from silk banners, the hardware shop just a few strands of tatty tinsel looped above the electric drills and toasters. The bookshop, a cosy independent Rebecca was fond of, had filled the window with children's picture books on a Christmas theme – Raymond Briggs and Alan Ahlberg and the nativity story in gentle, soft-edged pastels.

I've really got to do the cards.

Each year Rebecca had a batch of Christmas cards printed from her own designs for her friends and family, and for business contacts and clients. This year's were sitting in a box in the studio, but she had yet to write any.

Tonight. I'll do it tonight. Or tomorrow, latest.

She felt wearier than she ought. Rebecca usually enjoyed the run-up to Christmas, her gift-list not too long to be arduous – her stepfather, Aunty Edie, a handful of friends – but this year it was difficult to focus. The World Invisible was hogging her energy.

What on earth was going to happen? They couldn't keep the tallixer in the walled garden for ever, and meanwhile Connor was just wasting his life away at the Ferry House.

I'll need to give Connor a present.

Rebecca wanted to groan. How should she handle this? He'd be embarrassed, she'd be embarrassed, she didn't have the first idea what to get him or what price range she should be thinking of, but at the same time she couldn't *not* get him something either.

Too difficult, too difficult.

She had never been in this position before, having to buy a gift for a – well, not that Connor was, but...Anyway, she had no experience to draw on.

Steph, she'd ask Steph. Not that Steph had ever met Connor, and he wasn't exactly...run of the mill.

Portland, Foster had said. But it couldn't be Portland because they had already been over it and ruled it out.

Rebecca shuddered, the same old sensation she was getting used to now, as into the forefront of her mind leapt the memory of Connor tearing across the stones to throw himself into the icy waves. This sort of thing happened all the time these days and she seemed powerless to squash it.

Has everyone been through this? she wondered, scanning the faces of the passers-by. Is this what it's always like?

She had experienced a touch of it, like a trial run, when she first met Michael, with his astonishing looks and intriguing Anglo-American accent and vocabulary. But that had been only a shadow, a ghost-image of what she was suffering now. A premonition: *this is what it will be like, this is how you will feel, only much, much more…*

Rebecca pulled up short and got the footplate of a baby buggy in her ankles.

'Sorry!'

She'd give him a book – books. Obvious, really. Of course he had read masses, but he would never have been able to buy books before, only borrow them from public libraries. It wouldn't matter that she was giving him stuff he already knew, the point was that he would now possess them.

The bell over the door jangled as she pushed it; the bookshop was warm and stuffy and smelled enticingly of paper. Rebecca opened her coat and loosened her scarf, shaking off the raindrops.

Fiction and children's books were downstairs, non-fiction on the upper floor. Rebecca climbed the creaky staircase.

Half an hour later she had an armful of editions that she was fairly confident with, and was making her way back to the stairs when her eye was caught by a display on a table: geology and ancient history – reading the landscape, reconstructions of Roman settlements, and early English vernacular architecture.

Amid the stacks, one book was propped on a vertical stand to face her: a large, glossy, coffee-table book in a square format, no doubt full of atmospheric pictures of mists and sunsets and aerial photographs of crop circles.

But the cover stopped Rebecca dead in her tracks.

Chapter Thirty-Eight

'This one.' Foster laid his index finger along the narrow line of metal. 'See? The short one.' He used his nail to extract the short, wide cutting blade from the shiny red handle, opening it out and then pressing it closed again.

He handed the penknife to the boy. Jack turned it over in his hand, found the short blade and pulled it out.

'That's right,' Foster said.

'Ta.'

How old had he been when he fell out of the world? Two? Three? Geoffrey Foster was vague about the speech development of small children.

He watched the boy set off down the path, armed with more pencils and the penknife in his pocket. Good thing Michael was well stocked with drawing materials. He hadn't been able to find a pencil sharpener but there was a Swiss Army penknife, a slim, simple version, lying on the desk next to a mug of graphite pencils with chiselled tips.

Artists! And it looked like this Jack was the same. Well, it gave him something to do since he couldn't read, or at least not English.

Geoffrey opened his laptop. So far, it looked like Cambridge would be a likely start point for getting Passenger's knife analysed; they had labs running both dendrochronological and radio-carbon dating analysis.

He would wait for Michael's input first, though.

He had found a book on wood identification on Michael's shelves – pages of coloured detail shots of textures and grain belonging to more tree species than he had known existed – Cocobolo and Snakewood and other strange names. None of them looked like the grey wood of Uriel Passenger's knife but he acknowledged his eye was not educated; Seward's opinion would be useful if he was not to come across as a complete novice when he approached the labs.

He reopened Google Earth, without a great deal of enthusiasm. After his calculations with the bearings there was no doubt that one line hit Portland and others hit absolutely nothing. Well, some tiny rock off the coast of north Wales, but hardly what you would call an island, and certainly nothing that could house a 'place of captivity'.

He drew the lines in again, anyway. With Portland on one line, another line almost – not quite, but within a possible margin of error – touched Lindisfarne.

Foster frowned. He had already discounted that after finding that the Lindisfarne Priory Stone, deeply carved on both sides and believed to be a Viking grave stone, was in the Priory museum.

And anyway, a monastery?

But there wasn't anything else which looked remotely possible falling anywhere near the bearings.

Discontented, Foster swooped the cursor across the map, skating over the mosaic of fields, the mortar lines of hedgerows. He pulled the map downwards, heading north towards the horizontal line of the M4, his old tramping ground from the city to his parents' home in Bristol, reading the names of the towns and villages he had never visited because The Country did not appeal: Salisbury, Chippenham, Marlborough... He moved in, enlarging the scale to get an impression of the sizes of these settlements.

And then he frowned again and zoomed in closer.

There was a circle outlined on the screen, but it wasn't Stonehenge. He made it grow, and the village names popped out of the landscape: West Kennet, Beckhampton, and Avebury.

Foster selected the ruler tool and measured: nearly half a kilometre across. He sent the program to find Stonehenge and measured again.

'My God.'

Avebury was more than ten times the size.

'He'll need Latin.'

'He will not need Latin. The University no longer stipulates Latin these days.'

'If it did, it would never fill the places.'

The Vulture managed to convey disapproval almost every time he spoke, but Connor had realised it was habit rather than bad temper.

The names Rebecca had allotted the Dons were disrespectful but unfortunately very apt, and they had stuck.

'Latin?' he said now, mostly in order to counter the impression he was merely a bystander in this conversation they were having about his future.

'*I'll* teach you,' whispered the Tortoise reassuringly.

They were planning: Professor Peregrine had a four-step programme for him.

Step One: Enrol in the local tertiary college for two years of A-levels – or rather one and a half years. *('Not a problem; you'll catch up.')*

Step Two: Apply to Oxford. They seemed to think it a cert that he'd get in. (*'There is no question you have the ability. There is always an element of luck in the interview stage, I fear, but there we can help,'* said Professor Peregrine, and the Tortoise added, '*Glamour!*')

Step Three: Three years as an undergraduate at Oxford. That was the part that threw a scintillating cloak of excitement over Connor, full of sparks and dazzle; the bit he couldn't get past.

The Dons could though. Step Four: A doctorate and then post-doc positions leading to tutoring, a lectureship and ultimately a permanent faculty position. That was when he would be deemed a safe, guardian for the gap that lurked inside the plinth.

'But it isn't guaranteed. It can't be guaranteed that I'd get a permanent position here,' Connor protested.

'It's called *tenure*, and we can do something about that.'

Two of the Dons looked vaguely shifty; the Tortoise beamed.

Connor said slowly, 'This...glamour...You aren't telling me you can work magic over here?'

'It isn't *exactly* magic,' Professor Peregrine said, cagily.

'But it isn't exactly *not*,' Professor Viator said.

Connor fell silent. Had it not been for meeting that estate agent, Geoffrey Foster, at Michael's cottage he might have queried it further, but having experienced the difference himself he thought he understood.

Working his little bit of Skill on the doorstep had been like pushing a car uphill, or wading thigh-deep in the sea off Chesil Beach – there seemed to be a great weight of resistance which hadn't been there in the other place. Of course you'd expect the Dons to be far better at it than he would ever be, but still…It seemed magic knew its place, and this wasn't it.

Yet they must have kept in practice, at least a bit.

'Has no-one ever suspected anything?' he asked.

'Oh, once in a while, here or there.'

'We have – generally – been careful,' the Vulture said, with a glare at Professor Lloyd.

'It is true we do seem rather to have stirred up imaginations,' Professor Peregrine said, his fingers laced comfortably on his lap.

'Imaginations?'

'The Merton chap, with his made-up languages. Did awfully well out of that book.'

'Exeter,' corrected the Vulture.

'I mean his professorship.'

'Oh well, yes.'

'And his Irish friend.'

'Univ.'

'Taught at Magdalen, though.'

'Oh well, yes, *taught* there.'

'And then that boy from Cheshire – Alderley Edge wasn't it?'

'Yes, and him. Where was he, now?'

The Dons fell silent, all frowning.

'He was Magdalen too, wasn't he?'

Connor asked slowly, feeling the metaphorical ground insubstantial beneath his feet, 'Are you talking about–'

'And Deadly Dodgson of course,' said the Tortoise with glee, and everyone let out a guffaw of exasperation.

'Dreadful man.'

'Such a nuisance.'

'Had to be so careful.'

'Dodging Dodgson, that's what we called it.'

'Nearly onto us back there in – what was it? – Sixty? Sixty-one?'

'Fifty-eight,' Professor Viator said heavily. 'The March the shed roof blew off.'

'The shed roof blew off in nineteen fifty-eight?'

'No, no, *eighteen* fifty-eight.'

'The so-and-so. Knew there was something about a hole, you see, and assumed it was a hole in the ground. Ha!'

Connor changed tack. 'Do you mean Lewis–'

'That's right. That was his nom-de-plume, in case his stories didn't sit well with his lectureship.'

'Didn't sit well with Christchurch, more like,' the Vulture said.

'A regular terrier, he was,' the Tortoise put in. 'Sniff-sniff-sniff. Got hold of the thing about the mirrors *and* the cards. Barking up the wrong tree with the chess, though.'

'But,' Connor tried again.

'Very awkward. Christchurch just across the river, you see. Altogether he found out far too much, so we had no option.'

'No option but what?'

There was another pause. Then Professor Viator said, 'We took his diaries.'

'*Confiscated* his diaries,' said Professor Peregrine.

'Snuck in and whipped 'em,' said Professor Lloyd. 'Four years' worth. He lost heart after that.'

'But no need to dwell on the past,' Professor Peregrine said. 'Time to light the lamps.'

Connor closed the curtains in the drawing room. He heard the slap of the cat flap and Milly, the tabby, sauntered in from the hallway and made her way to the hearth.

Professor Viator went out to the kitchen and began to clatter pans; he was going to bake something which would no doubt be delicious – he had after all been practising for over a century.

Professor Lloyd flipped through the pages of the Sunday magazine to find the television schedule.

'How are your riddles coming along?' Professor Peregrine asked.

'Hopeless,' Connor said. 'They don't seem to work, but no-one can think of an alternative island of glass or great circle.'

'And you've tried Glastonbury and Stonehenge?'

'Yes.'

And the Tortoise said, 'What about Avebury, then? Oh good, Doctor Who is back on.'

Chapter Thirty-Nine

'It's Avebury!' Rebecca said. 'It's the circle that has to be great, not the stones!'

'I know,' Connor said.

'Has Geoffrey Foster–'

'Yes.'

'And?'

'We think it's Skye,' Connor said.

The weather stayed fine.

The red Mini took her from Trentham Road to the Ferry House to collect Connor, and then to Ashendon, where Michael had still not returned and Foster had become weirdly domestic. He cooked a risotto for supper and washed up afterwards.

The next day they zipped along the network of motorways northwards, crossed into Scotland at Gretna, and then got horribly snarled in traffic around Glasgow so that they arrived at Loch Lomond just after dark. Rebecca drove it in one go, and was happy to crawl through the village roads of Balloch looking for the Bed and Breakfast she had booked.

'There – just passed it.'

'Which one?' Rebecca reversed into a turning.

'Next to the post box.'

She tucked herself into the gravelled yard of a low white house with an old-fashioned lantern in the porch, and they climbed out into the sharp, sweet air to find out what the Bed and Breakfast would be like. Always a gamble, booking on the strength of a website.

On Skye it would be different. Astonishingly, they had a contact. After well over a century of teaching, the Dons had collected an impressive database of past students.

'Cameron, that's the fellow. Donald.'

'Dougal,' said the Tortoise.

'Douglas,' said Professor Peregrine. 'He has a farm, if I recall. He'll be delighted to help.'

And, surprisingly in Rebecca's view, he was. Rebecca emailed the address the Dons gave her, so that the poor man would have a chance to invent an excuse if he wanted one, but received a reply the same day: *Always a pleasure to meet Oxford friends. Very welcome to stay – plenty of room. ETA nearer the time?*

She felt a little uncomfortable about the assumption that they were 'Oxford friends', but it would have been churlish to refuse such hospitality, even if it did mean staying on a farm. Rebecca knew about farms.

'Oh but they're quite modern these days, you know,' the Tortoise said. 'They have machines for milking the cows!'

'I know,' Rebecca said. 'I grew up on one.'

The second leg of the journey, from Loch Lomond to the Kyle of Lochalsh where the Skye Bridge took them onto the island, was a chain of twisting roads over hills and between mountains that impressed Rebecca, who had not seen nature so vast before. Steph had been the one who went on the school skiing trips. It would have been too banal to comment on how big the mountains were, but still…they were so *big*. Surely it was the first time for Connor, too?

'There were mountains in Vermont.'

Oh yes.

'With tree cover right to the top. Amazing.'

Maybe, but Rebecca found these white-capped mountains amazing too.

They passed a loch where the water was so still and so clear that it mirrored the mountainside perfectly; if you had seen a photograph of it, Rebecca thought, you would suspect it had been Photoshopped.

By the time they reached the Skye Bridge, she was tired from concentrating on taking the car round hairpin bends and up and down such steep inclines.

The road they had been following for miles continued on the island. Sometimes mesh sheep fences marched alongside; other times the sheep lay tucked up placidly on the crumbling tarmac edges and watched her drive cautiously by. They passed low white houses set on squares of mown grass amongst moorland, and occasional clusters of hairy red cattle with unlikely horns. And after they had turned onto a new road there was water on their left, a sheet of pearl grey, the horizon misty and insubstantial. It looked cold and clean and somehow timeless.

And then at last there was a turning on their right with a fingerpost directing them to Carnbeag and, thankfully, Rebecca drove along the tipsy, bumping lane to the home of the Dons' old student.

Douglas Cameron's house was a long, simple affair set in front of the outbuildings and farm yard, and inside it reminded Connor instantly of the Colvins' farmhouse in Antler Hollow – honey-coloured wood, rag rugs, and the sharp, back-of-the-throat smell of wood-smoke. A dog emerged at the end of the hall, something small and whiskery, toenails clicking importantly on the floorboards, and strains of what sounded like Radio 4 drifted through the door.

Douglas Cameron himself was tall and spare with sloping shoulders and a receding hairline. He shook hands and took Rebecca's bag from her with old-world charm.

'Why don't I show you your rooms so you can freshen up? I've got coffee on. Did you have a good drive?'

He wasn't Scottish and he didn't sound like a farmer – more like a politician or financier, Connor thought, admittedly vaguely. At any rate, someone moneyed and secure, very English, and…faintly louche.

The rooms they were taken to were at one end of the long upstairs passage, opposite a bathroom. 'This is all yours,' Douglas Cameron said. 'I'm at the other end.'

Connor waited in his room so that Rebecca could use the bathroom first. He knew she'd want to.

How accurate had Foster's calculations been? Skye was an island, but it was pretty big – six hundred and forty square miles, although there wasn't really a top-to-bottom measurement because of its peculiar shape. That was a heck of a lot of ground to cover if the riddles didn't pinpoint the spot.

It did contain a place of captivity, provided you were allowed to interpret the words creatively. One of the mountain clusters included a strange formation that had been called 'The Prison' for generations, and was believed to have been used as a protective enclosure for cattle. However, they still had to identify which stone they needed to face. It looked to Connor, from the maps they had bought, that there were several contenders.

But he didn't doubt that they had come to the right place this time. It was hard to be specific about what he felt, but since they had crossed the water and headed north on the island he had sensed that they were on track. There was a kind of frisson, like a low-level tingle in his guts, like excitement...or possibly fear...

Rebecca approved of Douglas Cameron's kitchen instantly. It was a proper farmhouse affair, with the cooking stuff at one end and a sagging sofa covered with a rug at the other – a patchwork of woven squares, navy and violet and bottle green. The terrier and a lurcher were curled up together there, and flopped their tails sociably when she and Connor entered.

There was an inviting smell of ground coffee, and something savoury was in the oven.

'Mutton stew,' Douglas said, bringing the coffee pot to the table. 'Got a sheep out of the freezer.'

He told them he had retired from the Civil Service and bought the croft ten years ago, after his wife died. It sounded to Rebecca like he ran it as a hobby, although he didn't call it that. *'Always liked sheep.'*

'Now tell me about Oxford,' he said, sliding onto the bench seat next to Rebecca. 'Peregrine's still there, is he? Amazing old bird!'

You don't know the half, Rebecca thought. She smiled and said, 'Well, he's very old of course,' and saw Connor's mouth twist.

'Wonderful lecturer. Great stories. Very charismatic. I count myself lucky to have had him.'

Not that lucky.

'We've a little while before we eat; would either of you care for a drink?'

They didn't, but their host went ahead anyway. Rebecca thought it looked routine, the decanter on the dresser less than half full and far from dusty. Douglas Cameron poured the drink with a fluid, practised manner. 'Talisker,' he said, bringing his glass to the table. 'Our local distillation. You should try some while you're here. Why are you here, by the way?'

'We're looking at landscapes,' Rebecca said, as they had planned. 'I'm an artist.'

'Are you? Do I know you?'

The old charmer. 'I doubt it,' Rebecca said. 'I work mostly in illustration. Children's books, usually.'

'Fascinating! And you're on the lookout for backgrounds, are you? Like the movie people looking for locations?'

'That's right. Well, kind of.'

'Wonderful.' The man took a sip of whisky and turned to Connor, facing him. 'And you are…?'

'I'm looking for fairies,' Connor said.

Chapter Forty

The roads on Skye went on and on and to Rebecca they all looked very similar. You could get seriously lost if it weren't for the fact that there were hardly any turnings, so if you stayed facing forwards you'd eventually end up back where you began with a tour of the whole island behind you.

There were some junctions, though.

'Looks like we turn right here for Portree.'

Rebecca indicated *(to whom? Sheep?)* and took the road signposted to Portree and also to Port Righ. The road signs were all dual language.

The day was dry but with low cloud, hence the tour; there was too much mist to go as high as the Prison in the Quiraing, which was the wonderful name of the rock formations in the north-east of the island. So instead they were running through the itinerary Douglas Cameron had drawn up for them – drawn up with a raised eyebrow and a sardonic smile.

'Whatever made you say that?' Rebecca had asked, incredulous, as they climbed the wooden stairs at the end of the evening, leaving their host to his third nightcap. He did rather knock it back.

Connor smiled, turning her insides to pulp. 'Why not? Look at all the information we got.'

'Well, I suppose…'

Fairy Glen, Fairy Pools, Fairy Bridge, not forgetting the Famous Fairy Flag. Fairy wives and fairy babies…

'Do you think all this is real?' Rebecca asked uncertainly, and was relieved to hear Connor's casual, confident reply.

'I doubt it. It's myth. People make things up, take simple coincidences and embroider them, boast about being special or knowing someone special.'

That was good, then.

'And you'd only need one person crossing over every hundred years or so to build up quite a tradition.'

Or maybe not.

'One person a century is a lot,' Rebecca pointed out, with feeling. Look at all the trouble she had inherited just from Uriel Passenger!

However, Douglas Cameron had now concluded they were both in the Loony New-Age camp and accordingly pointed them at the best-known paranormal sites, and for want of anything else to do they were obediently ticking them off the list. At least it gave them a good impression of the island.

Which was beautiful. By daylight, even a misty, damp daylight, the water that was everywhere cast an atmosphere both calm and wild at the same time. The coastline was incredibly frilly, the island consisting almost entirely of peninsulas with the middle bit filled up by mountain, and there was very little traffic. Rebecca soon relaxed about driving on single-track roads; she even stopped worrying about the sheep, stoically chewing the cud inches from her wheels.

'Isn't it beautiful,' she said, apropos of nothing except the build-up of emotion inside her.

'It's different,' Connor said, and Rebecca shot him a glance.

'But *beautiful!*'

'It's okay. It doesn't really appeal that much.'

Rebecca felt slightly irritated.

They had driven to Dunvegan Castle first, as it was the closest venue on their list to Carnbeag. They wound their way up the long drive between giant fir trees, silent and wintry and trapping the misty air, to the great, grey castle on the hill, imperious and gloomy. Inside the walls were darkened by wood panelling and made spiny by antlers mounted on plaques.

The Fairy Flag lay in a glass-topped cabinet, a square of faded, grubby silk, not very impressive.

Rebecca read the label. 'Given to the fourth chief around 1380, according to this. I thought Douglas said it had been dated seventh-century or earlier?'

'Fourth to seventh.'

'Isn't that a bit of a discrepancy?'

Connor said, 'It means there's time for it to have been somewhere else in between.'

'You mean the fairy wife was returning it?'

Connor shrugged.

'Returning it after it having been taken to – there – a few centuries earlier?'

Connor turned round. 'I don't know, Rebecca. I've been there but that doesn't make me an expert on history and folklore. How would I know about a tatty piece of silk in a Scottish castle? Or what happened to a Macleod chieftain six hundred years ago?'

Point taken. Rebecca gave herself a mental slap round the head. Stupid.

They finished the tour and returned to the Mini. Next up was the Fairy Bridge, where horses, Cameron had told them, balk and ditch their riders into the foaming waters of the Bay River.

The bridge was dour, a tall arc of stone, although Rebecca thought she had seen it, or a bridge very like it, before. No horses were in sight, so there was no prospect of entertainment.

From the bridge they had to drive miles to go not really that far because the sea cut so deeply into the coast, and Connor suggested they see what the capital of the island looked like.

They parked, and then investigated the harbour, where a row of pastel-painted terraced houses faced out over the sea and a cluster of fish-and-chip shops lined the harbour wall. Someone was running an engine in a small fishing boat with an enclosed wheelhouse at the bows, and there was a lifeboat, startlingly orange, moored farther out.

They walked to the end of the quay, looked out to sea for a minute or so, and then returned and climbed the slope to sit on a bench near the town square to eat their sandwiches. Douglas Cameron had provided granary bread and some nice, runny Brie and cherry tomatoes.

Near the square was a shop that had been calling to Rebecca since they arrived, almost tugging on her sleeve, its window full of jewel colours that she was unable to resist, and when she'd finished eating she surrendered.

The inside of the shop was a golden cave of coloured cloth, woven and dyed and printed, and despite the suspicion that she was conforming to stereotype, Rebecca succumbed and bought a jacket of kingfisher and emerald, and a soft-brimmed hat to match.

Then she bought a bag, a gloriously random affair with every pocket a different colour, and, ridiculously, was given yet another bag, of screen-printed calico, for her purchases to travel in. Wild!

'Sorry,' she said to Connor, without feeling remotely apologetic. 'Where next?'

The cloud was breaking up and fingers of brighter sky appearing here and there, but it was no day for climbing. Still, the atmosphere was less dank, and the sheep no longer wore their morning veils of dewdrops.

The road towards the top of the island ran alongside a loch for much of the way, and the high ground on their left brought shadow as the sun began to sink. Ahead Rebecca saw the startling silhouette of a pinnacle, a column of rock, wider at the girth than at its base.

'I think that's the Old Man of Storr,' Connor said.

They drew closer, the road curving and dipping and then climbing. The Old Man grew larger.

'What do you think – our landmark stone?'

'Might be.'

Or it might not. They still had a lot of work before them.

They drove on through settlements of low white houses and occasionally a petrol station or a general store. Between villages there was only grass and sheep and here or there an isolated homestead.

'I think that's it.'

Rebecca looked where Connor nodded and saw the dramatic, irregular silhouette of the hills, or mountains, or whatever they were here. It looked somehow familiar – one face almost vertical, the other sweeping up in a curve...The cloud had lifted, and the tops were clear.

Too late to do anything now, though.

'Well, we know where to come tomorrow.'

They carried on round the top of the northernmost peninsular, and then south towards the wonderfully named Uig, and Connor said, 'The Fairy Glen is along here, the other side of the village.'

Rebecca followed the road, squinting when the low sun emerged from cloud to dazzle her, strangely not the least bit irritated when it did. She was looking forward to the comfort of

Carnbeag and whatever Douglas Cameron was cooking tonight; the mutton yesterday had been fabulous.

Looking forward to tipping her shopping out on the bed, too, and trying everything on again in front of the mirror, especially that hat.

'Here,' Connor said. 'This road.'

They climbed out, stretching. Connor set off and Rebecca followed, happy to take a break and uncrease her legs. She watched the track, stepping where he had stepped, and only looked up when he stopped.

'Amazing.'

Rebecca looked too. 'Well, yes it is…but…'

She stared. The glen was a series of strange, conical hills, grassed over but with visible horizontal rings on the slopes. They were far, far too big…

'These are…'

She faltered.

'What?'

Rebecca said, 'These are my molehills. Connor, I *drew* these.'

Chapter Forty-One

'Yes, very rare. The first to be imported to this country, in fact.' Geoffrey Foster embellished the rubbish he was spouting. 'There are a couple in Somerset, I believe, and I heard someone has started up in Scotland. The Grampians.'

Detail always helps; detail and a smile. He saw the woman waver and dredged up another line to press home his attack.

'The history of the breed is unique. Apparently they–'

'Dear me, it's all quite fascinating but I'm afraid I need to get back…'

'Of course.'

At last! Foster watched the woman retreat. He waited until she was through the gate, and then called pleasantly, 'Any time!'

She waved acknowledgement and vanished round the hedge. Thank God he had the blarney. And thank God the tallixer sounded, if it sounded like anything, then more like a dog than a lion.

The noise it produced was weird and it was hardly surprising that people had noticed and asked questions. The trick was to appear enthusiastic and keen to impart more information than was truly wanted. He was quietly pleased with the Mongolian Forest Wolfhound that he had invented.

'A misnomer, of course, they come from Tierra del Fuego. I wish I could introduce her to you, but they're very sensitive when they're in whelp, and this litter will be worth a fortune.'

Foster closed the front door and pulled out his phone, which had buzzed in his pocket while he was fending off the hotel manager. Michael Seward had called.

Geoffrey hit Return Call and took it into the sitting room where there was a pad of paper to jot down the details.

They had to tramp about the glen a bit before they found a signal. Then Connor watched Rebecca make her call. She stood frowning into the distance, the breeze throwing her hair across her cheek first, and then, when she turned, sweeping it back from her forehead so that she looked almost as he remembered her from before, when she wore her hair cropped.

He saw her speak, and pause, and speak again, frowning at her feet now, taking little steps backwards and forwards, unable quite to keep still. When he couldn't bear to look at her any longer he stared across the glen instead.

Finally she pocketed the phone and crossed the peculiar, grassy ridges to him.

'Done. I told him to send them by special delivery. We'll have them tomorrow morning.'

Thank God. One more night, and tomorrow afternoon he'd be away.

Foster stuck shop pizzas in the Aga and opened a bottle of Shiraz. One more meal sitting across the table from the weird kid, watching him shift about on the chair, shovelling food into his mouth. One more attempt to shower under that pathetic trickle the system could manage. *No* more excursions to the supermarket to fetch trolley-loads of raw meat; there was a small flock's worth of leg joints crammed into the freezer.

He'd go across to the bar for an hour or so later, tell the guys he was off tomorrow, and the next time he started the engine it would be to head south.

Geoffrey grabbed the torch and went to fetch Jack.

'Ah. 'Fraid not, you see.' Douglas Cameron ladled soup into Rebecca's bowl. 'Tomorrow, possibly. Probably. But definitely not by nine.'

Connor saw Rebecca's mouth open as if she were about to argue – her default position – and said quickly, 'Yes, you are very remote up here.'

Rebecca shut her mouth, and Connor watched her think.

'We are. Although the climate is surprisingly kind. We don't get much snow, you know, even when the mainland is impassable, which always amazes visitors.'

Connor recalled the posts lining the highway through the Highlands and the depth markings on them. Snow there could clearly drift ten feet deep and more.

Douglas replaced the lid on the tureen and nudged the bread basket in Rebecca's direction.

'However,' he went on, 'the weather should be clearing in the next day or so. I don't think you'll have any trouble getting up the Quiraing. Although if you take my advice you will get yourselves some walking boots before you try.

'Now, I suppose neither of you happens to play chess?'

Douglas was right, of course.

The parcel turned up just before five the next day, ending hours of frustration on Rebecca's part, which was very apparent to Connor through her snappiness and her inability to settle to anything.

She was overwrought. So was he, but he handled it differently.

At last the doorbell rang and Cameron came into the room with a gigantic padded posting bag.

'Your drawings, I believe,' he said lightly, and Rebecca lunged.

Roly Pidgeon had carried out Rebecca's instructions to the letter; the pile of paper that slid out of the bag included sketchbooks and notebooks and loose sheets of paper, some as large as A2, some no bigger than a postcard. Most of it was in pencil, but there were pastels and watercolours too, and ink sketches. Rebecca had asked him to gather up absolutely every bit of drawn-on paper he could find in her studio, and the harvest now poured itself out over the coffee table: mountains and forests and streams and castles and bridges.

'Here,' Rebecca said, pouncing. 'You see? I'd thought they were molehills!'

Connor took the page. She was right. With nothing included for scale, the conical hummocks did resemble molehills. But they had ridges on their sides and were densely packed.

'Well, well!' Douglas said. 'The Fairy Glen!'

'Yes. And here, too.'

Rebecca slid a smaller sheet towards them and carried on shuffling.

'And I'm sure...Okay, here!'

Connor took the new sketch, this time of a stone bridge over a small river.

'I wondered at the time why I hadn't made it prettier. Well, now I know!'

It was the Fairy Bridge.

'Well, well!' Douglas said again.

'Hold on – I think – Connor, isn't this...'

Rebecca passed across a small pen-and-ink study of a tree, split just above the ground into five slender trunks.

Connor frowned. 'There's a tree like this where the Cherwell, joins the Thames. On the north bank, near the boathouses.'

'I knew it. I always knew it.' Rebecca didn't know whether to be pleased or afraid. Her eyes lit on another page and she pulled it out. 'And here.'

It was a long, horizontal sheet with a spidery horizon drawn in ink – hills rising to a rocky outcrop with a silhouette that was still fresh in Connor's mind.

Not only Connor's. Douglas Cameron nodded appreciatively. 'There you are,' he said. 'That's the Quiraing.'

Chapter Forty-Two

Walking boots definitely helped, Rebecca decided, once you got used to the feeling of your ankles being encased in something so rigid.

She had put them on in the parking area, leaning against the side of the car to lace them up, and had immediately noticed she couldn't feel the ground anymore. It was there to stop her falling through the earth, but all the textures had disappeared and grass or rock or stones all felt the same. Very odd.

She zipped up her jacket and set off, acutely aware of her feet but otherwise unencumbered – they only needed one rucksack and Connor was wearing that. Rebecca had tried lifting it earlier and been surprised at how heavy it was.

It was another clear day at last and without much wind either. On the mainland there had been snow but Skye was dry and bright.

There was another car in the clearing when they arrived, a Volvo estate with a dog net behind the seats, but the footpath ahead was empty and it was very quiet. Once again Rebecca felt the pull, the attraction of living somewhere so – untrodden; Douglas had told them the island received visitors all year round drawn by the scenery and the climbing, but Skye was too remote ever to be touristy. Even Rebecca's home county of Suffolk, out on a limb and bare to the east winds, had more holiday-makers than this place.

She paused and looked back the way they had come, taking in the distance and the fall of the land, and the soft greyness that was the ever-moving sea beyond. She opened her mouth, and then shut it again. Every time she commented on the island's loveliness Connor said 'Mm', and it was getting boring.

The Quiraing seemed steep enough to Rebecca, who had never scrambled about in the foothills of mountains before, but not so steep as to be scary, and the feeling of gaining height with every step was invigorating. She felt fizzy. The bits she enjoyed most were where she needed her hands to help her over the rock, so that her whole body was involved in the task of moving along; it was utterly different from walking on the level.

When Connor halted, she came alongside him grinning. 'Fantastic, isn't it?'

'Mm.'

Rebecca looked at him, at his profile while he scanned the way ahead. He was frowning. Perhaps it was just that he was preoccupied; but then, so was she yet she felt energized too, excited that the search might be nearly over and the final stages of the task upon them. Connor seemed reluctant, which she didn't understand.

'With luck this'll soon be over,' she tried, 'and you can go back to Oxford and the Vulture's cheese scones.'

'Mm.'

So that hadn't worked either.

Half an hour later they were in the Prison. They had reached a kind of hollow, an amphitheatre almost, of grass and rocks between sheer cliffs that had been formed, according to their host, by prehistoric volcanic action. Legend had it that the Macleod clan had driven cattle in here to protect them from raiders, and Rebecca thought that if so then the cattle must have been a sight more nimble of foot than her father's hefty British Blues.

Still. A compound formed by ancient natural forces and used by past generations to protect livestock from theft *possibly by fairies* seemed more in keeping with the riddle and the quest than Portland's bricks and mortar and barbed wire.

Fairies, apparently, harboured a desire for cattle which was almost as strong as their desire for human babies and for young mothers to act as wet-nurses. From her admittedly unusual standpoint, Rebecca found all this rather disturbing.

'Do you think that's what really happened?' she had asked Connor, only to get back the usual shrug.

'I doubt it. Maybe once or twice. Who knows?'

It occurred to Rebecca that hiding cattle in a compound close to a fairy portal might not have been the greatest idea.

Then it occurred to her, with a jolt, that the proximity of the gap was probably the very reason the people around here needed to keep their livestock hidden in the first place.

Patterns, and elements falling into place. It was like Ashendon all over again – the incredible becoming actual in her very presence.

Connor unzipped the rucksack.

'We need the map.'

They were standing in the place of captivity and now they had to face the stone. The question was, which one? There were several on offer, including the dramatic perpendicular pinnacle to the side of the compound, named the Needle.

But that was too close. If the gap was located between them and the Needle, then they were practically in it already. Possible – and alarming – but perhaps unlikely, or you'd hardly bother to leave directions about which way to look.

Moving farther out, the biggest, the most famous, the most startling stone on Skye was unquestionably the Old Man of Storr, visible from the road that ran north to south along the eastern side of the island and the star of many a postcard and holiday snap.

Rebecca had drawn that, too.

'I wondered why I had,' she admitted. 'It's not something I'd ever use as a background; I thought it looked unrealistic.'

Which it did, with its base like a waist, narrower than the bulge of stone above.

Now Connor oriented himself to face the Old Man of Storr, invisible beyond the layers of ridges, using the map and compass. Rebecca shuffled through her sketches one more time, committing to memory what she could. They had extracted everything they recognized – the bridge, the giant molehills of the Fairy Glen, the Old Man of Storr himself – and brought only those unidentified landscapes. Now Rebecca aligned herself with Connor and scoured the landscape for something she might recognize.

And found it.

'Your father too? I'm sorry. My condolences.'

Damn. Going to have to hang about a bit now – maybe have a coffee. Can't really shoot straight off.

Not caring to check his wrist watch in front of Michael, Geoffrey Foster shifted fractionally and got in a swift glance at the clock on the mantelpiece instead: nearly two twenty. Away by three?

He put the kettle on and leaned on the dresser, drumming his fingers, while Michael Seward brought his luggage indoors. Not much of it – the one holdall and his coat, but there was a box as well, which Geoffrey did not recognize. He had seen Michael leave and it hadn't been with him then. Something of his parents' then…

Nice-looking box, and not one of Seward's make. It was smooth but not polished, with a carved lid and sides, and looked old…

His hand slid into his pocket and his thumb stroked the worn wood of the knife. He'd have it identified soon. Or rather, hopefully *not* identified.

He smiled, then quickly wiped it away as Seward entered the kitchen. He suspected Michael's response to losing both his parents in the space of a fortnight had been somewhat different to his own on hearing about Aunt Margaret, and he was going to have to tiptoe about for half an hour.

From the distance it looked to Rebecca like a cattle shed: a byre, or a barn, or whatever you would call such a thing – a small, low, four-sided building of dark grey stone rising from the grass. A scrubby bush affair was growing around one end, a mess of tangled stems and serious thorns. The interesting thing was that there were no windows, no holes of any kind, not even a door, which was why it only passed as a barn from a distance.

A pointless building. Except that it had a point, of course.

The roof had collapsed, which meant that light could now get in. And out.

Climbing over was easy – the walls were only six feet high or so, and Connor got up with a heft and a scrabble, and then came back down and boosted Rebecca up instead.

She sat astride the wide wall and looked through the rafters. The floor was beaten earth. There were drifts of dead leaves in the corners and dried droppings and feathers. Something had been using it as a bolthole.

She slipped down inside and Connor scrambled over to join her.

'Here, then, I suppose,' she said.

'Mm.'

He was very tense.

Rebecca said, 'So I guess we'll have to hang around and find out whether the half-light bit means dusk or dawn.'

They had discussed this already. On the assumption that the gaps all worked on the same principles as the Ashendon one – a few minutes of interaction at a set time each twenty-four hours – then all they had to do to confirm that the gap was here was to wait for the light from the invisible world to be revealed. It was blindingly obvious, and she had only said it for the sake of saying something.

And all she'd got was 'Mm'.

Rebecca sighed.

'Okay. Well, let's hope it's dusk, eh? Then we can have a lie-in tomorrow. Now, what about lunch?'

At ten to three Geoffrey Foster crossed the threshold for what he hoped would be the last time, at least for a few weeks. He had had enough of sweeping out hearths and washing up; central heating and the dishwasher beckoned.

He watched Michael head down the path towards the locked garden.

And mythological beasts, he'd had enough of them, too.

Michael's Honda was parked tidily alongside his BMW. Boring car, but Seward was a non-driver at heart, Geoffrey suspected – hadn't even owned a car when he lived in London, he believed.

Geoffrey swung his case into the boot. Six hours and he'd be home.

He was opening the driver's door when Mrs Dixon trotted across the gravel.

'Mr Foster, I'm glad I caught you. I have a request. Several of our guests are life-long dog-lovers and we are all fascinated by your beautiful lady Mongolian Wolfhound. So might I ask – would you do us the honour of giving an after-dinner lecture one evening this week?'

Chapter Forty-Three

It was early afternoon and the sun would be set by four. Connor, who had spent his life down south, found himself surprised that the distance between Skye and London, small as it looked on a world map, could make so much difference to the length of day.

In view of the general dirt and droppings in the hut they elected to wait in the car. Using the Ordnance Survey map and the compass and helped by his own innate sense of direction, they explored the possibility of getting the car closer. Rambling about on the hillside in the dark was not an attractive prospect.

After a couple of abortive attempts, one along a drive leading to a crisp, modern house and one using a lane that simply petered out in the face of increasing gradient, they found a narrow stretch of broken tarmac and bumped along it for half a mile before turning a corner and finding themselves in front of a ramshackle cottage. The grass grew high right up to the door step and the shutters and windows were broken; it was clearly deserted.

The tarmac finished there, but a rough cart track wound on in what looked promisingly like the direction of the hut.

'I'm not driving up that,' Rebecca said.

So they walked, one either side of the overgrown central patch, boots crunching on loose stones. Not more than a hundred yards along they stepped over a tiny burn, parted more of the thorny bushes, and found themselves facing the back wall of the barn.

Connor glanced back, gauging the distance to the empty house.

'Do you suppose they knew?' Rebecca asked.

'Perhaps. Perhaps it was built there so that someone could look after the gap. Or perhaps they had no idea.'

The hollow was completely hidden from the modern house that was its nearest neighbour. The lie of the land probably acted as a sound baffle too. You'd be hard pressed to notice the place amongst the thorns and stones unless you were looking for it; they would have missed it themselves had Rebecca not previously drawn it.

'I'm not sure I like this,' she had said. 'Already knowing it, I mean. Drawing things that exist but which I've never seen. It's like the V and A all over again.'

True…the solution to that riddle had lain in her sketchbook too.

Longer ago for him than for her.

Connor sighed, and then wished he hadn't. Rebecca was looking at him again, sideways on, studying him. He shook himself mentally, tried to dig up some energy from somewhere.

'Okay, what have we got here…How are we going to seal this off afterwards?'

They had talked about this as well. Connor realized he had been expecting a monolith to be the problem – a great rock planted right on the gap, an impenetrable barrier to any alien light beams. Instead they had a structure, like the secret, windowless room in Ashendon Cottage and the Dons' brick plinth. And like the plinth, the integrity of the structure had been destroyed, not by fire this time but by neglect.

Rebecca said, 'I think we should repair the roof, sure, but we need to block off the gap in the meantime too. So we have to find our own monolith.'

They killed time roaming the hillside, leaning on stones to test for potential movement. It was something to do, and it kept Rebecca from paying attention to him. He had no idea how much she would have noticed anyway, but it was definitely better when she was looking in a different direction.

None of the stones on the hillside looked promising, though, and when the shadows became too deep for searching they returned to stand beside the broken walls, half-watching the reddening sky, half-watching the roofline, as it darkened to a silhouette.

Breathe.

Connor flexed his hands. Rebecca was saying something, but he had no idea what – his ears seemed to have turned off. He made an effort to hear.

'Connor? What do you think?'

'I...'

But the light had almost gone. When is it half-light and when dark? His heart was clunking.

'It'll be dawn then. Rats.'

'Pardon?'

'Dawn,' Rebecca repeated, exasperation evident in her voice. 'We'll have to get up horrifically early.'

Dawn, not dusk. The gap hadn't opened, and they had to do it all over again in a few hours.

Rebecca said, 'Mind if we go back through Portree? I need chocolate.'

His house in Wandsworth was cold and smelled of electrical cable and carpet instead of the wood smoke Foster had become used to at Ashendon. Perhaps he should have spent a day or two at Aunt Margaret's place instead, which probably still smelled of furniture polish and flowers.

Foster turned up the thermostat and unloaded the contents of the carrier bag into the fridge: milk, butter, orange juice and sliced salami. He cut into the loaf straight away, and ate bread-and-butter, folded over, while he shuffled through the mail – mostly junk, of course; investment statements and a quote for the new kitchen at Camden Square; that gave him pause for a moment, but he'd get the money back when he sold.

He went round downstairs, switching on lights and closing curtains, and when he was confident no passer-by in the street could see inside, he lay Passenger's alien knife on the table and woke up his laptop. He had already narrowed the likely sources of information to three or four in the UK – the Natural History Museum was one, and there was a division of the Materials Institute near St James.

So let's make some appointments...

They didn't need to get up particularly early; Douglas told them sunrise wouldn't be until nearly nine o'clock.

'But if you want that grey quality, you'll need to get out earlier, of course.'

Rebecca's line about photography had been inspired. It was extraordinary, the way she always managed to produce a solution, on the fly, as if from some inexhaustible store of neat ideas. Nothing ever fazed her. It was one of the things he loved about her.

They walked up from the derelict cottage through the cold dark. Connor tried not to shiver, and failed.

At least she couldn't see him.

Next to the broken walls, Rebecca switched off her torch.

'Save the battery.'

'Yes.'

Breathe.

'Thank goodness Michael's back,' Rebecca said. 'And thank goodness he actually let us know!'

'Yes.'

'Because I really didn't want to have to drive down and then all the way back up again with Jack and that tallixer.'

'No.'

'Although it's pretty awful that his father died.'

'Yes.'

'Well, awful that his mother did, too, of course, but I mean, even more awful that his father then...'

Her voice trailed off.

'Connor, are you alright?'

The hut was visible, which meant that the sky was lightening.

When does dark stop being dark and become half-light?

It was freezing.

'Connor?'

Deep inside him, Connor felt a pulse start – not his own but something other, something extraneous that nevertheless had somehow got inside his skin and was filling him with vibration: unpleasant, like the ache you get after a limb wakes up from numbness. His guts trembled.

The air was trembling too. There was a low-frequency thrum now, but he couldn't move his head to detect where it was originating from because he didn't seem able to move at all.

The quality of the light had changed; a soft, pale glow had appeared above the broken wall, and it flickered.

Something beyond the wall of the barn was sucking at him, turning his legs to string and his heart to a hammer. With a huge effort, Connor turned towards Rebecca. His hands were shaking, so he clamped them down on her shoulders.

'What's the–'

His voice croaked, but he managed to get the words out. 'Rebecca, I'll be straight back. Wait for me.'

He released her and drove his feet forward, forced his body to move towards the barn and his hands to reach for the jagged top of the wall.

How long would it remain open? It was like climbing in sand – he had to be quicker…

He hauled himself to the top and swung his legs over. The pulse beat inside him and against him as the light in the barn rippled below like the water in the marina, pulling at him with its promise of secret depth.

Rebecca's voice sounded from far away.

'Connor! What are you – wait – *Connor!*'

But the barn was filled with wavering forms and the rustling of growth and now all he had to do was slip down into it.

'I have to check it,' he said, desperately, with no idea whether his voice made any sound. 'I have to check that it's safe.'

And then he jumped.

Chapter Forty-Four

'I have to check that it's safe,' he had said.

He had been so afraid.

In the cold dawn light, which was pearly and misty and utterly bleak, like death, Rebecca walked back to her car and sat behind the steering wheel, her hands in her lap.

I've done it again. I didn't see it, and I've done it again.

'I have to check that it's safe.'

Of course. He was Connor. He had been through into the World Invisible before and been held captive for four, five, maybe even six years. He knew each gap took you to a different place and he knew they had no idea where this one led. Connor would never send Jack off without knowing he would be alright the other side. And so he was checking that it was safe.

After a while Rebecca covered her face with her hands.

Quite a long time after that, she put on her seat belt and started the engine.

She had a day to get through. At dawn tomorrow, he would be back. At dawn he *would* be back. He would be back, and they would let Michael know and Michael would bring Jack and his pet up to Skye and everything would be fine. Jack would go home, the stupid tallixer would go with him, and they would all have mince pies and brandy at Douglas Cameron's.

Mince pies and whisky. Scotch. Talisker, the island's own, famous, blend.

Talisker, tallixer, she had said to Connor that first evening, when Cameron went out to start the vegetables. 'Any connection there, do you think? The sound 'ks' gets transposed easily, doesn't it?'

'Alexander the Great was called Sikander by the Persians,' he had said, and she had thought, Might have known he'd come up with something like that.

She found she had driven to Portree, so she parked in the square. Christmas lights were strung along the shop fronts and the batik shop was glowing.

He'll be back tomorrow.

People milled about, busy with affairs that were not hers, ignorant of what had happened, untouchable beyond the brittle shell that encased her.

Her feet took her down to the harbour, where the lifeboat was moored far out, sickly orange against the frightening, hostile sea. Oily water slapped against the quay, heedless and horribly deep. There were ragged heaps of tarry rope and dented cans and, further along, lobster creels like cages, and she knew nothing about how any of it was used. An alien world.

He was being alive, somewhere. Whatever the rules that affected the relative times of the two worlds, in Connor's own personal time, he was doing something, being somewhere.

And what if time slipped about? What if the 'five years there to three here' had been a one-off? Was that what the Dons had meant about everything going wrong if you came back through the same gap you went through? *A few days,* Professor Peregrine had said, and after that something so bad they hadn't wanted to tell her.

Was a gap between the worlds the source of Rip van Winkle and the host of similar legends? What if he came back tomorrow an old man?

Oh God.

And what was she going to say to Douglas?

Michael rang while she was driving, which meant she didn't have to answer. Couldn't answer. She pulled into the side of the road, though, and checked the screen in case…Well, she didn't know in case what, really.

But it was Michael, and she thought about calling back, her thumb hovering over the button, but then dropped the phone on the seat Connor should have been occupying and drove on.

What would I say? Tell him we've lost him again? Add to the grief?

Was it grief? It felt like grief. She sat in the car, preparing herself as best she could before she went indoors.

She had a story. He had run into a friend in Portree, a friend up here on holiday who was just about to go home for Christmas, and had decided to spend the night at the hotel.

Preposterous, of course, but Cameron wasn't to know.

'But I'll be catching the dawn again tomorrow,' she told him.

'My word! I'm afraid it's going to be wet.'

Wet doesn't matter.

It was wet, and Rebecca stood by the thorns with the water pouring over her in the dark, running off her jacket and into her jeans as the sky turned to iron, and all through the play of unearthly light above the broken walls, and even until the clouds had turned white and begun to break apart and drift away, by which time only her tears were still falling.

Chapter Forty-Five

One of his books on timber identification was out, lying on the table next to the saucer Foster had been using as an ashtray. Michael tipped the ash into the bin and put the saucer in the sink, and then slipped the book into its place amongst the others he had brought up three years ago from London.

Not many, but highly specialized; should he leave them here, or give them away? But who to? There was nothing that his fellow cabinet makers would not already have. A student? An apprentice?

The thought led inevitably to the workshop. Perhaps he should have advertised a year ago: *Master cabinetmaker offers apprenticeship with prospect of future partnership in box-making business.* And what about the rest of it? *Successful applicant will have open mind and interest in mythology.*

Too late now. There could be a free-for-all, the tools and equipment auctioned off, the workshop reduced to storing lawnmowers and fertilizer.

Rebecca would take care of it. She was good at organizing.

Michael felt that he had organized enough and wanted no more. Wrapping up affairs at Aberfeldy after his father had so suddenly, so shockingly, followed his wife to the grave had used up all his capacity for administration.

The strange, lost boy behind the garden wall would have to put up with his silence and inertia. Thank God Foster had gone quickly.

But there was one task he had to see to, and before five Michael rang the solicitor in Matlock and made an appointment to talk about the trust managing Connor's share of the moneys. Then he called Rebecca and learned that for the second morning running Connor had not returned.

'Still not back, then?'

Rebecca shook her head. Douglas Cameron moved about the kitchen, adjusting saucepan lids and wiping the counter. He wore a tea towel jauntily over one shoulder.

'Well that's going to be alright for ten minutes or so. Care for a drink?'

Rebecca didn't really, but felt she should try to play the part of a normal, rational guest. It was the minimum level of politeness, but she dreaded the prospect of questions.

She had dragged her way miserably through another day, unable to focus or plan, weary from the effort of trying not to imagine what was happening to him, not to dream up horrors that might be preventing him from coming home.

Michael's long-awaited participation was less help than she had expected. Having spent weeks irritated that he was out of contact, now she found herself wishing him away again. There was nothing he could do to help her, and having to speak to him, having to voice any of her thoughts, made her tremble. If she could only ignore the possibilities, not think about what might be happening, then the image of Connor walking back into the world retained some degree of credibility, and that was all she had to cling to.

In the meantime she had to seem normal.

Supper was more of Douglas Cameron's home-raised mutton. The sheep were kept for wool, and only the old, barren ewes were butchered. 'You have to cook it slowly,' Douglas had told her. 'And I do mean slowly. Twenty-four hours in the coolest oven. But then...'

And he was right; the meat was meltingly tender and so full of flavour that it seemed to be from a different species entirely from that sold as 'lamb'.

'You said your family farms?'

'Yes, mostly arable, a few British Blues. Suffolk.'

'Must have been wonderful for you growing up.'

It was the common, romantic and entirely false view of agriculture – haystacks in the farmyard and white ducks on a pond. Her stepfather's farm was a factory, with industrial units housing grain produced by state-of-the-art machinery. She hadn't been allowed anywhere near the yards as a child, and the only advantage she had ever been aware of was being already competent with the basics of driving before she had lessons to cover the highway stuff.

Which jolted her memory.

'Douglas, your tractor, it has stone forks.'

She had noticed it round the side of the lambing barn.

'It does.'

'Would it be possible, would you mind, could I perhaps borrow it for a day?'

The fourth morning was dry, and there was a crisp frost to sparkle in the beam of Rebecca's torch. With no clouds, the sky was a deep, beautiful navy blue, and as the eastern horizon beyond the wide water became tinged with pink and the sun began to rise, it gained colour as if it were paint in a palette with Rebecca adding drops of white to it.

She waited, watching the stars go out one by one and the day trying to begin, and when the hissing, rustling noise emerged and the hollow flashed with writhing light she turned her back and kept her eyes on the sky and tried very hard not to start crying again. It would soon be over; the gap was never open for more than a minute.

She had no idea where she was going to go today.

And then the light shifted again as the way between the worlds closed, and the night had gone. Rebecca faced the slender arc of the new sun, and in that instant her skin turned icy and her heart contracted.

There was a sound behind her, close by, something scuffling on stone, and she turned, her mouth stupidly open and her fingers spread, and saw Connor slip down from the wall. And he was whole.

She was only six feet away. It took her two strides to reach him, and then her forehead was against his canvas jacket and her hands were on his back and her arms were gripping him at last.

Chapter Forty-Six

The phone rang while Michael was smoothing beeswax into the box on the workbench; he wiped his hands and checked the screen.

'Rebecca.'

'He's back. He came back this morning.'

Michael checked his watch; it was three-thirty. 'How is he?'

'Oh, he's…fine. He's fine.'

'And what about the gap there? Can we use it?'

'The gap's perfect. Connor said it put him in a kind of gigantic pasture area, quite a lot like Vermont actually, only without the mountains. And there are farms nearby who are perfectly friendly – the people, I mean – and Connor thinks Jack will have no problem at all. They're used to tallixers as well, so no problems of any kind really, he reckons.'

'I see. Good.' Michael hesitated, sensing something not quite right. 'And Connor's definitely okay?'

'Yes, he's fine.'

'Why did he stay so long?'

'Ah.' Rebecca's voice became businesslike. 'We had heavy cloud. There wasn't enough light from here to get over to there, not even moonlight. It was featureless that side, and without strong light he couldn't find the place.'

'Good grief.'

'I know, something we never thought of! Not enough photons crashing because not enough photons!' She sounded very bubbly.

'And are you alright?'

'Me? I'm fine. Fine.'

'Right. Okay. Well, I'll leave tomorrow, then.'

Michael finished the call and stared at the box before him, half-polished and sweet-smelling. It needed its label on the base, the vine leaves framing his name and the unique number of the piece: 324…or simply, 'last'?

* * *

Rebecca put her phone away. She had the idea she might have made an idiot of herself. *Fine, fine, fine...* Would Michael have picked up on it?

Did it matter?

She surprised herself by laughing, and then felt serene and smiled mildly at the girl in the mirror over the chest of drawers, who smiled back.

'And you'd better not turn into the Queen of Clubs either,' she said, mock-severe. 'No more magic!'

She had been avoiding mirrors for weeks. She must have undergone a sea change to be talking to herself like this.

Is this what it's like, then? Is this how you're supposed to feel?

Maybe; probably; how would you know?

Any moment Connor would be through in the bathroom and they would go downstairs and rehearse for Douglas Cameron's return from counting the legs on his sheep or whatever he was doing. Quite how they were going to manage she didn't like to guess.

It had been okay – just about – earlier. They had sat in the Mini outside the derelict cottage first, while Connor explained how he had found himself stranded the other side of a gap he couldn't find. The once-in-twenty-four-hours thing applied there too, although of course it wasn't exactly twenty-four hours. Connor hadn't replaced his watch, so there was no way to be sure, but he said it had felt like a short day.

Short in some respects; achingly long in others.

He had made for the nearest settlement, hoping against hope, fearing the worst, and – thank everything holy – had found himself among people to whom the prospect of a stranger from farther away than they could ever have imagined was not alarming or even particularly interesting.

They fed him and gave him a bed for the night, and when he couldn't find the gap to come home, they had accepted that too. So he hadn't needed any of the supplies he had packed into that heavy rucksack, not even the writing materials he'd taken just in case.

In other words, they had been as different as they possibly could be from the people beyond the Ashendon gap.

He had even dug a bit. *Do you get any tallixers around here? How do you deal with them?*

Shut up the livestock and wait for them to move on.

And if one was being kept as a pet?

'They'd come across that before,' Connor had said. 'Lots of "ooh, ah, no accounting for folk" stuff.'

'And you could say all this?' Rebecca asked, always impressed by linguists having given up French after scraping a GCSE.

Connor pulled a face. 'In a manner of speaking. Slowly. They were very polite, but I think I amused them.'

So Jack would be fine. It crossed Rebecca's mind that had Connor landed amongst such people from the portal in Ashendon Cottage he would probably never have come back. Her stomach made a little downward dive.

Afterwards they had driven back to Carnbeag to find Douglas about to set out to view his flock, and simply had to hope he'd accept that Connor had walked out of Portree to rendezvous with Rebecca at that morning's destination. It was debatable whether Cameron let it lie unchallenged because he believed it or because he wasn't interested, but he told them to make a late breakfast and said he'd be back in the afternoon.

Neither of them had wanted to eat.

The truly miraculous thing, Rebecca realized, was that they both wanted each other. All these weeks while she had been stealing looks when Connor's back was turned or his attention elsewhere, he had been doing exactly the same; had been for longer, in fact…in New York, even.

'But I knew you thought I was just a kid. And anyway, there was Michael.'

He had seen how things stood. Rebecca felt a blush ought to be in order, but somehow one didn't seem necessary. 'No luck there. He was untouchable.'

'I know. Poor you.'

'No,' Rebecca said, propping herself up on her elbow to look at him properly. 'Not poor, not now. And not even then, really. It was a just crush.'

They had slept afterwards despite the clear, white light coming through the curtains, and it was only after they had woken, and talked some more, and kissed again, and finally got up to shower, that Rebecca had remembered she must tell Michael that Connor was safe.

And fine. Very, very fine.

Chapter Forty-Seven

Rebecca thought that with a mixture of natural acting ability and a degree of conscious effort she was managing to behave unremarkably. Connor also looked normal to her – wonderful, but normal – and there were no quizzical looks from their host, so they had got away with it.

Michael would be on his way, driving overnight in order to arrive at the Quiraing well before dawn to tip Jack and the tallixer into the shifting light inside the hut. He was leaving himself plenty of time for the journey because the last thing they wanted now was an extra twenty-four hours with the two alien beings shut in the van.

'I'll hire a Transit,' Michael had said. 'I can't drive with an animal like that on the back seat.'

How perceptive. Rebecca had had to learn that lesson the hard way.

'And I'll stay in a hotel in Portree,' he went on. 'Don't mention me to your host. I can't impose.'

So there was little else to be done.

'We still have to make it safe afterwards,' Connor reminded her.

'Sorted.'

'Sorted? How?'

She had surprised him. She grinned smugly. 'I've found a monolith. *The* monolith, probably.'

It was in the thorn bush, smothered by the tangled stems, and she had discovered it that dreadful first day, in the half hour after the sun rose. Unable to think where to go or what to do, and not yet able to surrender hope of a miracle, she had kicked about around the barn and ended up peering into the thicket and seeing stone that wasn't another section of wall. A lump of rock, perhaps four feet high and as wide around as a fridge, stood alone in the hollow as if rolled there and abandoned.

'I reckon it was used to seal the gap before anyone thought of building a hut,' Rebecca said. 'All we need to do is move it back into position. Then we can take our time in having the barn rebuilt around it as a second layer of defence.'

'But how are we going to move the stone?'

Rebecca smiled even more smugly. 'Douglas is going to lend me his tractor. He's got stone forks for it.'

'Stone forks?'

'Like a forklift. Heavy-duty.'

'And what are we going to tell him when he asks why he's moving rocks?'

'We won't be telling him anything. He won't be moving rocks. I will.'

'*You!* Rebecca–'

'Connor, I grew up on a farm. I could drive a tractor before I could drive a car. And forklifts are fun!'

'I'll leave you two to turn the stove down,' Douglas said, taking his mug upstairs at ten minutes to midnight. 'You'd better close both doors because the cats will go in if a bedroom's empty.'

So they hadn't got away with it after all.

The Transit van rolled into the car park soon after six, and pulled up a few feet from the Mini. Rebecca watched the driver's door open and a figure just a little blacker than the surroundings step down. He walked towards her, and she recognized his shape and his way of moving.

'Michael.'

He was tired. It was a long drive, and unlike Rebecca, he had not been able to do it in two hops. Bed and breakfast with a tallixer in tow was not an option. But there was something else too; he seemed restless as well as weary. Tense.

'Is everything okay?' she asked. 'Jack?'

'Yes, all okay.'

Rebecca elected to let it pass. 'It's only five minutes from here.'

The car park for the Quiraing was signed and reasonably findable even by a stranger in the dark; the overgrown track to the derelict cottage was not. Michael climbed back into the driver's seat for the final step, and Rebecca drove carefully to the turning, keeping the headlights of the Transit in her rear view mirror.

'This place is empty?' Michael asked, peering into the dark.

'Yes,' Rebecca said. 'Don't worry.'

'It would be better if it wasn't here. Someone might decide to renovate. It's too close.'

Rebecca said, 'I've had an idea about that.'

'An idea?'

'I'm working on it.'

She sensed Michael's doubt, but he didn't pursue the point, which was a relief as she didn't feel ready to commit quite yet. She had done some internet checking, though, and the signs were promising...

Forget renovation, though; she'd want to rebuild from scratch...

And still they had time to kill.

For safety's sake, Jack climbed into the hut, coaxing his wild beast over the wall with him. When the light came, they would be in position and ready for it.

'Where's that cat?' Rebecca asked, suddenly remembering.

Michael shook his head. 'Chose not to come. Last seen heading west. Time for a change of scene, I guess. You can't own a cat.'

Rebecca found she was relieved. Since Professor Peregine's remark, cats had made her feel uncomfortable. If there were cats over there as well, how could you be sure which kind you had? She had been a little afraid Biggles might start talking to her.

It was cold to be standing still, but it wouldn't be long now.

'I suppose he will be alright?' Rebecca asked after a pause.

'Biggles?'

'No! Jack.'

'It's the best we can do.'

'If he heads for those farms, he'll be okay,' Connor said.

'Yes.'

Somewhere there was a mother who would never forget the toddler she had lost, but they say time heals, at least a little. Would it really have been kind to seek out the home he had come from and present them with a fully-grown alien? And it might have proved impossible anyway; he never had given them a surname.

'Not necessarily even his real Christian name,' Connor said. 'It's quite possible they gave him that over there.'

'Really? They have the same names as us?'

'No. But *Jack* is like a label, shorthand for one of us that has strayed. Anyone from this world that ends up there could be called Jack – a bit like 'Jock' for a Scotsman or 'Joe' for an American. I would have been called Jack if I hadn't told them my name.'

He meant before, as well as this week. Rebecca gripped his hand, held between them where Michael would not see.

Not that it would matter if he did. And he seemed preoccupied anyway.

'Jack...It is the archetype of fairytale heroes, isn't it? Jack and the Beanstalk; Jack the Giant-Killer.'

'Jack and Jill; Little Jack Horner.'

'Little Jack Horner is supposed to be based on a real bloke,' Connor said. 'Something to do with Henry the Eighth and Glastonbury.'

Glastonbury again.

'But there are so many,' Michael said. 'Jack-in-the-Green, Jack-in-the-box...Rebecca, you still have your box?'

'Of course! It's beautiful.'

'Would you...'

Rebecca waited. Then she said, 'Would I what?'

'No. Nothing.'

Some time after eight Rebecca realised the roofline of the barn was visible against the sky.

Michael called, 'Jack? Ready?' and the boy's head appeared above the stonework, where he had hoisted himself up to see over.

'When the light comes, okay?'

'And make sure Gira goes first!' Connor added.

Michael lowered his voice. 'You know why she's called Gira?'

'No.'

'Bagheera from The Jungle Book. He must have had it read to him, or maybe to a brother or sister. His one overriding memory of this world: a story about a lost boy.'

'Lost and found,' Connor said.

After so long waiting, it happened very quickly. Suddenly above the broken barn there was a halo of shifting, twisting light and the echo of shadows that moved, and Rebecca felt in her flesh the heavy beat of sound just beyond her hearing, the hiss of noise from outside of existence.

There was a brief sound of movement on the other side of the stone wall, a scrabble of feet, and then nothing.

Rebecca locked eyes with Connor. 'Have they gone?' She tightened her grasp on his warm hand, just in case.

Then the thrumming was still and the light vanished, as if snuffed out, and there was only the grey dawn in the sky, and the silence of the open air.

Michael was leaning with his palms on the crumbling stone, as if listening and feeling for what lay behind.

Connor hoisted himself up to look.

'Gone. Empty.'

Rebecca filled her lungs and stretched and smiled. It was done! Now she had just to drive the tractor here, push down a bit of wall and move the stone into place.

It was Christmas Eve and she was on Skye; she had found Connor, and incredibly, Connor had found her; and if she really pulled her finger out and set to, she'd even get those illustrations ready in time as well.

And there was only Michael, staring bleakly at the barn, to give her pause.

Chapter Forty-Eight

Douglas Cameron was impressed.
'You've driven one of these before!'
He meant the make, of course; he had already accepted that she had driven the generic machine.
'My father's is an earlier model. Yours is much nicer.'
Her experience of earning a living had taught her the value of blarney; three years ago she wouldn't have bothered.
Out of the corner of her eye she caught the expression that slipped briefly across Connor's face.
He knows I wouldn't have bothered too.
She grinned. Being understood by someone was novel and immense fun, her bad points every bit as much as her good ones. And it was going to be fun driving a tractor again, too.
The logistics were working out nicely, thanks to Cameron's easy attitude. It was Connor who had pointed out that if they wanted to place the monolith accurately they needed to do it immediately the light had ceased, while the position was fresh in their minds, which meant the tractor would need to be at the barn waiting overnight.
'No problem,' Cameron had said, surprising everyone. 'Why, though? If you don't mind my asking.'
And Rebecca had drawn breath and embarked on the story they had prepared.
'It is the most extraordinary place.' That much was certainly true. 'The way the light falls at dawn is astonishing. I don't hold with computerised effects, I want to photograph the actual scene as it truly is, and if only the monolith could be shifted a few feet...'
'Unusual way to spend Christmas day.'
Yes, it was. With fingers crossed that Douglas Cameron would put it down to artistic eccentricity, she said, 'Oh but the rising sun on Christmas day is the very *essence* of what I'm looking for!'

Cameron waved his whisky tumbler. 'If you say so. And no, I'm not going to worry about the tractor out there overnight – this is Skye, people here leave their doors unlocked.'

He had told them that the crime rate on the island was practically non-existent: the occasional cycle theft and once a year a punch-up. It sounded romantic in the extreme and a far remove from London, or even Oxford, where bikes padlocked to railings frequently ended up minus a wheel. Steph's gel saddle was stolen once, and she had to ride two miles to get home standing on the pedals.

A deep, low thrill had started in Rebecca which was quite different from the one set off by Connor. She was going to buy the derelict cottage and have a new house built on the plot – people were doing it all the time, according to Douglas, and he had named three companies who specialized in one-off builds for private customers, like her.

'Wouldn't I need to get planning permission?' she had asked.

'Of course, but that's not likely to be a problem if you're replacing an existing dwelling. A solicitor will handle that for you.'

And he'd given her the address of his own. This was going to be *easy!*

The tractor trundled along the narrow lanes to the barn, where Michael met her. Handling the levers with a skill that quickly returned to her, Rebecca first pushed the wall down – it fell easily in the face of the gorgeous modern tractor – and then drove the stone forks into the depths of the thorn bush and extracted the monolith, bringing most of the briars with it. She manoeuvred the stone ready to position, and left the tractor with the forks down ready for the final stage tomorrow.

The *final* final stage.

Michael then drove her back to Carnbeag. He wouldn't come in, and dropped her at the foot of the drive.

'I'll see you tomorrow.'

'If you're sure,' Rebecca said. 'If you'd rather start back, Connor and I can manage by ourselves from here.' She loved saying his name.

'I'll be there,' Michael said.

* * *

Rebecca had expected their host to have wanted them out of the way for Christmas but Cameron was easy about that too: *'We don't make so much of Christmas here; we save all that for Hogmanay'*

Douglas had not attempted to decorate his house, but Rebecca, unable to resist, found some greenery with berries on – cotoneaster rather than holly, so not traditional but good enough – and set up a few jugs in effective places. Douglas had a party to go to that night (*'Just a gathering at the local, you're welcome to join us'*) but they had declined, and had the firelight and the sofa to themselves.

Tomorrow they would be getting up before dawn one final time.

'Then we really have to go home,' Rebecca said. 'I can start the house thing remotely, I think. We can't impose on poor old Douglas any longer, and I have really got to get back to work.'

They'd drive down on Boxing Day, when the roads would be empty, and make the break at Loch Lomond again. Michael might well set off at once, she thought, doubting that Christmas featured much in his solitary life.

Oh Michael…

The cloudless, frosty weather was holding, and the ground crunched under their feet as she and Connor trod the path to the barn. The tractor loomed, massive and modern and industrial in the midst of the tumbled stone and tangled briars, waiting to finish the job, and Michael was there too, his hands in his pockets, his features invisible.

'Hi.'

'Hi.'

Rebecca climbed into the tractor cab and started the engine. It turned over beautifully; nothing had died overnight and everything was going to be fine. She turned off and got back down.

'So.'

'Yes.'

Rebecca cuddled her coat close around her neck and stamped her feet. Connor had been quiet on the way over, and as usual it seemed to be down to her to find things to say.

'We're leaving tomorrow. I was afraid we'd be imposing by staying today but I think Douglas is quite happy to share his turkey with someone, don't you think?' She looked at Connor for support.

'Mm. Probably.'

'Michael, when are you–'

'It's getting lighter.'

Rebecca glanced at the eastern horizon, over the sea that was as yet invisible. 'I suppose. A bit. A few minutes to go yet, though.'

Connor said, 'Michael...'

But Michael seemed to have jerked into motion and spoke over him. 'Rebecca, take this.' He was holding something out to her. An envelope?

'What is it?'

'An explanation. You'll find everything else you need in the van.'

'Explanation of what?'

She had yet to take the envelope. Michael pushed it at her chest. 'You'll see when you read it.'

Something had begun to stir in her mind, deep down, like the inkling of a very bad migraine.

'Michael,' Connor said again, and suddenly Rebecca knew.

'You want to go through,' she said.

Of course he did. He had wanted to go through three years ago and she had stopped him. He must have carried on wanting to go all the months and years since.

She had known for a long time that the complicated arrangement of prisms and props at Ashendon made it impossible for him to close the gap behind himself, and had been relying on that to prevent him from trying; that and, possibly, Connor's disappearance.

But Connor had returned, and moreover had now given the all-clear to this portal, and to the invisible world on the other side of this particular gap.

'You can't,' she said, knowing as she spoke that he could. He didn't even have his parents to hold him any more.

'Rebecca, the envelope.'

She took it.

'And here's the key to the van.'

Connor took that; she didn't seem able to move.

The sky was definitely lightening now, and for the first time she noticed that Michael was wearing a backpack. What do you take to Fairyland? In Connor's case it had been food and water and writing paper.

She watched him step over the rubble of the wall she had knocked down and stand, feet wide apart and balanced, on the beaten earth floor of the hut.

How could he do this? How could anyone do this? It was a terrible prospect, insane and petrifying, yet crazily she was the only one of them who seemed to think so.

'Your boxes,' she cried suddenly, with no idea why they should seem so important.

'You decide. Do whatever you think best.'

He didn't even turn to face her, all his attention now on the air before him and the next few moments.

And then the light broke and Rebecca gasped. It was shocking, green-blue and wavering, and once again Rebecca formed an impression of snaking tendrils and shapes not quite fully formed. The sub-audible throb beat against her, hissing in her ears, sickening her stomach, and for an instant it seemed to her that even Michael hesitated.

And then he stepped forward and was gone.

Rebecca felt Connor's hand holding hers, and the slight backwards pull, but it was not needed; the one thing she knew she could never do was walk into that light. She wouldn't even have followed Connor, had he madly gone again. She had her limits, and this was far beyond them...

When the sound and the light had left too, the normal world seemed strange and unearthly. The tractor was waiting. She knew where to place the stone now.

He wasn't coming back. Ever.

'Rebecca.'

'I know.'

'He wanted to go.'

'I know.'

Connor folded his arms around her. The light, the proper light, was stronger now, and from far away drifted the sound of church bells.

Rebecca began to cry.

A World Invisible

by

Joanna O'Neill

"You're telling me the Victoria and Albert Museum only exists because seven Victorians needed to hide a handful of objects for a hundred years?"

Finding she can draw nothing but vines, Rebecca reluctantly puts her ambitions as an illustrator on hold when she is drawn into the machinations of a Victorian secret society founded to make safe an interface between parallel worlds.

But first she has to grow up.

Dragged into helping a cause in which she barely believes, Rebecca finds herself playing Hunt-the-Thimble amongst England's oldest institutions. Over one summer she will break a code, discover her astonishing ancestry, and half fall in love – twice.

But what begins as a game will shake her to the core.

A World Invisible begins the story continued in *A World Denied*.

Available from booksellers: ISBN 978-09564432-0-5

ABOUT THE AUTHOR

Joanna O'Neill is a textile artist and horse whisperer, and the author of many articles for both textile and equestrian magazines. She lives in Berkshire, England.

A World Denied is the second book in the trilogy which began with A World Invisible.

For more information, visit www.joanna-oneill.co.uk.